Natalya,
God's
Messenger

Natalya, God's Messenger

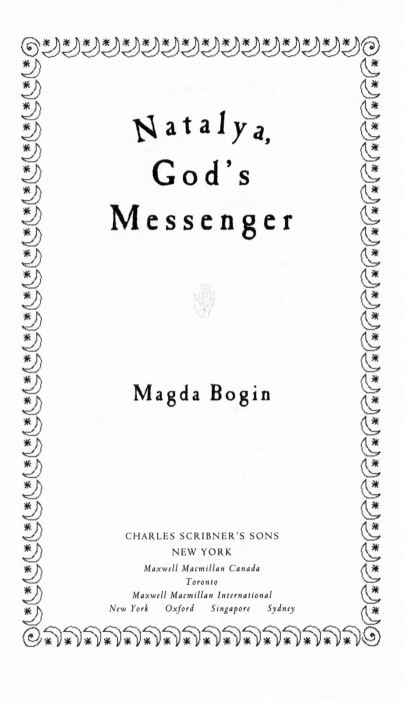

Magda Bogin

CHARLES SCRIBNER'S SONS
NEW YORK

Maxwell Macmillan Canada
Toronto
Maxwell Macmillan International
New York   Oxford   Singapore   Sydney

The author is grateful to the New York Foundation of the Arts for a grant in the early stages of this work. She would also like to acknowledge the encouragement and support of her colleagues at the Writers Room, in New York City, where the first draft of this novel was completed.

Charles Scribner's Sons
Macmillan Publishing Company
866 Third Avenue
New York, NY 10022

Maxwell Macmillan Canada, Inc.
1200 Eglinton Avenue East
Suite 200
Don Mills, Ontario M3C 3N1

Macmillan Publishing Company is part of the Maxwell Communication Group of Companies.

Library of Congress Cataloging-in-Publication Data
Bogin, Magda.
Natalya, God's messenger: a novel / Magda Bogin.
p. cm.
ISBN 0-684-19624-7
1. Jewish families—New York (N.Y.)—Fiction. 2. Palmists—New York (N.Y.)—Fiction. 3. Family—New York (N.Y.)—Fiction. 4. Aunts—New York (N.Y.)—Fiction. 5. Jews—New York (N.Y.)—Fiction. I. Title
PS3552.04394N3   1994
813'.54—dc20   94-4608

Book design by Richard Truscott / PIXEL PRESS

10 9 8 7 6 5 4 3 2 1

Printed in the United States of America

For my parents, Ruth and George Bogin, who got me started, and for the little Messenger, who helped me finish.

*

And with special gratitude to Elaine Markson, who made it possible, again and again.

Natalya,
God's
Messenger

We slip through our lives like water, says my aunt. What we know is a blur. But history does not repeat itself. Little by little, knowledge is passed on. Fish to fish, we press small morsels of the truth into each other's mouths as we swim past.

Is that all? I ask.

All? In the scheme of things, darling, it's a lot. In the scheme of things, the least understanding is a lot.

You have an advantage, darling, because you were foreseen. You know things that happened before you were conceived. But some day you'll have to learn what you already know by other means.

*

Ever since I can remember, I've known exactly what would happen next. Thanks to my Aunt Rita, life was a book I had already read from back to front. Like the triumph of good over evil or the essential wisdom of mankind, who I was, and who I would become, were a foregone conclusion. Still, that doesn't mean the things that happened didn't take me by surprise. They did.

So much so that for years I was too stunned to be the chronicler my aunt had always prophesied I would become.

When I finally began to write the story of her life, we both believed her prophecy had been fulfilled. But now that it's complete, neither of us is so sure. Is it her story or mine? Did she help me write it, or did I help her tell it?

Perhaps, in the end, it doesn't matter who did what. What counts is what remains. My aunt says nothing vanishes without a trace, and I believe her. How else could we read the hand we're dealt?

One

Natalya, God's Messenger, is my aunt. It was her lucky break right after the war. One Friday afternoon the summer of V-E Day rumors began to fly, and no sooner had paychecks been handed out at the Universal Tool & Die Co. at the corner of West Fourth Street and Sixth Avenue, than she and the other girls who worked as turret lathe machinists got the news: the boys are coming home and veterans are going to have priority; you girls better look for something else. It was the end of June, and the war in the Pacific was still on, but the first soldiers from the European theater had already been sent home. For women like my aunt, the handwriting was on the wall.

On her way to the subway my aunt stopped to buy a copy of the *Daily Mirror.* She flipped to the help wanteds, but before she could focus on the listings for machinists her eye stopped short: "Natalya, God's Messenger, retiring. Established palm-reading practice for sale. Two hundred dollars. No experience necessary." Destiny's own sturdy arms, as she would later put it, propelled her across town, and ten minutes later she was standing at the corner of East Seventh Street and Second Avenue from where, looking east on Seventh, she could see the palm-shaped sign halfway down the block.

"I saw your ad," she said when the door to the tiny store was opened by a stooped, beturbaned woman with the bluest eyes my

3

aunt had ever seen; and sure enough the original Natalya, a Ukrainian reader adviser, was packing up her tarot cards and heading south after a lifetime of reading the outstretched palms of the weary immigrants who worked nearby and the wealthy matrons who came to see her from uptown. "You'll make a lot of money and meet many interesting people," she told my aunt, who, after a brief negotiation, wrote out a check in the amount of $140, her entire savings, for a sequined turban, a fake ruby with adhesive backing for the middle of her forehead, a crystal ball, two framed pictures of the Bay of Naples, a fringed red lamp, a folding table with four matching chairs, and a blue damask tablecloth.

"Sit down, darling. I'll tell you everything you need to know."

While Natalya was sweeping up, pressing her broom around the tiny store like a cat meticulously licking itself clean, she distilled her vast chiromantic knowledge into a fifteen-minute course for her successor. My Aunt Rita didn't know a life line from a crack in the sidewalk or the Plains of Mars from the Steppes of Central Asia, but by the time Natalya had finished sweeping, she knew that the left hand was the slate you had been born with and the right what life had written on it. She knew that a thumb could tell you more about a person than a little finger, and that the rarest hand, the elegantly tapered philosophical hand so prized in Europe, had never been seen in the United States. "And remember, darling, always feel the pulse before you start," Natalya said. "The pulse will tell you if they're going to believe the rest of what you say. If it's fast they will. If it's slow they won't. It's the middle ones you have to watch for: they expect to hear something interesting."

Natalya showed my aunt how to wrap the turban tight enough so it would stay, how to center the adhesive ruby exactly an inch above her eyebrows, and how to gaze into the crystal ball without losing sight of the front door, because you never knew who might walk in. It was almost dark by the time Natalya had packed her bags and tied her flowered scarf around her chin, and it had begun to drizzle. "You'll be fine," she told my aunt, tugging on the light string in the middle of the room, and by then Rita knew enough to suffer only mild stage fright when a customer walked in just as Natalya, God's Messenger, was walking out. Staring through the crystal ball as the man took off his coat, she saw Natalya waving at her through the plate glass window. She looked up at the customer and back into the crystal ball but by then the old Natalya was gone.

*

Her first customer was wearing a baggy suit and a slightly wet pearl-gray fedora. He had shut his black umbrella and was nervously twisting its tip into the floor. His bushy eyebrows reminded Rita of her father, but her father would never have appeared in public with a fine gold chain around his neck, from which hung the letters of a name: Sylvia. "You read palms?" he asked. She nodded, unsure how a palm-reader should speak. "How much?" She held up all the fingers of her right hand. "Fifty cents?" the man asked, his eyebrows shooting skyward. "That's pretty steep. Could you make it a quarter?"

My aunt nodded all right and motioned him to take the empty chair on the other side of the small table. She cupped her hand over the crystal ball and circled it three times as Natalya had told her to before a reading. "Your palm," she said in what she hoped might sound like faintly accented English, pointing at the man's right sleeve. From across the blue damask tablecloth a hand appeared before her. She reached out and turned it so the palm was facing up, deftly sliding her right hand down his wrist and holding it there as she scanned his palm with the fingers of her left, just as Natalya had said she should. For a fleeting moment she felt like the blind girl in Charlie Chaplin's *City Lights.*

"How's my life line?" the man asked. "Tell me the unvarnished truth. I gotta know." His pulse was racing.

My Aunt Rita stroked the man's fleshy hand, which was sectioned into little pads like the quilt on her parents' bed. His life line loped around through the center of it and disappeared in the cushy hill below his thumb. Remember the pulse, she heard herself think as she drew in her breath. "Long," she said, with a suitable sigh.

"How long?"

"Seventy-five. Maybe eighty."

The man smiled. "Really? Hey, that's swell. Listen, let me ask you something else. See any romance in there?"

The future would bring other, more genuine examples of clairvoyance; this one was born of sheer good will. "Romance?" my aunt replied. "I see marriage! I see a woman who can't wait to tie the knot."

The man beamed. "Hot dog," he said, standing up. "That's exactly what I needed to know." He reached in his pocket and drew out a dollar bill. "Keep the change, miss," he said. "I never been inside a joint like this before, but I guess there's a first time for everything."

As the man went out the door my aunt blew him a kiss he didn't see.

Suddenly she was exhausted. She had already put in a full day at the factory and here she was sitting in the middle of a store whose lease she had just acquired, with a turban on her head and her hand on a crystal ball. It was almost eight o'clock and if she didn't close up fast, another customer might walk in the door. She didn't want to push her luck. She jumped up from her chair, drew the spangly red curtains across the front of the store and, noticing the cardboard OPEN sign that was propped on the ledge facing the street, flipped it over to read CLOSED. Then she unwound the turban, carefully folding it and laying it on one of the shelves inside the tall oak cabinet in the back corner of the store, where she also placed the crystal ball in its special felt-lined box. As she bent to wipe the dust from the bottom shelf she noticed a thick brown book that was almost invisible in the dim light. She picked it up and carried it into the center of the room, beneath the naked bulb. It was *The Practice of Palmistry for Professional Purposes,* by the Count of St. Germain. So that was where the old Natalya had learned her tricks. She blew the dust off the cover and dropped the heavy volume into the leatherette tote in which she carried her oil-spattered turquoise jumpsuit back and forth from work.

Her hands were black with grime. When she went to wash them at the tiny sink in the back of the store she caught a glimpse of herself in the cracked mirror just above it on the peeling wall. She had forgotten to unstick the dimestore ruby, and her thick black hair, coated with oil as it always was at the end of each day at the factory despite the special cap she had to wear, was flat as a pancake. "A sight for sore eyes," she said aloud, smiling to herself as she wondered what her friends in the Party would say if they knew how she was going to be making her living from now on. On Monday morning she would stop by the factory and tell the foreman she had found another job. She wouldn't tell him where.

*

"It was the best of times, it was the worst of times . . ." she heard her father declaiming in his thick Yiddish accent as she stepped into the darkened foyer of the three-story house on Essex Street, in Forest Hills. She was just in time to catch the beginning of her parents' nightly ritual, an island of calm in the long days of a stormy marriage. Each evening after the dinner dishes had been washed and dried, Chaim, her gentle, book-loving carpenter father, read aloud to her irritable, irascible, illiterate mother, Gittel, who by the time I was old enough to read had become a tiny shadow of a grandmother who spent her final years staring out the window at the hydrant across the street, which she insisted was a poor unfortunate woman in a bright red dress hawking newspapers that nobody would buy. But while my grandfather was still alive, Gittel's evenings were filled with knowledge: the terrible knowledge of those years, which Chaim patiently and slowly transferred from the printed page into his wife's aging but still agile brain. During the week he read to her from the *Daily Forward,* but on Friday nights, in the name of a Sabbath which as atheists they scrupulously refused to honor, they paid joint homage to the classics of world literature.

"So what else is new?" Rita heard her mother interrupt as she threw the bolt on the front door. "The more things change the more they stay the same. Terrible, terrible . . . This Dickens—he was Jewish?" My Aunt Rita peeled her damp raincoat off and tiptoed past the living room into the lighted kitchen. She hadn't eaten dinner.

Her brother Abey the Baby, just back from liberated France, was sitting at the kitchen table with their moon-faced sister Esther, Esther's potbellied husband Maurice, and the Three Mosquitoes, Gittel's name for Esther and Maurice's three perpetually scrapping redheaded daughters, who were still up even though it was nearly ten o'clock and long past their bedtime. Esther, Maurice and Abey (later on in life and this account to become my father) were drinking beer and the Three Mosquitoes were sucking the life out of a jar of sourballs, carefully eyeing each other to make sure neither of the others got ahead. This too was a nightly ritual, and on almost any other evening but Tuesdays, when she had her Russian class, my aunt would have been sitting there among them instead of looking at them from the doorway. Chaim's unmarried sister Fay—Feigel in another life long past—had probably already gone to bed; she lived upstairs across the third-floor hall from Rita in her own small apartment, and led a solemn, mysterious life as a bookkeeper in an insurance company around the corner from Penn Station. She suffered from emphysema, which kept her awake at night, and generally retired early, as she put it, to get a head start on the arduous task of falling asleep. Fay too had been renamed by my grandmother, whose ripsaw tongue spared nothing in its path: she was the Lump, a dual reference to her potato-like appearance and the fact that Gittel considered Chaim's entire family to be beneath her. Their father's family were lumpen, she ceaselessly reminded Esther, Rita and Abey while they were growing up; it was written all over their faces, and on none more clearly than on slightly stupid Fay's.

Before my aunt could say anything the Three Mosquitoes were swarming around her. "Rita, Rita, Uncle Abey says you're going to lose your job!"

"Because from now on veterans get priority. And you're not a veteran!" crowed the littlest Mosquito, whose real name was June but whose name in the family, once again courtesy of my grandmother, was the Snake.

"We heard it on the news," little Brenda said. "They said all women welders and machinists are going to lose their jobs." At eleven Brenda was the oldest Mosquito. My grandmother called her the Bedbug, because she got under everybody's skin.

My aunt had already made up her mind not to tell a soul that she had just become Natalya, God's Messenger. It had been hard enough for the family to accept her left-wing politics, but that at least was rational, the logical conclusion to which any intelligent man or woman might be led after reading the paper every morning and trying to figure out what the *New York Times* had not found fit to print. Their daughter's Marxism, while unsettling, was something Chaim and Gittel could understand and even, in their way, respect. Fortune-telling, however, would run a swift chill down their upright spines, causing them to wonder whether Rita had lost her mind. And the mind, as Gittel never tired of repeating, was a Jewish girl's most precious treasure after her virginity. Especially after her virginity was lost, my aunt would silently reply.

Rita didn't answer the Three Mosquitoes. "I brought you something," she announced, bracing for the fight she knew would automatically ensue. From her navy pocketbook she drew three candy lipsticks she had bought on her lunch hour in Greenwich Village. True to form, the Bedbug, the Snake and the Slug, their sloe-eyed middle sister, immediately went to war over their booty, jockeying to see whose lipstick was thicker, whose longer, whose redder. While the little girls preened and pursed their cherry lips, the grown-ups tried to have a conversation.

Esther rose to light the stove. "We saved you some roast. You had a meeting?"

My aunt nodded, grateful for the perennial excuse of politics. Whenever she was late for dinner, the family assumed she had a meeting, unless she told them otherwise.

"Hell of a lot of meetings you've been having since I got back," Abey the Baby said.

"Didn't she tell you? She's on the Central Committee," Maurice cut in. He was Russian-born like the rest of them, but he never missed a chance to take a swipe at Rita's politics, which he considered unbecoming and potentially fatal in a people that had found safe haven in America only thanks to the compassion in capitalism's heart.

"Daddy says maybe now you'll get—" the Snake began.

"Be still, Junie," Esther cut her off. "Let Rita eat in peace."

"Married!" the Slug said in a stage whisper.

"To L-e-o," the Bedbug spelled in her smug way.

"Oh, that reminds me, Leo called," Esther said. "He said to tell you tomorrow's on. Same time, same place. You don't have to call him back."

Leo was my Aunt Rita's boyfriend. He and Rita had met at a benefit for Russian War Relief the day the Japanese attacked Pearl Harbor, and had been keeping company ever since. Leo had fought with the International Brigades in Spain and had been wounded in the leg at a place called Jarama, but although he walked with a slight limp he was one of the lucky ones, because most of his buddies had been blown to pieces on the same olive-covered hillside where Leo's kneecap had been shattered by a burst of shrapnel. Because of his politics and his limp he had been rejected by the Army and had spent the war years driving a taxi called La Pasionaria, a rolling monument to the Spanish Republic that was his home away from home. Leo practiced what he preached. He charged the rich and drove the poor for free, lived in a shabby rooming house off Central Park, cooked dinner on a hot plate and owned a single pair of worn brown shoes that he repaired himself. He loved holding forth from behind the wheel, delivering long speeches on the virtues of socialism while a pale-faced banker or businessman sat captive in the back. And when the spirit moved him, which was often, he would roll down the window, lean his head out and offer his front seat to a pedestrian in overalls or chinos while the passenger already in the cab clutched his leather attaché and shook his head in disbelief.

Every Saturday at three o'clock La Pasionaria pulled up along the curb at Fifty-third and Third with Leo at the wheel and waited for my aunt to emerge from the Lexington Avenue station of the IND. For the next few hours Rita rode in the front seat with a pair of castanets dangling in her face and portraits of Roosevelt, Marx and the real La Pasionaria, the fiery orator of Spain, staring at her from the dashboard, while Leo engaged his passengers in intense political discussion and collected enough fares to cover two standing-room tickets to that evening's concert in Carnegie Hall. Leo was crazy about classical music, especially the Russians Rachmaninoff and Moussorgsky (he had heard *Pictures at an Exhibition* sixteen times and still found it enthralling) and the Spaniard Granados, whose suite of Andalusian songs always made him cry; but they went no matter what was on the program. Afterward they ate at the Automat on Fifty-seventh Street, marveling at the transcendent skill of the cashiers who always dealt a perfect hand of twenty nickels for a dollar. At eleven-thirty Leo drove my Aunt Rita back across the bridge to Forest Hills, where they could feel Gittel's eagle eyes peering at them through the white organza curtains as they said goodbye.

Chaim and Gittel, although not impressed by Leo's occupation, felt he was a suitable match for Rita, since he shared what they referred to as their daughter's "outlook." They couldn't understand why there were still no signs of a formal engagement. But although Rita was charmed by Leo's curly black hair and gap-toothed smile, his generosity toward the working class and the way he would unconsciously begin to whistle *"Los Cuatro Generales"* whenever they got stuck in traffic, she had steadily resisted his attempts to place marriage on their amorous agenda. For the past two years she had been studying Russian at the Workers Forum, inspired by their mutual friend Vera, an older woman of allure and independence who had been the first to speak to her of Alexandra Kollontai and the other extraordinary women of the early years of the Revolution. Vera believed in free love, and so, after reading Kollontai, did Rita. She and Leo had had endless discussions on the so-called woman question and on the nature of the relationship between the sexes, with no resolution yet in sight. Marriage, Rita felt, was a bourgeois institution; she could see no point in enlightened people of her own generation chaining themselves to one of the last pillars holding capitalism aloft. Leo held that by definition the marriage of two comrades was exempt from the taint of prior systems; however, if Rita preferred, he was willing to call their marriage a union or an association. But my aunt would not be swayed; marriage by any other name was still a set of chains. "Free love or nothing," she would say whenever Leo broached the subject.

Unfortunately, the war had put a damper on her plans: men were few and far between, and she had dated no one else but Leo for the past four years. On the other hand, everybody knew that all the best men were at the front. In the back of her mind, much as she admired Leo, she was saving herself for the rush of new prospects she had no doubt would come clambering over the horizon as soon as the war was ended.

"Can we be your bridesmaids?" the Snake wanted to know.

"Jesus," Rita said. "How many times do I have to tell you Leo and I are only friends. I am not getting married."

"Then how're you going to live when they give your job away?"

"That's for your Aunt Rita to worry about. Now will the three of you please do us a big favor and go up to bed?" Maurice said. "Vamoose!"

"It's too hot to sleep. Anyway, we're not tired."

"Then pipe down and let the grown-ups talk."

"I hate to be the bearer of bad news," Abey began, "but it's true about women getting fired. We heard it on the radio. They're going to be filling every job they can with vets."

"Which is the least you can expect after everything those men did for their country," Esther interrupted.

Rita was going to say something but decided against it. It wasn't worth it. Her sister always took everybody else's point of view instead of hers, no matter what the subject. Besides, hadn't she already found another job? Wasn't she as foresighted as the next person, if not more so? Which of the other girls at Universal Tool & Die could possibly have taken their boss's warning so to heart? Who else but she was now Natalya, God's Messenger? It might be crazy, but it was a job, and from what the old Natalya had told her it might even pay more than her present one.

Just as Rita put her fork down they heard Chaim's husky voice round the bend of his last paragraph. Then there was the thud of the heavy leather book being shut, and a moment later the two old people shuffled into the kitchen. They were already in their long European nightgowns, the sight of which invariably sent the Three Mosquitoes into peals of laughter.

"How was your meeting?" Gittel asked my aunt.

"Fine."

Chaim poured himself and Gittel a cup of tea and sat down at the table. "Leo called," he said, sipping his tea through a lump of sugar.

"So I heard."

"Date tomorrow?" her father asked.

"I can't," she said. "I have to work on a report."

"A report?"

"Yes, a report."

"Imagine that," said Maurice. "A report so important that she can't see Leo. If you ask me, she's definitely on the Central Committee."

Who's asking you, Rita said to herself. If they only knew that by Monday she had to memorize the fourteen intersecting lines of the hand and learn the order of the mounts. If they had only heard of the Count of St. Germain, the Albert Einstein of the palm. Not only would she not have time to go out with Leo, she wouldn't be able to tell him why. Neither he nor any of their friends in the Party, except perhaps for Vera, would understand. How could they, when it was hard enough for her to understand what had possessed her to follow up Natalya's ad? For a while at least she would have to keep her new profession to herself.

Two

By the time I was born in 1953, Rita was an old hand at reading palms, and almost the entire family took for granted that that was what she did. She had already predicted the exact hour of my birth, was positive that I would be a girl and advised my parents to choose a name that began with M because, she said, I would be cursed with a turbulent intelligence and would need to have my feet kept on the ground by any and all means available. My parents had hoped to name me Ellen after a childhood playmate of my mother's, but when Rita explained how unsettling it would be for me to have a name that began with E, a letter forever on its side, they were persuaded to change their plans. But that's jumping ahead, because the summer my aunt took over the palm-reading practice on East Seventh Street, I wasn't even a gleam in my father's eye (although my mother, squinting through her telescope at Hunter College, is convinced she saw me as a glint in the night sky).

The night she answered Natalya's ad, my aunt dreamt she had been called to Russia to deliver a message on behalf of all the riveters and machinists in America. The sky over Moscow was a brilliant blue and she was standing on a platform overlooking a crowd of tens of thousands of Soviet workers who had come to hear her. "Comrades," she called out over the sea of faces, and her words, simultaneously translated into Russian, belled out larger than life from the huge loudspeakers on either side of the enormous square. She had wanted to speak words of hope and promise, but in the dream it was 1941 again and she could hear the boots of Nazi soldiers pounding the flatlands outside Moscow like a drum. She backed away from the mike and ran toward the wooden stairs at the edge of the platform, trying to escape, but someone pulled her back and she was forced to continue with her speech. What could she tell them? "We have no way of knowing what the future holds," she said into the mike, terror-struck. "Every age is a creature of its own imagination." The crowd burst into a frenzy of rage and disappointment and the next thing she knew she was crouched in a dark forest, waiting to be hidden in some sort of hut by people who could speak her language. In the dream it wasn't clear what her language was. When she woke up it was a sticky Saturday morning in July. The air was gray and heavy and she could hear her Aunt Fay's labored breathing in the room across the hall.

My Aunt Rita has never been an ambitious person in the ordinary sense of the word, but she's always set high standards for herself. That doesn't mean she has no flaws—to this day she can't boil an egg, and her inability to read a train schedule is a story in itself—but when she decides to do something she does it well. If she had stopped to think about it, she might have wondered how a reasonably educated woman like herself, with a thorough understanding of class struggle and the evolution of the human race, could have suddenly immersed herself in a pseudoscience that had been categorically discredited centuries before. Fortunately for all of us, my aunt has always had this strength: she doesn't look before she leaps. She leaps, and then she looks. That's the way she's always done things. So it was only natural that the day after she took over the storefront on East Seventh Street and saw herself in the mirror with a turban on her head and a dimestore ruby on her forehead she should be curled up on the bed in the stuffy little third-floor room of her parents' house in Forest Hills, doing her utmost to acquire the rudiments of her new trade.

She spent that whole weekend poring over *The Practice of Palmistry for Professional Purposes,* going downstairs only for meals, whose imminence was announced at regular intervals by the delicious odors wafting up the stairs that separated her and Fay's floor of the house from everybody else, and by the almost nonstop screams of the Three Mosquitoes, who slid up and down the banisters like chimpanzees or banshees, shouting out the names of the dishes being readied by the Witch (as they had vengefully renamed their grandmother) and Esther, the only other woman Gittel allowed across the threshold of her kitchen.

It was not the first time my aunt had studied while her sister cooked.

All her life Gittel treated her two daughters like two halves of the same coin: herself. "I have two precious treasures," she had told the principal at P.S. 4 through an interpreter when she enrolled Esther in third grade less than a month after the *Mauretania* sailed into New York harbor: "Esther is my body, and Rita my soul." The principal, a ruddy church deacon from northern Maine, rolled his eyes at the interpreter, but it was true that Esther at nine had already acquired the same doughy shape as her mother and that Rita, a babe in arms who had learned to walk on the voyage to America ("She's maybe the Messiah," Gittel had told the astonished captain; "she walks on water . . ."), already showed the same lively intellect that had won Gittel a place in the girls' academy of Shtebsk until the rector realized she was Jewish, and which eventually put such an edge on Gittel's tongue.

Still, my aunt reflected as the aromas rising from the kitchen grew more irresistible by the hour, she had always been the apple of her mother's eye. If Gittel had refused to let her cook, walking her firmly to the door whenever she wandered into the kitchen to see what her big sister was concocting, it was because she expected greater things than *kreplach* and potato *latkes* from her younger daughter.

"This one," she would say when Rita came home from school bearing this prize or that, "can read anything."

"Within reason," my aunt said aloud, looking down at *The Practice of Palmistry for Professional Purposes* and pushing her reading glasses up her nose; because at the rate she was going it seemed highly unlikely that she would ever get her bearings in the chiromantic world. There were so many lines, so many ways they could etch themselves into the surface of the hand. In chart after chart the crucial furrows intersected in a thousand undecipherable forms. How could she be sure that a strong diagonal was a line of fate slightly awry and not a twisted line of liver? When was a fork in a line a star, and when a branch; when was it just a sharp bend in the same old path? Which lines should she look at first? Which ones counted— which ones didn't? As she studied her own hands, she noticed that her left palm was more deeply creviced than her right. Was that because she was left-handed?

If only she had thought to ask the old Natalya for her address in Key Biscayne. Now there was no one she could turn to for advice.

She wondered if she was the first Jewish palm-reader in New York City. Or ever. A ghostly echo of the Ten Commandments swept through her unbelieving mind: no graven images. Was reading palms, graven as they were with life's own scribbles, a way of cheating God? Then why the name God's Messenger? One thing was clear: no gypsy fortune-teller would give her the time of day if she came in with all her questions. She needed human hands to practice on, but whose? All Friday night and Saturday she racked her brains in vain.

Not till Sunday morning did she think of Leo, whose hands she had held through innumerable concerts and political rallies and who would certainly be willing to oblige. Kind, dependable Leo, whose quick, reassuring hands would raise an umbrella high over her head when it was raining or catch her when they did the tango at this benefit or that (despite his limp he was a first-rate dancer and refused to partner anybody else, even though my aunt tripped her way through all the latest steps); whose broad, calloused hands were warm as chestnuts on a winter night; whose powerful hands lay as lightly on the steering wheel of La Pasionaria as they rode on my Aunt Rita's body in the dark—but of course: Leo was the perfect solution to her problem.

My aunt sat up in bed. There was still time to reach him. She would arrange to meet him at the Eclair, on West Seventy-second Street, where he had breakfast every Sunday with his mother; or, if he preferred, somewhere in the Village later in the day. Or at his room just off the park on Sixty-eighth Street, which would be filled this summer day with the scent of fresh leaves up the block; except that when they went there it was always to make love, and today it was his palms she wanted, nothing more. Naturally, she would have to tell him: "I've just become Natalya, God's Messenger, and I have until tomorrow morning to memorize the fourteen intersecting lines of the hand and learn the order of the mounts. I need your hands." Ah, there was the rub; because she would rather crawl into a hole and die than let Leo know, at least just yet, what in God's unmentionable name she had gotten herself into. So much for that idea.

She stayed in bed, puzzling over the palm prints of nineteenth-century actresses and statesmen that the Count of St. Germain had copied straight from nature and laughing aloud at his observations on such matters as "the seven attributes of true clairvoyance" and "the blind spot that confers a fatal dignity on every chiromant's pronouncements," until she could no longer resist the smell of fresh-baked bread rising from the kitchen.

Meanwhile, unbeknownst to my Aunt Rita, luck was just around the corner. Moments after one o'clock that afternoon, while the family gathered in the living room to hear Mayor Fiorello La Guardia read the comic strips aloud on the first day of a massive newspaper strike, inspiration arrived in all its glory: she would use the Three Mosquitoes.

After the dishes had been cleared away and the much-loved mayor had bade goodbye to the children of Manhattan, Brooklyn, Queens, the Bronx and Staten Island, prodding them to do their homework and urging their mothers to be sure they ate enough fresh spinach, my aunt summoned the Snake, the Bedbug and the Slug to her third-floor room and held out a jar of sourballs.

While the little girls smacked their lips and compared the color of their tongues, she drew them into her secret plan. She wanted to crochet them each a pair of eyelet gloves for summer but she needed a pattern. Mere tracing wouldn't do the trick; the fit had to be exact. She took a stamp pad from her desk, spread a large sheet of paper on the floor, and had each of her nieces press her right hand first onto the jet-black cushion and then onto the sheet of paper. Delighted at the prospect of flaunting their new gloves at the Irish girls across the street, the Mosquitoes readily agreed to Rita's one condition: they must swear to keep the offer of the gloves a secret. Why? Simply because. Which was enough for the Bedbug, the Snake and the Slug, who adored their Aunt Rita and respected her authority. Unlike their vacillating mother, who changed her mind six times a day and rummaged in their drawers while the treasures of Jewish cookery were baking and bubbling away, Rita was a figure to be trusted: when she promised something she delivered, and if you told her a secret she would keep it. It was flattering to be entrusted with a secret in return, so they gave their solemn word, rubbed their palms with turpentine, and disappeared down the banisters before their prints were dry. Rita could hear them shrieking in the yard while she studied the inky road maps of their future.

Like her own, their life lines safely rounded the base of their thumbs, a sure sign they would each reach eighty. She imagined three ancient ladies still riding the banisters of Essex Street at breakneck speed, raising their white-gloved hands to wave at the ghost of their Aunt Rita as they passed. Then, with a pang, she noticed that the line of Fate on the Slug's small hand stopped abruptly at the line of Heart. She flipped to page 283: "persistent despondency caused by love troubles; will often culminate in insane morbidity." Could this really be what lay in store for bright-eyed Marilyn, the last one up in the morning and the slowest eater the family had ever seen? Of course not. It was all a farce, irresistible perhaps, but a farce nevertheless. The old Natalya had practically said as much: hadn't she admitted that she made it all up on the spot? You went by the pulse; the rest was history. Or lines. Exactly: lines you made up. Like an actress, you put on a good show. You cheered, cajoled, counseled or consoled; in short, did your utmost to give your customers their money's worth. That didn't sound so difficult. Still, just to be on the safe side, my aunt continued studying deep into the night.

On her own hand the line of Fate sailed straight up to the Mount of Saturn, ending in a star. "Will I really marry Leo?" she heard herself ask aloud under her breath, wondering as she did so how anyone in her right mind could possibly expect a book, least of all the dusty tome that lay before her, to answer such an unfathomable question. "When I was your age," Gittel frequently reminded her, "I was already married with three children. What are you waiting for?" My aunt knew perfectly well what she was waiting for, but she couldn't tell her mother: a man her whole body ached to be with, so that when he nuzzled toward her, as men are wont to do at any time of day or night, she wouldn't shut her eyes the way she did with Leo.

She looked up "stars" in the index of *The Practice of Palmistry.* She didn't want to believe that her middle niece was doomed to a life of heartache, but it was hard not to rejoice when she read that her own hand, with or without Leo, augured "a life of exceptional good luck."

*

On Monday morning she left the house as usual at seven forty-five to avoid suspicion. Watching her from the front stoop, Gittel would never guess that at the bottom of Rita's imitation pigskin tote lay a chiromantic classic by the Count of St. Germain, which her farsighted daughter had already read from end to tattered end.

All the way into Manhattan my aunt wrestled with her conscience. Should she call in sick, or should she go straight to Universal Tool & Die and tell them she had found another job? When she reached into her pocketbook and felt the keys to the storefront her heart gave a little leap. It was exhilarating to think that after all these years of waiting—for the war to end, for love to drop into her train pulled into the Lexington Avenue station, she stepped onto the platform with unexpected pride in her new job.

*

In the crush of people on their way to work, my aunt imagined going down to Universal Tool & Die. She knew that if she told the foreman she was quitting he'd expect her to return her uniform, a prospect which filled her with dismay. Because if Chaim, Gittel, Abey, Fay, Esther, Maurice and the Three Mosquitoes didn't see her turquoise jumpsuit hanging on the line, questions would rain down on her ad infinitum unless she could reassure them that her livelihood was still intact. Why pull the rug from under them? She walked the two blocks south on Lexington to Fifty-first, stopped at a phone booth to call in sick, and caught the downtown local to Astor Place. Later in the week she would phone again to say that she had found another job; she would promise to return the jumpsuit on her first day off.

When she emerged from the subway it was so hot she could feel her leg makeup trickling toward her heels, the penciled seam line turning to a rivulet of grease. "Hot enough to fry an egg on the sidewalk," said a bum leaning on a lamp post as she waited to cross the street. The clock in front of Wanamaker's, already warping through the heat, said twenty to nine, early enough for my aunt to stop at the corner of Third Avenue for a ten-cent glass of fresh-squeezed orange juice. Swiveling back and forth on the dark red leather stool, she wiped her calves with the cotton handkerchief Fay had brought her from a long ago once-in-a-lifetime trip to Montreal. ("Yours till Niagara Falls," the embroidered legend read, capping a diminutive blue version of the mighty cataract.) Then, leaning her elbows on the cool glass counter, my aunt absently

Half missionary, half performer, she was ready for her first week on the job.

*

My aunt's heart leapt again as she unlocked the door to the storefront, which was bathed in hot red light after a whole weekend without air. In the back of the store, standing before the small cracked mirror above the sink, she pressed the artificial ruby to her forehead and wrapped the sequined turban tight around her head. Emma Lazarus, here I come, she thought, feeling like the Statue of Liberty without her torch.

She lifted the crystal ball from its felt-lined box in the oak cabinet and placed it gently, almost reverently, on the blue damask tablecloth. Then she took a long, deep breath, walked toward the front of the store and flipped the cardboard sign around to OPEN. With a tug on the pulleys, the spangled curtains jumped to either side and the light from the street poured through the plate glass window. Break a leg, she whispered to herself, smoothing her turban and checking one last time to be sure the artificial ruby was perfectly centered an inch above her eyes.

No sooner had she sat down to wait than the door opened and a heavy-bodied woman in a flowered housedress crossed the threshold. "I never got the chance to ask your aunt about this little line right over here," the woman said before my Aunt Rita had a chance to catch her breath. "Maybe you can tell me." The woman introduced herself as Lucy, the superintendent of the building, and explained that she knew all about my aunt, and wasn't it nice to keep things in the family. Natalya had told her that a niece would be taking over the business, and she and José were sure they would have just as nice a relationship with Rita as they had had with

Natalya. "We'll miss her," Lucy said, "but I'm sure you'll carry on in her tradition."

My aunt was floored. She had thought she was prepared for her new role, but it had never crossed her mind that the preceding Natalya would saddle her with yet another false identity. What if people expected her to act Ukrainian? She wouldn't know where to begin. But then, being Rita, she decided to cross that bridge if and when she came to it; if worse came to worst, she would say she had grown up in a Jewish neighborhood in Queens and didn't know the Ukraine from a U-boat or a ukulele.

My aunt said she would be more than happy to look at Lucy's hand. "But don't expect me to be as good as Natalya," she said. "I'm not as experienced." Lucy told her not to worry, placed her hand face-up on the table and pointed to a small fork on her line of Fate.

"You never had this little line before?" my Aunt Rita asked solicitously. "That's right," Lucy replied. "It just popped out on me about a week ago. I would have asked your aunt, but when she told me she was moving to Florida I didn't have the heart."

My aunt was learning fast. She stroked the crystal ball three times and stared into it raptly, half hoping as she eyed the door that the real Natalya would suddenly appear like a fairy godmother to offer her a few last tips. She wrapped her right hand around Lucy's wrist and stroked her palm with the fingers of her left. The super's pulse was going a mile a minute. All that cramming over the weekend hadn't been in vain; neither had her revelations on the way to work. "Your line of Fate is long, which shows long life and fulfillment," she began, Joan of Arc, Emma Lazarus and Sarah Bernhardt all rolled into one. "This little branch doesn't cut across it, which could have meant bad luck, but extends it sideways into the Mount of the Sun, which shows a warm and extroverted personality." It wasn't perfect, but it was a start, and it seemed to do the trick. Lucy was beaming.

"What a relief," she said. "I was hoping it would be something like that. You're a nice girl. Just like your aunt. She told me you wanted to keep the name Natalya. Why not? It's all in the family. I wish you a lot of luck at this location."

"Thank you," my Aunt Rita said, wondering at which location she was supposed to have read palms before.

By noon she had had six customers not counting Lucy, including the middle-aged masseuse from the Tenth Street Baths, to whose delight she promised "a steady supply of fat old men," and the man with the gray fedora, who introduced himself as Al and brought along "one of the boys from the garage," a thin, hollow-cheeked mechanic named Francesco, in whose grease-blackened palm Rita read "a change of job in the near future," which made Francesco's face light up with pleasure while his companion's darkened in a scowl. She had made three dollars and was almost faint with hunger.

*

On her lunch break my aunt discovered the famous B & H Delicatessen, which served the best vegetarian chopped liver sandwiches in New York City, and the B & H discovered Rita, "a fruitcake dressed as a nut," as Jack, the counterman, described the girl in the blue dress to Nat and Manny in the kitchen when he gave her order. "What are you, some kind of gypsy?" Nat, newly arrived from Hungary, asked my aunt, emerging from the kitchen to slap down a bowl of ice-cold borscht with a slice of challah and contemplate the strange new customer. Rita looked surprised.

"He's just kidding, miss. You can wear whatever your little heart desires," Jack assured her. "It's a free country, ain't it?"

In her haste to close up shop my aunt had forgotten to remove her turban and unstick the artificial ruby. She was mortified, but she was also fast on her feet.

"You work around here?"

She nodded.

"Actress?"

She smiled, keeping her mouth too full of bread to carry on a conversation.

*

For the next few weeks Rita stuck to her routine. She left her house each weekday morning at seven forty-five, opened for business on the stroke of nine, and was home for dinner by six-thirty. Every evening she washed her turquoise jumpsuit and hung it out to dry in the backyard, and every morning she ironed it and carried it to work in her imitation pigskin tote. She told no one of her new profession, not even Leo. *The Practice of Palmistry* was relegated to the tall oak cabinet in the far corner of the store, exactly where Natalya had kept it. It was too heavy to carry back and forth to Forest Hills. Besides, business was booming, and for the moment my aunt felt she was managing just fine without the Count of St. Germain's encyclopedic treatise; Natalya's advice about the pulse and her own talent for improvisation were holding her in perfectly good stead. She knew that sooner or later she would have to tell her friends and family what she was doing for a living, but she had made up her mind to wait as long as possible.

At the end of July she was astonished to discover that she had earned a total of $317 after expenses, more than twice what she'd been making at the turret lathe. She could tell no one of her sudden fortune, which she piously deposited in her account at the Amalgamated Bank, but by August 1 she felt well heeled enough to walk into Saks Fifth Avenue and buy each of the Three Mosquitoes an exquisite pair of white lace gloves from Italy.

Three

For years it was a broken record. If Rita could see deep inside her crystal ball and halfway back to Russia, Gittel used to ask, how come she couldn't see what was right under her nose?

Namely Leo, a good man if there ever was one.

Not so fast, a voice whispers at my side. What do you think, you can squeeze a life like an accordion and beautiful music will come out?

She's right, of course, but what am I supposed to do? Bang the drum slowly—take a deep breath? Even now, after everything that's come to pass, my aunt sometimes forgets that the two of us have more in common than either one of us can tell. We both have a weakness for the future and a tendency to overlook the present in our haste to leave the past. We'd rather leap every hurdle in our path than cast a single backward glance.

Don't give away the store, my aunt insists.

As if this were a store, or an accordion, or anything but the simple story of her life. Trust me, I say. We'll take it one step at a time. What does she think—I was born yesterday? I know you can't roll out the inside of a carpet without first showing the rest.

After a whole month of carrying her turquoise coverall back and forth between Manhattan and Forest Hills and washing it out each night as she had for the two preceding years, it was becoming

increasingly difficult for my aunt to pretend that she was still re-
porting in each morning to her oil-spattering turret lathe in Greenwich Village. Instead of holding the accumulation of grease to a
minimum as it had before, her daily laundering had rendered the
unused garment suspiciously clean, and by early August she was
sure it was only a matter of days before Gittel waved the scrawny
finger of doubt in her direction. So on the radiant morning of August 6, instead of going straight to her storefront on the Lower
East Side, she headed down to Universal Tool & Die, where she returned her pine-scented uniform and cast a final backward glance at
the rows of girls in their protective caps, which were already slick
with oil half an hour into the morning shift.

She wondered what would happen to them all once final victory had been declared. Her friend Vera was convinced the revolution
was just around the corner, in large part due to the tens of thousands of women riveters, solderers and machinists, including Rita,
who were about to lose their jobs; this traumatic event, Vera opti-
mistically believed, would transform women, Negroes, Jews and
other disenfranchised groups into the vanguard of a new, revolutionary society. My aunt wasn't sure how women would react, but
she knew her friend was right about the facts: in July alone the U.S.
Employment Service had found jobs for 160,000 returning vets,
and the drums of Madison Avenue were right behind them, pounding out the message that a woman's place was in the home.

In place of the tool-wielding heroines of months before, the
ads showed women beatifically returning to their prewar roles.
"Square gives way to round," *Life* magazine joyfully proclaimed,
ushering in the new "womanly" look.

Ads for soap showed bell-shaped mothers bathing rosy babies
while the infants' fathers, still in uniform and haloed in light,
floated in the background; ads for power tools showed rugged men

sawing, hammering and plastering back together an America that had presumably fallen into disrepair while they were gone. In ad after ad, grateful wives watched from the sidelines, dreaming of postwar appliances the likes of which had never been seen before: featherweight vacuums in the season's new hues, avocado and puce; electric iceboxes; and, most amazing of all, a machine called the Laundromat, which could wash, rinse and dry a week's worth of laundry all by itself and even, according to the manufacturer, peel potatoes and double as an ice cream maker on the weekend.

Not to worry, Vera insisted. After World War I it had been different—women had returned to the fold like sheep—but this time they would not be taken in. They would not give up what they had fought so hard to win.

Besides, she said, it's all laid bare now; capitalism is an open book. When they need us they let us work for pay, but when they don't they send us back to cook and clean and make more babies so they have enough soldiers for the next war. If women worked, the country would produce too much and profits would drop; jobs would dry up overnight. It was a matter of months, at most a year, before women saw the light. After the terrible destruction of the war, hope was rising from the ashes. My aunt hadn't read the complicated pamphlets Vera had, but she hoped her friend was right.

*

Meanwhile, heading east on Eighth Street on the crosstown bus, she struggled with a more immediate dilemma: what to tell Chaim and Gittel she was doing for a living when they realized that her turquoise jumpsuit was no longer hanging on the line. In a family where jobs were scarce as hens' teeth and fear of persecution a hereditary curse, she knew she couldn't walk away from Universal Tool & Die without an explanation.

Esther, who seemed destined to spend her life staring out the kitchen window washing dishes, would doubtless be the first to notice, which meant that Gittel would not be far behind. A single word from Esther and the springs of anxiety would click into place in the steel trap of Gittel's mind. Chaim too would be undone by any change in their hard-won peace. My aunt had to invent a job that left no room for doubt.

Nearly thirty years after their arrival in America, her parents' dreams still rang with the shouts of saber-wielding Russian peasants slashing through the crowded marketplace of Shtebsk, where Gittel's mother and grandmother sold fresh bread and pastries and Chaim's father repaired boots. As children they had cowered beneath the stalls and seen old men beheaded and babies speared at their mothers' breasts. Despite the ocean that now lay between them and that distant past, the slightest creak of a floorboard in their house in Forest Hills sent them both into mortal terror. Age had only made their paranoia more acute. A Jew's joy is not without fright, Chaim repeated numbly at each toast or celebration, as if to warn his unsuspecting children of the hidden enemy that lurked behind the stage set of daily life. After all these years in the New World, America was not reality; it was a dream from which, with one false move, life might still cruelly wake them.

This was why Rita must not lose her job; she must not fall through the thin ice. Besides, the family depended on her paycheck. To say that Chaim and Maurice were partners in a business called Shtebsk Custom Cabinetry would be to misrepresent both the nature and the efficacy of their work: while Chaim dreamt of a better world and Maurice argued with prospective customers, the little money their carpentry brought in was barely enough to keep the Three Mosquitoes in shoes and dresses and the pantry stocked with the palatial amounts of honey and almonds Gittel needed for the stream of cakes and pastries that seemed to flow unbidden from the ghosts she had left behind in Shtebsk. Esther was up to her elbows in dishes and over her head with her three daughters and life in general, leaving only Rita, Fay and Abey the Baby, who had yet to find a job, to keep the household running.

Whatever she came up with, my aunt would have to give her parents a number where she could be reached during the day, "just in case." (In case there was a pogrom? she had asked one day when she was twelve, knowing it would make them jump.) This information Chaim would record in his indescribably cramped writing on a page of the small black book that never left his vest pocket, in which he had also inscribed the names and addresses of the two hundred and thirty-seven members of the Shtebsk Burial Society, whose solemn treasurer he was, an office that all too frequently required him to take his worn black jacket from the closet, fish the rolls of tissue paper from its sleeves and ride the subway to the farthest limits of the Bronx or Staten Island, where his graying friends were laid to rest.

As the bus neared Astor Place, Rita realized that she had no choice: like it or not, she would have to give Chaim and Gittel the number at the storefront. No one else but she would ever answer if they called. From there it was a hop, skip and jump to what she calls "the job I didn't have before I could read palms." Much as she hated the idea, she would tell them she had started work as a receptionist, a highly respectable position for someone who could fill a stenographer's pad in seconds and type eighty words a minute if she had to—a valedictorian, after all. But a receptionist where? And how to explain the informal way she would answer the phone, the lack of a company name? Finally, inspiration struck: she would say she was working for a professor on sabbatical who was writing a book.

This cover-up was so successful that years later, long after everybody in the family knew that Rita was a palm-reader and when Gittel, dressed like a gypsy with a turban of her own and a pair of Macy's curtain rings dangling from her ears, was taking tickets in the thriving storefront on East Seventh Street, the family continued to believe that for several years after the war Rita had helped a certain Professor Freundlich with a monumental treatise on the rise of the modern state, which only his untimely death at the age of forty-five had kept from publication. But as things turned out, the conversation that night at dinner was not about my aunt's new job, whose announcement would have to await a more propitious moment, but about the terrible new weapon that had been unleashed against Japan.

*

It was ten-thirty by the time she reached East Seventh Street that fateful Monday morning, and close to eleven before she was safely ensconced in her turban and had centered the adhesive ruby on her forehead. Inside the shiny crimson cloth, her hair was already clammy from the heat. My aunt remembers Lucy hosing down the sidewalk in her flowered shift, but to this day she cannot recall if she had any customers that morning, because the events of the remainder of the day were so tumultuous. She remembers looking down at the bone-white hand of Mrs. Harlan Bell III, an assiduous client of the previous Natalya, wondering what on earth to tell a middle-aged woman whose life line stopped abruptly at the age of fifty-two and whose pulse was almost catatonic, when Lucy burst into the store shortly after one o'clock almost speechless with the news: "It's over!"

Mrs. Harlan Bell patted her impeccable French knot and turned to face my aunt at the flowered housedress that seemed to fill the doorway. Rita knew immediately that Lucy was thinking of her son José Delgado, Jr., who was still in the Pacific and whose postcards of atolls and coral reefs were filled with words of false bravado that kept his parents awake at night.

Mrs. Harlan Bell did not appear to understand. "*What* is over?" she asked, her artfully plucked eyebrows rising to imitate the question on her lips.

Tripping over the words, Lucy repeated what she had just heard on the radio: that the United States had dropped a secret weapon on Japan and that the enemy was finished. "Finished," she said again for emphasis. No one knew yet what the bomb had done, but the first reports showed nothing left of a place called Hiroshima. If this didn't bring them to their knees what would, she asked excitedly.

*

Meanwhile, halfway around the earth, night had settled on the scarred remains of a city whose name was just beginning to make its way into the newsrooms of the world. In a single flash the atomic bomb, as it was called in the first dispatches to be filed, had turned the lush metropolis into a smoking plain. A hundred thousand dead lay rotting in the ashes, and an equal number of wounded were now walking, limping and crawling through the dark, too frightened to stay still and too dazed to know where they were going.

My aunt saw it all. A group of men who had been clearing a field when the bomb exploded groped their way through a stand of trees, no longer able to tell night from day: their eyes had melted straight out of their sockets. A woman whose infant daughter had been strapped to the back of her kimono sat before the ruins of her house, cradling the tiny body in her arms, stroking its bloody head and singing a lullaby about a tiny boat on a tiny lake, as if her house, her child and her mind were still intact.

Across the city, in one of the few hospitals left standing, a single doctor, the only member of his staff to have survived the blast, tended to the stream of wounded who managed to find their way to his beleaguered ward. He too wondered what had hit the city. But when people asked, he only sighed and repeated what they had already heard: that the Americans must have dropped a cluster of bombs that had somehow—perhaps because of the high winds, the doctor thought—spread like wildfire across the city.

In a few more hours, when the sun came up again, the survivors would be able to observe the full extent of the destruction. Of ninety thousand buildings, sixty-two thousand had been turned to ash; in the center of the city, only five modern buildings were still standing. Bridges and railroad cars had been crushed like so many bits of tin, telephone poles charred like roasting spits, and rocks and minerals turned to glass from the heat of the explosion. In time, other details would be noted: how the bomb had scorched the shadow of one building onto the flat roof of the building next to it; how the silhouette of a couple fleeing across a narrow footbridge had been projected on the wall of a house across the way; and how dozens of women had been branded for life with burns the shape of flowers, the pattern of their own kimonos seared into their flesh.

*

For a fraction of a second, three women in a tiny storefront on East Seventh Street in New York City froze in time: one, dust rag in hand, stood just inside the doorway in a beam of light in which particles of dust were delicately, aimlessly floating toward the ground; the other two sat face to face across a bright blue tablecloth on which the upturned palm of the tall, well-dressed one with the chiseled face and elegant chignon rested in the extended hand of the other, whose green eyes shone like a cat's beneath her sequined turban.

And then it happened. My aunt looked down at the palm before her on the table and for the first time in her five weeks as Natalya, she saw what she would see in thousands of hands for years to come: perfectly framed by the lines of Life, Fate and Heart, a vast triangle had opened up in the palm of Mrs. Harlan Bell III, into which my aunt appeared to have a limitless view. She saw the life and death of Mrs. Harlan Bell III and all the memories that would die with her in the spring of 1952 when cancer of the liver overtook her, and she saw as if she could touch them the sweeping forces that had made this woman who she was: her love for her mother, who had died of an overdose of ether in a Staten Island hospital during World War I, her fragile marriage to investment banker Harlan Bell III at the age of twenty-one to escape her father's gambling, the strange brother whose lifelong battle with insanity had consumed a substantial part of her inheritance, the dashed hopes of a career in opera that had made her one of the most sought-after patrons in New York City and the secret love for her son that would pursue her to the grave. But this was only the beginning, because the hand of Mrs. Harlan Bell III held more than her own life; it had become a translucent screen on which one set of images yielded to another and another and another. My aunt was spellbound. For a moment she even thought that she saw Leo leaning up against the stoop outside the storefront, but he was older and he had gray hair, and in the end she wasn't sure. Without realizing at first what she was doing, she began telling Mrs. Bell everything she saw, speaking faster and faster until her words were almost an indistinguishable hum. Suddenly Mrs. Bell looked up at her: "What do you mean nothing will ever be the same?"

Rita didn't realize she had spoken. "I see the end of one war and the beginning of another," she continued. "I see the holocaust in a time capsule. I see the monster Death divided into tiny dreams that fit a child's sleep. An age has begun . . . that marks the greatest divide in human history since Adam and Eve. Auschwitz belongs to the past, Hiroshima to the future. The knowledge of what we are will cling to us like a snake."

"It must be the heat," Lucy said in a stage whisper behind her hand, as if in confidence to Mrs. Harlan Bell III, whose British chauffeur, parked in front of the store at a safe distance from the gushing hydrant, patiently awaited the end of her twice yearly consultation.

"I see you have all Natalya's gift and more," the opera patron told my aunt, ignoring Lucy. "I hope you are mistaken, but I shall be eternally grateful to you if what you've said is true," she added, handing Rita a carefully folded bill and gliding out the door toward her waiting limousine.

Only after she was left holding a fifty-dollar bill and noticed the worried expression on Lucy's face did my aunt realize what had happened. "I'm all right," she said immediately. "It's just that . . ." and she broke off, unsure how to describe what she had just experienced. ". . . I've seen the future," she finished to herself. It was true that nothing would ever be the same, but it would be some time before she realized quite how much had changed.

*

The rush hour subway that sweltering Monday evening was packed with people of every size, shape and color, most of whom were fanning themselves with the afternoon papers, which oddly contained no word of the event that had just transformed the world. It was too hot to read, but it was worth the two cents cover price to have a newspaper for the trip home. Those lucky enough to get a seat stared straight ahead, their *Sun*s or *World*s or *PM*s moving at a steady, soporific pace, while those unfortunate enough to board above Canal Street pressed as close as they could to a spot directly beneath the wooden ceiling fans at either end of the car, thanks to which the trains, however crowded, were always several degrees cooler than the street above.

For most of New York's citizens it was a summer evening like any other, but for my aunt the ride back to Forest Hills was a journey deeper into the world she had entered that afternoon. As hand after sweaty hand reached for the leather straps that hung from the ceiling of the lurching train, a vast screen, perfectly framed by the lines of Life, Fate and Heart, opened on each outstretched palm, giving off a translucent glow that drew my Aunt Rita like a magnet. Images of every conceivable description flew toward her almost faster than she could decipher them: the wife of the black man to her left, dead in a New Orleans hotel fire two years earlier while he was stationed overseas, and the infant son he didn't know she'd left behind, who would one day, map in hand, scale the stoop of a tenement in Harlem to light the days of his old age with grandchildren; the extraordinary career of the young girl next to him, not yet twelve, who would make a brilliant debut as a solo violinist and go on to play the great concert halls of Europe but would renounce it all to marry a Belgian physicist with whom she would have one autistic and one normal child before dying of kidney failure at the age of thirty-four; the long life of the young Irish woman standing straight beneath the fan, who had arrived full of dreams before the war to take a job as a nursemaid on Park Avenue but had fallen hopelessly in love with her employer, a politician twenty years her senior who would never divorce his wife as he had promised, leaving her to die unmarried and near ninety a decade into the next century; the fertile womb of the olive-skinned woman sitting by the door, who was already the mother of five blue-eyed sons and would go on to bear two more, and whose aptitude for mathematics would remain a secret even to herself but would be passed down in the family as a recessive trait to surface in the final decade of the century in a great-granddaughter she would never know; and the smile that would light the face of the sad young man across from her, who had just been fired from his job as a packer in a Brooklyn brewery, when he learned that he had won the lottery years hence, enabling him to take his wife and their three children back to Puerto Rico, where they would spend the rest of their lives in a pink and yellow house with a sweeping view of the sea.

Then there were what my aunt would later come to call "loose" images, those that came rushing at her in no apparent order and which only with the greatest effort she was able to retrace to their palms of origin: the burning building collapsing like a house of cards that turned out to be from the hand of a dark-haired woman at the far end of the car, whose husband had died trying to pull his brother from the flames; or the astonishing paintings full of violins and moons that were the work of the mother, dead in Treblinka, of the thin young man beside the door, next to whom, a copy of the *Daily Worker* folded underneath his arm, stood an old man whose palm was just visible enough for my aunt to glimpse a boat pulling into New York harbor, and the elation on the face of that old man as a young boy catching sight of his bearded father, who was waving wildly from the pier.

Strangest of all were the filaments of light that shot across each outstretched hand, vanishing as soon as they appeared. In their brief wake, visible only for a second against the opaque canvas of each palm, were piles of grenades and bombs, a whole hidden cache of weapons lit like antlers caught in the headlights of a speeding car.

What had begun as an intriguing game had quickly become a nightmare my aunt could not control. The images came faster and faster, colliding and overlapping as they hurtled toward her from hand after hand. Finally, in a moment of despair and curiosity, she glanced down, discovering by sheer coincidence the shield that would protect her again and again in the years to come: her own palm, unlike those around her, was as empty as a field of freshly fallen snow.

*

She walked the final block from the subway as if it were a gangplank, wondering how on earth she would weather the coming assault on her new skill. In seconds she would be face to face with the flapping, never-stopping, endlessly upturned and shrugging palms of Gittel, Chaim, Esther, Maurice, Abey, Fay and the Three Mosquitoes, which centuries of fear and wit had powered with the hidden motor of gesticulation.

As she turned the key in the door, she braced herself for the inevitable. She raised her right palm to eye level, took a long deep breath and stepped inside. She knew the Three Mosquitoes were lying in wait. Sure enough, with a single whoop, they came careening down the banister, practically landing on her face, their red hair flying up like brooms. "The war's over!" they shouted in unison. "We just dropped the biggest bomb in history on Japan!"

"I know," my aunt replied. "Can I please get through?"

"But the war's over—don't you care?"

The Bedbug insisted on reciting the news exactly as they had just heard it on "Report to the Nation," and the Snake tugged at Rita's pocketbook, desperate for Chiclets she knew she wouldn't find. When the Slug blocked Rita's path to the stairs, my aunt knew she didn't stand a chance.

"What's the matter with your hand?" the Bedbug asked, pointing to the raised right palm which, like an object independent of its owner, was still floating in mid-air. But before my aunt could answer, a piercing shriek echoed through the house. "Thing!" Gittel shouted from the kitchen, addressing Chaim by her favorite epithet for him, her voice dripping with venom. "Can you walk or do I have to come and carry you?" Saved by the bell, my aunt thought to herself, as the Three Mosquitoes dashed into the dining room.

This nightly summons from wife to husband was the sign that great platters of food were at that very moment being conveyed from the kitchen to the dining room by compliant Esther, and that the scattered members of the family should converge from their far-flung quarters with the full force of their collective appetite. No one else had to be called by name. Nor did Rita have to glance into the living room to know that at this very moment her father would be slowly rising from his frayed plaid armchair, that he would then take a last sip from the glass of seltzer that never left his side and then, like the dreamer that he was, glide toward the enormous radio across the room and turn it off. Soon his gravelly voice would send a return greeting to his wife, which nightly crossed the house like the call of a bird across a lake: "I'm coming, Angel."

To my aunt's continuing dismay, Chaim's love for Gittel was as obstinate as Gittel's utter contempt for him. His wife's curses were of no avail: he was blindly in love with the twenty-year-old girl he had swept into his arms one moonlit night outside the Café Centrale in Shtebsk, and despite the intervening years and the separate beds that had made a gulf between their bodies, nothing Gittel said or did could convince him she was any different from the slender beauty into whose exquisite ear he had first whispered his love. Her jet-black hair had turned to snow when they crossed the Atlantic, her tinkling laugh to venom, but when he looked at her he saw the woman of his dreams. It was for Gittel he had played mazurkas and polkas every night on the violin that was his livelihood in Russia, and for her he played his heart out still, although none of his children ever heard him. Gittel had forced him to exchange his violin for a special practice instrument that made no sound. The old music gave her migraines, and even the scratching of the bow on the practice fiddle drove her half out of her mind.

"The maestro himself," she said as he shuffled into the dining room, his face wreathed in smiles and his bushy white eyebrows raised in half-moons that moved to an invisible song.

Dinner was marked by the usual mishaps—Fay nearly choking on the skin of a baked potato, the Three Mosquitoes knocking over the gravy and Esther tripping on a newly installed wire just as she was bearing out the roast, which had to be carefully rescued from the cracked remains of the platter Chaim's first employer had given him and Gittel on the anniversary of their arrival in America.

"A regular Pavlova you married," Gittel said to Maurice, inadvertently insulting her firstborn as she swept up the last fragments of white porcelain. My Aunt Rita bit her lip and tried to concentrate on her plate. After the longest, strangest day she could remember, she was exhausted.

"I said would you please pass the potatoes."

The voice, which was vaguely familiar, had a muffled tone, like a transatlantic phone call after its long trip across the ocean floor.

"Yoo-hoo . . ."

My aunt instinctively looked up. Esther waved triumphantly from the far side of the table, and the whole family began to laugh. To Rita's amazement and relief, the palm across from her was blank.

"What's the matter with Aunt Rita?" the Bedbug asked.

"She's probably tired," Esther replied, in a rare display of understanding.

"We would be honored to know what the Central Committee has to say about the latest developments in the Pacific," said Maurice, his mouth full of food. His voice was oilier than usual.

"How was work?" Gittel tried to change the subject.

"Fine," my aunt replied, chewing hard.

"Look at me, darling. I haven't seen you since this morning."

Just as my aunt looked up, her mother reached for a slice of bread; to Rita's astonishment, Gittel's palm was as empty as her own. Emboldened, she looked at the Three Mosquitoes, and then at Chaim. Eight palms as white and smooth as bars of Ivory soap.

"And since when does the Central Committee have no opinion on a major international event?" Maurice, true to form, had it in for her.

"Maurice," Esther pleaded.

"Rita doesn't feel well," the Slug chimed in, trying desperately to sound grown-up.

"Say what you will," Maurice continued, his forehead glistening with sweat, "it's a tribute to American ingenuity. The Japs may not know what hit them, but from now on they'll know a homer when they see one."

"How dare you!" my Aunt Rita said, jumping to her feet. "The United States has just committed one of the worst atrocities in history and you're treating it like a baseball game at Yankee Stadium."

"Ladies and gentlemen. . . . Miss Emma Goldman!" her sister's husband crooned, flinging his hands out to the sides. It was too late for my Aunt Rita to avert her eyes. She stood transfixed as the images streamed from her brother-in-law's palm: the face of the brilliant younger sister whose lifeless body he had pulled from the bloody cobblestones of Shtebsk; the passion for the sea and all living parts of it that would lead him year after year to walk alone along the beach at Coney Island with a bagful of fried clams in one hand and gulls pecking birdseed from the other; the Hungarian dance tunes that had accompanied his courtship of the once beautiful Esther; and, most surprising of all, the glow of a luminous intelligence that lay trapped within him like a coin he had swallowed years before, which would rise and fall on his garlic breath as long as he lived, forever opaque to all who knew him.

Once again my aunt felt the quicksand pull of fear that had gripped her on the subway when images began to hurtle at her uncontrolled. Once again she saw the filaments of light, and the rows of guns and bombs. Then she remembered. A single glance at her own hand and the phosphorescent screen on her brother-in-law's palm flickered and went out.

"I said here's looking at you, kid," a voice insisted to her left. It was Abey the Baby, doing his best to boost his sister's spirits. When she raised her glass to his, she saw his palm was blank.

It made no sense at all.

*

A week after Hiroshima my aunt and Leo were heading south on Seventh Avenue in the evening rush hour. They were on their way to a concert of Red Army songs, and they had taken fares for the past hour. The passenger in the backseat was a young lawyer who had just returned from overseas, where he would have left his skin had it not been for a buddy standing practically on top of him who received a German hand grenade between the eyes on a hilltop near Rouen, thanks to which supreme sacrifice this recent graduate of Harvard Law had entered Paris on the liberating tanks of the GI's and won the heart of the glamorous French schoolgirl who was now his wife. La Pasionaria was stuck in traffic, and the lawyer was growing edgier by the minute. He was already late for his appointment with Françoise, who didn't speak a word of English and was waiting for him in the lobby of the Algonquin Hotel, where she was doubtless draped against the bar, batting her Parisian eyelashes at everyone in sight. The lawyer was enraged by the political decor of Leo's taxi. He took it as a personal affront that this dark-haired cabby with the fervent eyes and gap-toothed smile should display his Marxist trinkets so offhandedly, as if they were no different from the lacquered baby shoes and St. Christopher medallions that hung in all the other taxis of New York. As La Pasionaria inched forward with a clack of castanets, the lawyer clenched his teeth and thought about Françoise, but when Leo started whistling "*Los Cuatro Generales*," he lost control.

"Why don't you go back to Russia?" he snapped.

"Because I'm an American," Leo replied.

"Not in my book you're not!" the young man shouted, leaning forward. "Where were you when I was busting my ass for this country?"

"Listen," Leo said, his temper rising, his voice measured. "While you were still in high school I was over in Spain trying to stop the fascists before they came to power. We were up on those hillsides practically starving while . . ."

My aunt was looking out the window at the stream of people pouring toward the square from every side street. Loose images hurtled at her from all directions, as they had ever since she looked down into the slender hand of Mrs. Harlan Bell III the week before; but tonight a new anxiety had joined the mix of curiosity and fear that had accompanied her from that extraordinary moment. What if Leo detected some change in her expression? What if he asked about her job? Worst of all, what if she accidentally caught a glimpse of his right hand? Then she remembered. A single, gentle tilt of her own palm, held before her like a medieval mirror, and nothing of this world could reach her eyes.

"If our government had understood what was at stake," Leo was saying patiently, "you and all your buddies might not have had to go to war." And he began to explain how thousands of men and women from all over the world had made their way to Spain in 1936 to help the Spanish people resist Francisco Franco's coup, and that among the hundreds of thousands who had fallen on the fields and hillsides of Castile and Aragon lay the bodies of French, German, Russian, Polish, English, Yugoslav, Italian, American and Latin American volunteers who had fought Spain's fight because they knew it was their own. "You know why they called us premature antifascists? Because we were ahead of our time. No one else saw what was coming . . ."

Rita interrupted them just as the lawyer stuffed a hastily scribbled note into his pocket. La Pasionaria had rounded the bend of Forty-sixth Street, and the electric ribbon on the Times Building had just come into view, flashing the seven o'clock news.

"It's over!" she gasped, and the headline wrapped around again: "Official—Truman Announces Japanese Surrender!" As my aunt threw her arms around Leo's neck, pandemonium broke out around them. From every direction people poured onto Broadway or Seventh Avenue to read the headline for themselves. Strangers hugged each other and wiped the tears from each other's eyes. As if led by an invisible conductor, hundreds of cars began to honk their horns in what became a single chord of celebration, and no one gave a further thought to destinations. For those trapped in the bottleneck that Tuesday evening, it was a moment they would remember all their lives. Many later said they would have been content to contemplate those same five words for all eternity: "Official—Truman Announces Japanese Surrender!"

Had he not slammed the door so hard, neither Rita nor Leo would have noticed the abrupt departure of their passenger, who disappeared into the undulating New York heat, attaché case in hand and jacket flaring as he rushed to find his wife.

Leo smiled. "I wouldn't have taken the bastard's money anyway," he said.

*

Years later Rita would recall the rush of blood between her legs as if it had happened only yesterday. She was not the only woman in the world that August night in whom the euphoria of peace unleashed a sudden menstrual flow, but she was the only one to whom the blood spoke so directly. "Blood relative," she said under her breath, and she knew it was the clue she had been seeking. She had finally understood, and it was a warning. The hands that were opaque to her were linked by blood; the ones she could read were not. If she looked, Leo's hand, like her brother-in-law's, would be an open book.

Four

Predictions, predictions. It isn't easy being Rita's niece. Because of her, I know more about more people than I can keep track of, and more than I can tell about the shape of things to come. I was rocked in the cradle of her foresight and raised believing that the future was as present as the past; nothing that has happened since has convinced me otherwise. In fact, thanks to Rita's galloping clairvoyance, the future was so present in my childhood that the news I heard about in school and read in the paper all seemed to me like part of some vast déjà vu. It was, because in her sight everything converged.

Two years before any of my classmates, I knew that John Fitzgerald Kennedy, the handsome man with the Ipana smile who was our country's president, would be assassinated on November 22, 1963, and I knew (or thought I knew) how that event would affect the course of history for years to come. My aunt had seen it in the hand of Lucy's cousin, Filomena Cruz, who worked the night shift in a Brooklyn Chiclets factory, mixing brightly colored coatings while we slept. Rita didn't breathe a word to Filomena, but she announced it to the rest of us over Thanksgiving dinner in the fall of 1961.

We were seated around the old mahogany table that filled the dining room in Forest Hills almost to the edges. By then Gittel was too senile to cook but still spry enough to keep getting up from her chair and wandering into the kitchen to throw salt in the soup whenever Esther turned her back. Two of the Three Fates, née Three Mosquitoes, were there with their respective fiancés, and my Great-Aunt Fay, frail, blind and still wheezing her way toward eternity, had been sent home for the day from a nursing home in Riverdale that had whole floors filled with other souls similarly stranded between life and death. Chaim was long since gone. I was eight years old, and it was the first time I was allowed to stay in the room when my aunt began to display her legendary powers.

As always, the grown-ups were talking about politics. They talked about a bay of pigs and a man with the same name as the store where we had bought our new tweed sofa: Castro Convertible. They argued about whether Kennedy was good or bad, liberal or reactionary.

My father called him a toady for the CIA. My Uncle Maurice called my father scum. The Two Fates groaned. My grandmother stared through her cataracts and her confusion, puzzling over the final question of her life: whether she was still in Shtebsk dreaming of New York, or the other way around. My Aunt Esther told my Uncle Maurice to leave my father alone. "Abey's entitled to his own opinions," she said meekly. "He's also entitled to go back to Russia," said my Uncle Maurice, who believed John Fitzgerald Kennedy was the greatest president America had ever had or ever would have, even though, in Maurice's opinion, he was "soft on communism."

"I have news for you," my Aunt Rita interrupted. "Good or bad, if he wants to leave his mark on history, he'd better hurry up, because on November 22, 1963, he's going to be shot to death in Dallas."

Everybody gasped, and my Aunt Fay began to wheeze. "Ha,"

said my Uncle Maurice. "You make me laugh. Where'd you see it—in some old lady's palm? Ha! What you call palm-reading is nothing but glorified propaganda. Agit-crap. Ha, ha, ha."

Suddenly everyone fell silent. My Aunt Rita was staring straight at Maurice but she didn't seem to see him. "History is time's worldly twin," she said, "memory its scribe." Her voice was barely audible. "In the well of time, Kennedy will sink like a simple coin. His death will open a fatal door in our side. New feet will claim yesterday's boots, the better to trample the corpses of today. Look, it's cleaner than a coup. The country mourns, everybody blames the mad assassin and after that people crave only one thing: security. They'll get it all right, but at a price. Escalating fascism."

Fascism. I didn't know the meaning of the word, but I knew it was something bad.

My own shy mother, whose patient explanations of the world of planets and stars were the measure by which I gauged the worth of all new information, came to my rescue. "If Rita saw it in someone's hand," she said, "it's going to happen."

"That's right, Maurice," Fay said in her half-whisper of a voice, staring into the darkness that now accompanied her day and night. "Whatever Rita says comes true. Remember when she told us Stalin would die on a Thursday . . . ? Mahatma Gandhi would be assassinated . . . ? Your sister Edith would have twins . . . ? Remember how she predicted the sinking of the *Andrea Doria*? The invention of the polio vaccine . . . ? Forrestal's suicide . . . ? You can't argue with her, Maurice. She has powers." I was dumbstruck, but not until two years later, when the voice of a school principal crackled through the wall of the chilly gym where I and two hundred other little girls in bright blue uniforms were jumping up and down in homage to that very President's appetite for fitness and announced that John

Fitzgerald Kennedy was dead, did I become convinced. From that moment on, my faith in my aunt's proclamations was unswerving.

It was then, at ten, that I fell madly in love with my Aunt Rita and began spending all my weekends with her in the storefront. In order not to disturb the customers, I used to sit, legs dangling, reading comics on the toilet, with the bathroom door slightly ajar so I could hear everything they said. Sometimes the customers had to use the bathroom, and I would come out rubbing my eyes like a gypsy. "Is that your daughter?" they would ask my aunt. "My apprentice," she'd reply with an enigmatic smile and that slight accent she's always had.

But that's neither here nor there, at least not yet, because nobody becomes Natalya, God's Messenger, overnight. Rome wasn't built in a day, as my Aunt Rita says, and talent is meaningless without hard work. Back to square one.

No magic wand was waved over Rita's head to make the transformation complete; no one anointed her. Alone in astonished silence she slowly groped her way through the fall of 1945, mesmerized by the scenes she saw in her customers' hands and by the words that leapt from her mouth as if by magic: the same dream-charged language that still takes hold of her whenever she recounts her visions.

All that fall, as she leaned across the blue damask tablecloth and whispered in the ear of Lucy, Francesco or the waiters from the B & H, who had become assiduous customers, she found herself saying things she barely understood. "Even a shelled egg won't leap into your mouth," she told Francesco, whose face was the very image of despair. The phrase haunted her for weeks. By the time she finally realized what it meant it was too late: Francesco had quit his job at the garage and gone back to the Abruzzi in defeat.

With Nat it was a different matter. After their initial encounter at the B & H, my aunt had avoided the little hole-in-the-wall with the best borscht this side of the Mississippi, preferring to buy herself a sandwich on the way to work and eat it in the privacy of her own store. The fewer questions she was asked the better. But by early September she arrived at the decision that would shape her life on the East Side for all the years to come: rain or shine, she would wear her turban in the neighborhood, and she would lunch at the B & H—vegetarian chopped liver and a slice of challah in winter, cold borscht with sour cream and sorrel in summer.

"I don't know what possessed me," she says now, "but I had to take the plunge."

On her next trip to the B & H, she was dressed in full regalia, with the artificial ruby perfectly centered on her forehead. "I give up," Nat said after several days of evasive small talk. "You're either an actress playing a palm-reader or a palm-reader playing an actress." My aunt, extracting a promise of the utmost secrecy, finally admitted she had taken over the palm-reading practice down the block. "I'm not Ukrainian," she said, "and my name's not Natalya."

"What's my name—Stupid?" Nat said.

When she saw his impish face peering at her through the plate glass window three days later, she knew she had a customer for life. Nat rolled up his shirtsleeves and presented his right arm as if he expected to give blood. "I promise, you won't feel a thing," my Aunt Rita said, waving him toward the table. "Relax. All I need is your palm."

My aunt stared into the crystal ball and circled it three times with her left hand. Nat could not believe his eyes. From one second to the next, her face had grown luminous with a look of profound concentration he had never seen before in someone wide awake. She took his broad, milk-white hand, cupped it in her own as if it were a priceless object and drew it palm-up toward her face. "Small boats on a wide, wide river . . ." she began. "Heart and head, house and heart divided. Go back for your son." Nat jumped. He wanted to interrupt her, but her expression told him she was barely aware of his presence. The sentences tumbled out pell mell, past and present and future becoming a single thunder in his ear as she finished with the words, "You hold the thread. The minotaur is dead."

It made no difference that my aunt didn't understand. Nat did. He walked up Second Avenue to Fourteenth Street in a daze, withdrew all his savings from the bank and disappeared into the thin blue air, causing his wife to suffer a nervous breakdown and the police to put out an all-points bulletin for his return. Two weeks later he was back with a scraped-kneed nine-year-old named Sandor, the fruit of a prewar romance with an innkeeper's daughter half a day's ride up the Danube from his native city. The child's mother and grandparents had been deported to Auschwitz, and the boy had spent the war years in a chicken coop behind the inn, smothered in lies and protective straw by the farm girls who had once tended tables with his mother.

Later the same day, a recalcitrant José shuffled through the door. He had agreed to see my aunt only as a favor to his wife, but he was disgruntled all the same. When he wasn't fixing the plumbing or patching the boiler, he was immersed in the complete works of Bolívar and Martí, which he had brought from Puerto Rico, and the idea of anybody reading anything but print filled him with suspicion.

"When is my country going to win its independence?" he asked in a gruff voice before he had finished sitting down. My Aunt Rita stared at the vast azure sky and swaying palm trees that had opened in the triangle that lay between the lines of Life, Fate and Heart on José's hand. She saw the sun come up over San Juan harbor and three tiny children running barefoot on the water's edge, followed by three more, then three again. She counted twenty-one sunsets, each more dazzling than the one before, and then the screen went blank. "Each sun a day, each week a generation," she said, halting over the strange words. José looked as blank as my aunt felt. "I wish I knew," she said, apologetically. "But I think the first part is about your son."

When José Delgado, Jr., appeared at the door exactly three weeks later with the glow of youth on his cheeks and none the worse for his stint in the Pacific, Rita's reputation was assured. My aunt didn't only *see* the future, Lucy told whoever would listen, she brought it closer. José Delgado, Sr., still reading Martí, reluctantly agreed.

Soon she had more customers than she could handle. While the longest Indian summer on record bathed the brick and stone facades of Seventh Street in sepias and ochers that reminded them of the Old World, dozens of men and women stood on line to learn what awaited them in this one.

To this day my aunt gets grateful postcards from the son of Gabriel Markowitz, a retired postman whose family was in despair: for months the old man had sat by the window of his fifth-floor walk-up, refusing to eat and waiting for a letter from Colombia where, he explained, he had a pen pal, a retired army colonel who would certainly write soon. His wife, at the end of her rope and convinced that her husband had lost his wits as well as his voracious appetite, brought him to my aunt.

As soon as he sat down my aunt saw the pen pal in her crystal ball. He had white hair and was a military officer, she said, though she could not detect his rank, and he would write, though she could not say when. Mrs. Markowitz shook her head and led her husband home to wait.

Six months later an envelope arrived with the photograph of a wizened colonel and a painstakingly lettered note apologizing for the long delay: the colonel's wife had had a bad attack of asthma; his pension check had not arrived; they had been forced to sell their last possession, a fighting cock; a friend had lent him paper and stamps. Markowitz, redeemed, lived another fifteen years, dispatching endless letters to Colombia with return postage enclosed and enjoying his wife's cooking till the day he died. "You gave him hope," says the son's most recent card, postmarked somewhere in New Jersey, "and you were right."

Then there was the famous bookie, Harry Gross, whose visits were an open secret in the neighborhood, where his outstretched palm had been a familiar sight long before the day he placed it, diamond pinky ring and all, on my Aunt Rita's damask-covered table. She had no choice but to tell him the painful truth: that those who devour dreams are one day devoured in return, that he would be hounded from his home for feeding off the hopes of others, and that, although he would avoid arrest, he would drug himself into oblivion years later, thousands of miles from the Hudson.

And there were more: the bachelor coalman Eddie Carney, born and bred in the neighborhood, who came to ask if he would ever wed and left with such a detailed picture of his bride-to-be that he recognized her three years later as she was entering St. Patrick's Cathedral and rushed across Fifth Avenue to offer her his everlasting love, which she accepted; the French princess exiled to Mexico during the war, who brought her little girl to shop at Bonwit's and Bendel's and was amazed to hear that the child would one day turn her back on her aristocratic past to become one of Latin America's

great writers; the doleful waitress Blanche DelBianco, whose plat-
inum hair was wrapped into a netted bun that would successfully
ward off all signs of age until the day she was handed her last paycheck, when she would disappear from the face of the earth like a
species that had suddenly become extinct; and the widowed teacher
Erna Sullivan, who lived alone above the florist's down the block,
nursing several ailing cats as well as rumors she had never married,
and who returned again and again to hear my aunt describe an elderly
couple kissing in a nearby park, clasping her flat palms together till
they blushed.

Day after day, week after week, my aunt sat at her table while the
palms before her brimmed with life. In the bright stillness of the
storefront, her voice rose and fell, filling and emptying with the stories that tumbled out at her across the table.

"Not just stories," my aunt cuts in, indignant. "Facts. Don't
forget—from day one I saw the future. And not just JFK. I saw the
Beatles years in advance. People taking to the streets. The White
House changing hands too fast. My Lai. I even saw Watergate,
remember? I had customers wrapped practically around the block."

My aunt is in her diva mode, and who can blame her? After all,
there's no denying her success. Business had more than tripled since
the day the old Natalya pressed a shiny key into her hand and disappeared into the gentle summer rain. In the space of a few months,
the storefront on East Seventh Street had become a neighborhood
phenomenon. "We ain't seen nothing like it, then or since," the
eggman two doors down recalls, shaking his head.

But on Tuesday nights, no matter how many people were wait-
ing to see her, my aunt closed shop an hour early, walked across St.
Marks Place and on toward Vera's house in Greenwich Village.
"Come back tomorrow," she would tell the disappointed crowd on

the sidewalk as she vanished in a headlong rush toward the revolving doors of Wanamaker's department store at Astor Place, which welcomed her into the whirl of shoppers, and went straight to the ladies' powder room, where she unpeeled the dimestore ruby, unwrapped the sequined turban and brushed the daylight back into her shiny hair.

*

Vera's ground-floor apartment on a tiny side street tucked behind Sixth Avenue did not smell like New York. There was thyme growing on the windowsills and garlic hanging from the ceiling. There was wine: the full-bodied wine from southern France that was as close as she could get to the wine of her beloved Spain—"red like stained glass, like revolution," she would shout, raising her glass to salute the advent of a better world—which had spilled so many times on every surface of the apartment that its presence was everywhere, invisible and pungent, like the trace of a lost river.

And there was ink: the special tints that Vera used in her work designing monograms for the city's finer stores. Vera's apartment was her office, and her kitchen table doubled as a desk. It was strewn with scissors, brushes, pencils, pens, stencils, swatches, spools of silk and satin thread, catalogues of lingerie and linen and dozens of small jars with rubber stoppers, all of which she pushed aside whenever someone came to dinner.

On Tuesday nights she and my aunt talked about everything under the sun, especially the latest news, which was almost always terrible and in need of immediate repair, and the less urgent but equally interesting state of their own hearts, which clenched and unclenched day after day like fists or flowers, unpredictable and bold. They talked so much and so fast that there was barely time for a plate of soup and a slice of bread before it was time for my aunt to run to her Russian class just down the street.

But by the last week in September, less than a month after Japan's surrender had been signed and sealed, Rita was tempted to talk about something else. It wasn't her new powers, though she longed to tell her friend about the images that flew from people's palms like reels of film. Nor was it her need to meet a man toward whom she felt more romantically inclined than Leo; this Vera already knew. What was bothering my aunt on this particular Tuesday evening was the fact that so soon after Hiroshima—while people were buying up Victory Bonds and making down payments on cars and houses, and while *Time* and *Life* and all the other rosy distillations of eternal truth were toasting the dawn of the American Century (*Life*'s September cover girl, the "Anatomic Bomb," had been the country's first self-conscious wink at the new age)—the fact that, wedged in between the lines that shaped the lives of the men and women who came to have their palms read on East Seventh Street, my aunt was seeing tanks and submarines and bombs. Maybe Vera, who had studied politics in Paris and been a nurse in Spain, could explain what it all meant.

But the minute her friend's eager, energetic face appeared in the window, Rita changed her mind. She would have to keep her wits about her if she wanted to steer clear of those two endlessly expressive hands.

"*Bon soir,* darling," Vera greeted her in French, as if it were the most natural thing in the world. She threw open the round oak door, which led straight to her living room, motioned my aunt to the table and poured her a glass of blood-red wine.

Vera, people said, had performed Shakespeare in Bulgarian—or was it Czech?—before fleeing the Nazis. She never spoke about her past, but the hint of Danube in her voice and her taste for sausages and wine led everyone to think that she was born not far from Budapest or Bratislava. Whatever her origin, and whether or not she had ever appeared on stage, her theatrical manner, resonant voice and flamboyant taste in clothes had long ago convinced my aunt that her friend was born to act.

"Cheers, babe," Vera proclaimed, raising her glass in a mock toast. "Here's to your roving eye."

"Cheers!" my aunt replied, raising her glass to meet her friend's irreverent clink. So far, so good.

Vera looked beautiful in the warm light. Her ash-blond hair, escaping as usual from elusive combs, was almost honey-colored in the glow of the chandelier, and her round cheeks were flushed as pears.

"You think I only listen to the speeches?" Vera said, answering my aunt's unspoken question. Her face was mischief itself. "I was watching everyone in sight—and so were you. Don't tell me no. So was Leo. He's madly in love with you, poor boy."

The night before they had been seventeen thousand strong in a salute to Spanish refugees at Madison Square Garden, and Rita, Leo, Vera and several other friends had found themselves in a section of the bleachers filled with freshly returned vets. It was true my aunt had spent the evening looking over the new arrivals; she hadn't realized she was being watched.

"A success in every sense of the word," Vera continued unperturbed. "We raised a thousand bucks for Spain and you raised eyebrows . . ."

"I thought the point was not to mix," my Aunt Rita laughed. "I thought . . ."

"My God, how many times do I have to tell you?" Vera interrupted with a laugh. "What happens between women and men is exactly what happens between the masses and the ruling class. Throw off your chains, kid. Take a lover."

My aunt's eyebrows must have disappeared behind her bangs. "I'm not saying replace Leo," Vera quickly explained, getting up to light the stove. "You know I think the world of him. I'm saying *add*."

My aunt wished she had one-tenth of Vera's savoir faire. She had met several of the men in her friend's life, and they were an impressive group—a fiery-haired painter who spoke only of marriage; an architect with ink-blue fingertips who could not make up his mind; and a young book reviewer with print-hungry eyes, at whose cold-water flat Vera often spent the night. There were others, including an aging sociology professor to whom she was devoted, but Vera offered few details and scrupulously avoided introductions. "You wouldn't understand," she said whenever my aunt asked. "He's strange and ugly and bigger than a closet."

Vera, who found much to love in all these men but not enough in any one of them, did not practice monogamy. "Life is too short to spend it with one man," she warned my aunt. "Too short, too interesting and too important."

"Besides," she added quietly, "it's not a good idea to put all your eggs into one basket."

Ironically, it was Vera who had introduced her to Leo, whom she had met in Spain, whispering that he was "unlike anyone you've ever known." They had talked politics and art, gone to concerts and clubs, driven up and down the island of Manhattan and explored the city's parks. From the outset Leo had impressed her with his eloquent descriptions of history's long march toward freedom and his impassioned concern for the ordinary men and women of the city.

He gave her perfume on their second date and invited her to meet his mother at the Eclair the week after. Two weeks later he proposed.

"Isn't it a little soon?"

"Why?" he said. "I love you."

Four years had passed since then, and they had settled into a rhythm that had all the hallmarks of a wartime courtship: slow, solid and moving toward marriage as surely as a troopship gliding through the dark Atlantic. Which was exactly what my aunt found so unnerving. "His heart's in the right place—but there's no mystery," she told Vera not long after they met. Vera, who knew more than she let on, thought my aunt was being too judgmental. "You're wrong, darling," she said on more than one occasion. "There's more to him than meets the eye."

Rita could see for herself that Leo was handsome, at times devilishly so. She knew his heart beat as strongly for the world as it did for his own life. And he was good enough in bed, once he got going. But his arms hung stiffly at his side, prickly with swirls of curly hair in spring and summer, awkward beneath thick sleeves and padded jackets in winter and fall. And when he ate he made little sucking sounds that reminded her of her Aunt Fay. These things bothered her, though she was not sure why.

"I mean it," Vera said, setting down two bowls of lentil soup thick with homegrown thyme. "Take a lover. But while you're at it, take another look at Leo. He's not what you think."

During dinner they talked about the newest shadows on the landscape. There had been more arrests, and there were rumors that the House Committee on Un-American Activities was planning to subpoena Charlie Chaplin, whom John Rankin, the congressman from Mississippi, had recently referred to as "the seducer of white girls."

"What do you expect?" Vera asked rhetorically, turning from the stove to face my aunt.

"It's not what I expect, it's what I see," my aunt said silently, biting her tongue. No. Tonight was not the night to tell her friend about the visions that leapt toward her when she peered into her clients' hands or about the threads of light that flashed across them.

"It's all going according to plan," Vera continued. The victory over fascism, instead of freeing the world from war, had only whetted certain people's appetite for more.

Vera understood the larger forces behind this new development. Like manna from heaven, she said, the war had lifted the United States out of the Great Depression and catapulted it to a position unique in the history of the West. France and England had been bled white; Russia had suffered indescribable destruction. Alone of all the major combatants, the United States was physically and economically intact. Ergo, Vera said, this was Washington's big moment. "Why do you think they're in such a hurry?" she asked my aunt, rolling herself a cigarette. "Because it's now or never, yes? If we have another depression, America is finished as a first-class power. And if Russia gets back on its feet, socialism might start looking good to workers here. Washington will never let that happen."

My aunt nodded. Both she and Vera knew that government officials and leaders of industry had met as early as 1944 to ensure that wartime profits did not evaporate in peace. They had heard about the ingenious solution proposed by Charles E. Wilson, the head of General Motors, who would soon become the Secretary of Defense: a permanent war economy.

From now on, the American dream would be powered not by manufacturing quality goods, which lasted, but by weapons, which were obsolete before they reached production. For the first time in U.S. history, a civilian economy would run on the momentum of military might.

"It used to be you had to wait a while between wars," Vera said. "Now the generals are chain-smoking.

"The god of war and the god of money—it makes Zeus look like a broken toy," she added bitterly.

My aunt had never heard her talk like that. "I thought you were so optimistic."

"I was."

"And now?"

"Now I see peace going to the highest bidder—war." Vera rolled herself another cigarette. "You can't have a permanent wartime economy without a permanent war psychology," she said. "That's what they're selling."

According to Vera, the strategists were leaving nothing to chance. All summer long the papers had swelled with stories aimed at convincing Americans that Russia—our ally of the past few years—could invade at any moment. Editorials that in preceding weeks had praised the Russians for their courage were now calling them a threat to peace, and maps that once showed Allied troops advancing on the Nazis now hinted that the enemy was further east. And just to be on the safe side, the hunt against domestic "reds" was in full swing. The House Un-American Activities Committee, revitalized by postwar zeal, had been given a new mission. The Russians were not only coming, HUAC warned the country: they were already here, and some of them were native-born.

"So much for peace," Vera said, slapping the latest headlines on the table: FBI Seizes Six as Spies, Two in State Department; Spy Queen Tells All; Arrest of Six Reveals Reds Got U.S. Secrets.

"If only Roosevelt were alive," my aunt and Vera said in unison.

"You can say that again," a man's voice said emphatically from just outside the open window. It was Arthur, a young organizer who ran his father's dry cleaning store by day and spent every waking minute of his evenings and weekends working for the revolution. Paunchy and already slightly bald at twenty-five, he often stopped at Vera's on his way home from Party headquarters on Twelfth Street. Vera stood up to let him in.

My aunt took a deep breath. Now there were four hands to avoid instead of two.

"We've been talking about the hearings," Arthur said, as Vera poured him a glass of wine. The following morning, HUAC was scheduled to interrogate Ben Davis, a Negro and one of New York City's two Communist councilmen.

"Hard times," said Vera, who agreed that the timing of the hearings was designed to exact the greatest possible toll on the left in the upcoming elections, the first since the war's end. By subpoenaing Ben Davis, HUAC hoped to sabotage his chance of reelection.

"It's a trap," said Arthur, banging his fist on the table. "They're trying to tie up all our energy. We have to defend Ben, but we can't forget the larger struggle."

"Defending Ben *is* the larger struggle, darling," Vera said softly. "It's not just a Communist issue. Davis is a hero to a lot of people who aren't in the Party. Especially Negroes. What do *you* think?" she asked, turning to my aunt.

Suddenly Rita felt shy. Who was she to discuss politics with Vera and Arthur, who had spent years immersed in complicated books? My aunt's beliefs came from her heart, and political theory was as foreign to her as Bogotá or Belgium. She listened with one ear as they continued to talk.

Arthur agreed that it was critical to mobilize a broad campaign.

"The important thing," she heard Vera say emphatically, "is for the people to make an educated choice."

"Faced with imminent strikes by millions of highly organized workers . . ." Arthur was saying. "The Committee's role . . . witch hunt . . . a three-ring circus . . ." He spoke with his hands, like an orchestra conductor, and the more excited he became, the more passionate the discussion, the more he moved them. "The real problems of economic conversion . . ."

Suddenly, before she realized what had happened, my aunt was murmuring the words that flashed past her on the living screen of Arthur's palm, where dozens of men and women were gesturing wildly for help as they were carried out to sea. "It's coming," she said, her face white as a sheet. "The left as we know it is going to be destroyed, and there are going to be loud and quiet deaths for years to come."

"Are you all right?" Vera was bending over her, stroking her forehead.

Arthur handed her a glass of water. "Too much wine?" he asked, and my aunt nodded. Soon, but not today, not in front of Arthur, she would tell Vera about the images that flew from people's hands like reels of film. She would tell her that she had become Natalya, God's Messenger.

When the doorbell rang they all jumped to their feet.

"What are *you* doing here?" Leo asked with evident delight, throwing his coat over a chair. For the first time she could remember, my aunt had forgotten all about her Russian class.

Still shaken by what she had seen in Arthur's hand, she sat silent as the others talked.

"What we really have to do," said Leo, jumping into the discussion, "is get rid of HUAC."

"*That* will be the day," Vera replied.

"Why not?" said Arthur. "All we have to do is prove that it's illegal. Look at Wood and Rankin for Christ's sake. I'm talking about Georgia and Mississippi. There's still a poll tax for the general elections. Negroes still can't vote in the primaries. You call that free elections? In other words, these guys are bogus. According to the Constitution, they aren't anybody's representatives . . ."

"The real un-Americans," Vera said with a wry grin, "are Rankin and Wood."

"You can say that again," said Leo.

"That again." Vera was an imp.

It was nearly eleven o'clock. Leo offered to drive my aunt back to Forest Hills, but once they were outside she thanked him and said no.

Leo held out his hands. "You look a little wan," he said.

My aunt jumped back. "I'm fine," she said. "I just need some time to think."

"About what?"

"The future."

"Ours?" he asked nervously.

"No, silly. The world's."

Rita was growing more seductive by the week, and more intense. Her Russian cheekbones were becoming more pronounced and her eyes had a light in them he hadn't seen before. Leo was proud to be her steady beau. He walked her to the subway at West Fourth Street and let her go.

*

A few days later, just in time for Rita's twenty-seventh birthday, the first ballpoint pens went on sale at Gimbel's department store, and Leo stood on line to buy her one for the extravagant price of $12.50—more than he could make in two solid days behind the wheel, even if he charged all his customers full fare. That Saturday night he presented it to her over dinner at the Samovar, a popular Russian café. My aunt had no idea what to make of this latest postwar marvel, which was guaranteed, among other things, to write under water. Being neither a writer nor a swimmer, she entrusted it to Chaim, who rolled it back and forth on his cracked Italian blotter, pronounced it a vast improvement on the fountain pen he had used since 1925 and promised not to say a word to Leo.

But her birthday dinner brought another, far more lasting gift. Two months had passed since her first visions, and my aunt was still playing for time. It was hard to keep her new identity a secret. It was even harder to look Leo in the face. But how on earth could she tell him that she had become a neighborhood phenomenon, that people stood on line for hours to have her read their palms, that she had seen the most extraordinary things (sad and beautiful and terrible all thrown together)—in short, that there was a whole other world in which she was not Rita but Natalya, God's Messenger?

Perhaps she momentarily forgot to breathe; perhaps, as the waiters came and went with plates of borscht and blini, she gulped her food too fast. However it happened, my aunt suddenly realized that she could control the flow of images from people's hands. Breathing only through her mouth, and thereby shutting off her sense of smell, she also shut down the luminescent triangle between the musicians' lines of Life, Heart and Fate. This trick, a vast improvement on having to stare at her own palm, was the source of immediate, profound relief: from now on she could sit across from Leo (or for that matter, she thought slyly, anybody else) without accidentally seeing what lay hidden in his hand. By blinking twice, she turned the images back on.

"A penny for your thoughts . . ." The voice came from far away. My aunt shook herself back to the present.

"Well then . . ." Leo asked, "will you—?"

"I can't," my aunt replied. "I really can't."

"Maybe someday you'll see things my way." Leo sighed with a hopeful shrug.

*

Within the next few weeks New Yorkers were shaken by a spate of anti-Negro riots; Ben Davis, the first black ever to stay in a hotel in downtown Washington, D.C., turned the tables on his questioners by demanding that the House of Representatives investigate John Rankin; Louis Budenz, one of the senior editors of the *Daily Worker,* the official paper of the Communist Party, became a media hero overnight with his surprise defection to the Catholic Church; and, in the Bronx, the nine-year-old son of an Italian garbage collector saw the Virgin Mary in an empty lot. He had just seen *The Song of Bernadette,* a cinematic paean to St. Bernadette of Lourdes, but that did not keep hundreds of faithful from flocking to the holy site.

Events were moving quickly, but in what direction?

"You see those fancy houses over there?" Vera asked my aunt and Arthur on the last Sunday in October, as La Pasionaria drove north through Central Park. They were on their way to a concert to raise money for Ben Davis's campaign. Her hand was jabbing at the mansions on Fifth Avenue. "Workers built them with their sweat and blood. But do workers live there? No! When the revolution comes they will."

"How soon?" my Aunt Rita wanted to know.

"Soon," Vera said.

Arthur, quoting from Marx and Lenin, agreed. Capitalism was in its death throes, and fascism, vanquished in Europe and Asia, was giving its last gasps in the United States.

Rankin and Wood could rail all they wanted; the tide was turning, and they would go down in infamy while the people rose on the splendid foam.

My aunt, still seeing guns and tanks and bombs in every outstretched hand, wondered who was right.

*

Meanwhile, Leo took up the guitar and became more ardent in his efforts to wrest the yes of comradely love from Rita's lips. He imitated Woody Guthrie and Pete Seeger, throwing his head back and closing his eyes to sing "This Land Is Your Land" as a backwoods twang crept into his speech. He imitated Paul Robeson, thrusting the words of "Old Man River" from the depths of his soul like Moses delivering up the Ten Commandments. Alone in his room on Sixty-eighth Street, he played and crooned for hours, barely sleeping as he learned his way up and down the fingerboard of his guitar which, like Guthrie's, was still stenciled with the slogan "This Machine Kills Fascists."

By the end of November, armed with the simplest chord progressions, he was ready to attack. On the Saturday after Thanksgiving, when my aunt emerged from the subway at the corner of East Fifty-third Street, she knew she was in for a surprise. Peering from the window of La Pasionaria, his Spanish beret tipped rakishly over his dark curls, Leo was grinning from ear to ear. He looked so handsome that my aunt jumped back, convinced she was looking into the wrong car. Suddenly a voice floated out over Lexington Avenue, filling the air with operatic sound: *"Si me quie-res es-cri-bir . . ."* If you want to write me a letter . . . My aunt turned around, instinctively seeking the source from which such music could be pouring. *". . . ya sa-bes mi pa-ra-de-ro"* you know where to find me . . . Leo leaned on the horn and Rita jumped. Still singing, he motioned her into the car.

That day they rode no more. Leo hung out his off-duty sign and, with the guitar lovingly propped in the backseat, they headed up Third Avenue and through the park to the rooming house on Sixty-eighth Street. Rita loved the smell of Leo's building, a heady mix of wax and flowers that blossomed from the polished dark wood banisters and floated upward in a timeless scent. But today she was on guard. Breathe only through your mouth, she told herself as Leo turned the cut-glass doorknob and they surged into his room.

They threw their coats on the faded armchair by the door and Leo switched on a lamp and poured them both a glass of bourbon. Rita walked to the night table and struck a match to light the pale blue candle in the wine bottle that was already encrusted with multicolored drippings. The flame cast its glow over the poster above the bed, a portrait of the real La Pasionaria, the fiery miner's daughter whose rousing speeches had made her a symbol of the Spanish Republic, which Leo had smuggled back from Barcelona, and which his mother had lovingly ironed flat between two sheets when he returned from Spain. My aunt unclasped her belt. Leo took off his tie. She kicked off her shoes and loosed her imitation nylons. Leo unbuttoned his shirt and Rita unzipped her cranberry wool dress.

He lifted it over her head, unfastening her bra, and she fell laughing on the bed. Leo shed his remaining clothes. For the first time Rita could remember, she didn't close her eyes.

Leo reached for his guitar. Naked as a prince in the light of the candle, he sat at the far end of the bed and began to sing. "Last night I had the strangest dream . . . I'd never ha-a-d before. . . . I dreamt that all the world agreed . . . to put an e-end to war . . ." His voice was honey, bourbon, wild bees, a dazzling ribbon of sound that pushed her to the edge of the precipice into which she was already falling, falling. No one had ever sung like that. The voice kept on, surer and surer of its power, and when my aunt came to, Leo had put down the guitar and was gazing at her with the brand-new face of a man who has been born to love.

He moved toward her on the bed, arriving alongside her with the grace of a fish and cupping his hands around her breasts as if he were seeing them for the first time. "I love you," he murmured, swirling his tongue around first one nipple, then the other, then looking up into the flushed alabaster of her face, the Russian jet of her hair, the cat-green of her eyes, the picaresque contours of her mouth.

Propped against the pillow with Leo's palms around her breasts, my aunt couldn't keep from smiling at the thought that his future—and perhaps even her own—was, momentarily at least, less than arm's length away. Which was exactly where it would remain, she told herself, because work was work and play was play. There were certain things best left to fate. Even if he begged her, Leo's was the last hand she would read.

"Let's make music," she said.

And for the first time in all the years they had known each other, instead of the wilted turnip that invariably adorned the place between his legs whenever they climbed into bed, she saw a perfectly formed swan gliding serenely toward her on the stillness of the sheets. Her hand moved toward it, and Leo's body tilted to receive her embrace. Hours passed—or were they minutes—and in the end the swan became a clarinet that Rita held in both her hands, playing its invisible keys while her lips brought forth from Leo's soul a final note that pierced the golden air as her shrieks joined his.

"Now will you marry me?" he asked.

"I can't," my aunt replied, shutting her eyes. "I really can't."

"Even now?" Leo asked, pressing his lips ardently to hers.

"Even now," my aunt sighed.

Time was closing in. Soon, sooner perhaps than she had hoped, she would have to tell him. Choosing her words with utmost care, she would tell him that she had become Natalya, God's Messenger. She would explain that she could see things that were hidden— past, present and future all rolled into one—and she would describe the strange, moonlit filament that laced back and forth in people's palms, like a comet tracing its own path.

"Maybe someday you'll see things differently," Leo said, gazing at her in stunned disbelief.

"No," said my Aunt Rita, without opening her eyes.

*

The following Saturday night they rode to the top of the Empire State Building, which still bore the scars of the B-25 light bomber that had slammed into its side back in July. They looked across the East River to Queens where Rita's house—with Chaim, Gittel, Fay, Esther, Maurice, Abey the Baby and the Three Mosquitoes wedged inside it like a family of circus midgets—was a tiny glow on the horizon. In the chill December air, the city lights spread out below them like a net of fireflies, Leo put his arms around my aunt and drew her gently toward him. Maybe this was her big chance. They were alone on the windswept edge an hour before closing, and Leo had never looked more handsome. "There's something I have to tell you," my aunt said, but when their lips met she jumped back. Static from the observatory had settled on their cheeks and the kiss had shocked them. They laughed and walked toward the western side of the deck to look for the clock tower around the corner from Vera's house in Greenwich Village. What they saw instead would stay with both of them forever: on the frosted air, a fine red snow was rising into the night sky in what seemed like a special message just for them. It was the strange, legendary snow lovers sometimes see above Manhattan's highest buildings, the product of updrafts and city lights. The red snow of revolution, Leo thought, still hoping against hope, the magic snow of a man and woman newly pledged to love. But to my aunt it was a warning. Blood-red, she thought, like the blood that had gushed between her legs when final victory was declared. Once again she understood: if she looked, Leo's hand would be an open book.

*

Juanita and Pavel's third-floor studio on West Eleventh Street was hung with bright balloons, and the liquor was already flowing when Rita and Leo arrived at nine o'clock on New Year's Eve. The apartment was filled with paintings—both Pavel's abstractions, thick storms of gray stacked against the far end of the room, and Juanita's self-portraits, which were propped against the walls in a kind of improvised exhibit. The same elongated figure stood in each, yellow hair rising straight up from her head and flying off the canvas. "She's experimenting with the frame," Vera explained, sensing my aunt's and Leo's confusion and taking their coats. "You know, trying to find out where art leaves off and reality begins."

"Not where—*whether*," Juanita said with a smile, sailing by with a tray of canapés.

Leo shrugged and his eyes met Vera's. "She's not political," Vera whispered apologetically. "But she's sharp as a tack. And talented. You'll see. Anyway, her heart's in the right place."

"On the left, where it's supposed to be," said Leo.

Vera and my aunt indulged him with mock laughter. "Very funny," Vera said. "The last time I heard that line I was a student in Vienna."

It was a large party, and everyone they knew was there, along with a number of people they had never met, including their hosts. Loose images came flying at my aunt from every corner of the room, but by then she was an expert in keeping them at bay. Vera introduced them to Pavel, whom she knew from Prague, and disappeared into the bedroom with their coats. My aunt was wearing her cranberry wool dress and a matching shade of Winged Victory lipstick. "Bourbon?" Pavel asked, already pouring. He had the same bushy eyebrows as Chagall, the same short legs and baggy pants, and the same wiry halo of gray hair. They shook hands with Juanita, whose long gray dress made her look as tall as her paintings, and waved across the room at Arthur, whose round face was lit as usual with the flame of political passion. He was deep in conversation with Charles, a silver-haired dress manufacturer admired even by Vera for his deft command of social theory, and Charles's wife Ann, a one-time debutante who had joined the Party while she was at Vassar, back in 1921.

"How's my riveter?" Charles shouted from across the room. My Aunt Rita rolled her eyes.

"Riveting as ever," Leo called.

"Thanks," she whispered. "I needed that."

"It's true," he said. "You look like a million dollars in that dress."

"Capitalist roader," Vera said with a wink, appearing at their side. She raised her glass to toast their happiness.

When the doorbell rang again it was Harriet and Jane, two fresh-faced girls from Minnesota—the Milkmaids, Vera called them—who worked at a hat factory on Twenty-sixth Street, just off Madison Square Park. They had just gotten out of work, because their boss did not believe in holidays. They were younger than Ted, Vera's angular book critic, who was twenty-three, and everyone adored them for their beautiful farm faces, their faith in the perfectibility of humankind and for being from outside New York.

As the clock inched toward midnight, the bourbon flowed more freely and the laughter and conversation rose in volume.

Had anyone heard, someone was asking, whether Robeson had been called to Washington? Was it true he was writing his autobiography? Had HUAC's budget really been raised to $125,000 for 1946?

Was Perón a fascist? Would there really be a cure for polio? Could the Greek resistance win?

"I saw it in the *Times*," someone said.

"Saw what?"

"That's what you always say . . ."

". . . so the little guy leans out of the boat and says . . ."

"You call that a joke?"

"All right, all right . . . How about the one about the little old lady who was walking by a pet store . . . ?"

In the background, Leo was softly strumming his guitar. "Here's to 1946!" Arthur shouted, raising a bottle of Russian vodka courtesy of Charles. "Not so fast," someone said in a slightly tipsy voice. "We've still got an hour and a half to go."

My aunt looked at her watch. Time was definitely closing in. She had finally made up her mind not to let 1945 slip through her fingers without telling her friends about the momentous change that had come over her ever since the warm June night six months before when she had signed the lease to the storefront on East Seventh Street and left her machinist's job behind. She would tell them all about the old Natalya, she decided, and then, when they were sufficiently intrigued, she would tell them that the new Natalya, God's Messenger, was none other than . . . " Surprise," she would say, summoning up all her courage. They would be shocked, but at least it would be done, and she would no longer have to lead a double life; except, of course, with Chaim and Gittel.

"Why so pensive?" Vera whispered beside her. My aunt, butterflies in her stomach, nudged her toward the empty bedroom, where the double bed piled high with coats and scarves loomed like some prehistoric mammal.

As soon as they had closed the door behind them, my aunt began to cry.

Vera could not believe her ears. How could anyone, she wanted to know, let alone a beautiful young woman in a cranberry wool dress, be so upset on New Year's Eve? Especially the first peacetime New Year's Eve in years?

"Well?"

My aunt was silent. Vera pulled a tissue from her sleeve and handed it to her.

"You're getting married."

My aunt shook her head.

"You're pregnant."

Rita shook her head again.

"You lost your job."

The door shot open and they were momentarily stunned by the glare and roar of the party. It was Pavel, arms outstretched like a shelf, bearing a pile of new coats. "Excuse me," he said, catching sight of my aunt and Rita and vanishing, ceremoniously backward, as fast as he had come, closing the door behind him.

"You lost your job," Vera repeated.

My aunt nodded. "Yes and no," she began, still sniffling.

"Meaning?"

And out it tumbled, beginning with the day she had answered the ad in the *Daily Mirror* and had found herself face to face with the stooped, beturbaned woman with the bluest eyes she had ever seen, and how she had discovered *The Practice of Palmistry for Professional Purposes* lying on the bottom shelf of the tall oak cabinet in the back of the store, and Nat and Lucy, and Al from the garage, and Mrs. Sullivan from above the florist's down the street, and Mr. Markowitz from around the corner, and Blanche DelBianco, Eddie Carney, Mrs. Harlan Bell III and the guns and tanks and bombs she had seen in all the luminescent, outstretched palms at which she had recently been staring.

"You don't expect me to believe . . ." The color had drained from Vera's face.

"It's not what I expect—it's what I see. I don't expect anything . . ."

"Really, darling . . . This is a delightful joke—for the New Year, yes?"

My aunt shook her head.

"You want to read everybody's hands?"

My aunt nodded.

Within minutes, the guests were lining up . . . They were drunk enough to think my aunt's parlor trick highly entertaining, a charming prelude to their midnight glasses of champagne; and she was far too nervous to see that in their present state they could hardly be expected to grasp the spectacular importance of what she was about to reveal.

Pavel, as befitted a host, went first. He grinned broadly and turned toward the others like a matador before a fight. Then, bowing to my aunt with consummate gallantry, he held out his flat, paint-splattered hand, which looked oddly like a palette. "Charge," he said with a daredevil twinkle in his eyes.

Two minutes later he had assumed a more thoughtful pose.

My aunt, cradling his palm in hers, was speaking so softly that only Pavel and those standing close to him could hear. First like a lullaby, then like a train, the words swept him along—"yellow star . . ." "oranges in wartime . . ." "lace curtains . . ."—tugging at places he hadn't thought about in years and losing themselves in a whir of fragments that finally settled into a single statement he would not forget: "Whatever is torn away must be sewn, whatever is sewn must be worn. Hate, like love, can be reborn."

As so often happened in those early days, my aunt had no idea what she was saying. But she saw Pavel swaying to the rhythm of her words, which came faster and faster—"dark nights . . ." "lost days . . ."—until the images exhausted themselves and a strange, excited look appeared on his ashen face.

"Speaking of riveting," said Charles, and everybody clapped. Everyone but Vera, who was laughing into her cupped hands.

Arthur's hand still bore the puffiness of youth, and at first glance my aunt was sure that it was blank. Years of handing coats and trousers back and forth across the counter of his family's dry cleaners had all but erased the lines on his palms which, like a bear's, had the feel of recently washed velvet. But when she looked again, the triangle between his lines of Life, Fate and Heart was bright and vibrant, and images began to hurtle at her uncontrolled. She saw the years roll back to his father's childhood on Staten Island and his grandfather's farm in the Urals circa 1885, and then she saw them catapult into the future like a movie in fast-forward, with glimpses of Arthur at all ages—newborn, old, then very old, then younger again, until at last the dizzying blur slowed to a halt and time, at least for a moment, stood still. My aunt began to speak of a time in the future when hidden energies would be revealed like water deep inside the earth, and no one's talents would be wasted. "No birth will be more significant than any other," she said, "because every child will be welcomed in. A lifetime anywhere on earth will be a harvesting of talent. The world will ripen like a fruit." She said she saw the march of decades,   strange overlapping flow that resembled the wooden escalator steps at Macy's with year folding into year in an endless sleight of hand that made her wonder if they disappeared for good or came again like spokes on a wheel. Without realizing, she had been speaking faster and faster, but now she stopped, appalled.

"What's the matter?" Arthur interrupted.

"Nothing," my aunt lied, staring down at the image she had seen at Vera's house a few months earlier: dozens of men and women gesturing wildly for help as they were swept to sea while still others, numbering in the thousands, watched in silence from the shore.

"I see you with a beautiful woman," she said, and paused for effect. "In Madison Square Garden," she added with a grin, and everybody cheered.

"Hear, hear!" they yelled, raising their glasses.

To this day my aunt believes she had no other choice. "First of all," she says, "I couldn't bring myself to tell him. Secondly, what would I say? Don't forget: I was still a babe in the chiromantic woods. I had no idea what I was looking at."

After that, partly to distract herself from what she had just seen, she resolved to lend the evening a lighter tone, and she dispatched the palms of Ted, Charles, Ann, Juanita and the Milkmaids with quick prognostications of revolutionary fame and fortune.

Ted was assured a brilliant career that would rival that of the legendary Christopher Caulfield, winning him a place in the pantheon of Marxist critics; Charles and Ann were told that they would live to see the revolution; Juanita that her portraits of New York garment workers would one day rank among the great works of the age; and the two young milliners were promised long lives, happy marriages to comrades not yet of their acquaintance and adorable descendants who would never lack for bonnets or berets.

It was almost midnight and the liquor continued to flow. Finally it was her brother Abey's turn. "Surely you jest," he said, giving her an incredulous look, which she returned with a wink. The joke turned out to be on him: Rita knew his hand would be as white as the muffled streets outside. "There's nothing here," she announced gaily, and everybody laughed, although moments later they would all be toasting his good fortune.

"And last but not least . . ." Leo's curly head emerged from the crowd, his face alive with anticipation. His gap-toothed smile was so winning that for a moment my aunt was tempted to read the hand that was nearly as familiar as her own. But she knew better. Whatever secrets Leo's palm contained, no good, at least not yet, could come of knowing what it held.

"I can't," she said, flashing him as dazzling a smile as she could. "There's a special rule about . . ." She caught herself mid-sentence. "Let's just say it goes against the rules."

"Let's just say you need a marriage license," someone said, and Leo blushed as laughter broke around them and lifted them into its redeeming arms. From the corner of her eye, my aunt saw Vera exchange a conspiratorial wink with Leo. Not until a few weeks later would she realize that, alone of all the guests, only Vera had managed to elude her probing gaze.

The last hand belonged to Helen, who roomed with Arthur's sister Ruth in a cold-water flat on Perry Street off Grove.

It was then, in a flash, that the room became electric, because Helen's palm bore word of a wedding and a birth: the following year she would marry Abey the Baby, whom she had met at the concert for Ben Davis in October, and on a warm June night in 1953 I would come barreling into life with all the garrulousness of a perfect Gemini, ensuring with my very first syncopated cry that my aunt—that Natalya, God's Messenger—would have a chronicler.

No one was more excited as the clock struck twelve than Rita herself, who offered the first toast. "To 1946! To Helen and Abey! To peace—and to my niece!"

Five

W hy anyone thinks April is the cruelest month I've never understood—and neither does my aunt. We both wish we had been born in Cuba or Curaçao and lived our whole lives in the tropics instead of in the sleet-driven slag heap New York becomes when February rears its ugly head. After all, what is New York in the depths of winter but a skyscraper-encrusted ice floe, a swirling, snow-bound, floating version-in-reverse of Dante's hell? Still, time presses onward and the rent comes due, which is why my aunt was hard at work one frigid February day, even though her electric heater had burned through its coils that very morning and the radiator in the storefront on East Seventh Street was thick with ice.

Anyone else would have called it quits and gone home hours earlier to wedge body, soul and socks as close to a red-hot stove or fireplace as possible. Not Rita. My aunt, dutiful and optimistic in her sequined turban, was huddled at the table at the center of the room, her knees knocking together and her hands cupping the crystal ball. ("Professional," she says today, and even now her hands revert to that exact position whenever we talk about her powers.)

Since New Year's she had entered a new phase. Confessions breed confidence, they say, and now that she had shed the burden of duplicity, disclosing her clairvoyance to everyone but Chaim and Gittel, she was daily feeling less like an actress or an Emma Lazarus manquée and more like the real McCoy: Natalya, God's Messenger.

Something had changed; something had multiplied. It would be years before she could describe how it had happened, but there it was, at once as strange and natural as breathing, as miraculous as the Virgin Mary's appearance in a North Bronx lot the fall before. She was Rita and she was Natalya. Not one and then the other, but both at the same time, separate, yet together. Disconcerting as it was—and decades on the job would do nothing to dispel my aunt's original amusement at what she likes to call her line of work—she knew that the ability to see was now a part of her, as unshakable as her own right hand or the green unblinking eye on the back of a dollar bill.

Where talent treads, guilt is never far behind, according to my aunt, and I believe her. You feel an obligation. In her case it was geometric. The more she saw in people's hands the more she felt she owed it to her customers to apply herself more scientifically to her new work, just as she had once, for victory's sake, devoted her attention to mastering the fine points of the turret lathe. The burden, to be sure, was not a light one. What if, in addition to the images that flowed like movies from her customers' extended palms, there were other truths still lurking in the hidden channels of their hands? Understandings that might change—who knew but even save—their lives?

This was why, as the sun moved slowly toward the west that Friday afternoon, casting a deepening chill over the island of Manhattan and an even deeper one over the unheated storefront on East Seventh Street, my aunt was staring fixedly into the crystal ball, in which there appeared to be a tiny replica of Leo's room. Like an Olympic skater adamantly perfecting her figure eight when everybody else has given up, my aunt was working on her powers. She was straining to read the words on the minuscule poster of La Pasionaria that hung above the small pine bed that floated in the luminous ice-world of the crystal ball. If she could read the legend on the poster, she thought, she could read anything; but it was hard to concentrate. Other images came swimming toward her in the ice-cold sphere—her father fleeing the czar's army, Gittel's hair turning snow-white on the boat from Antwerp to New York—and she lost track of where she was. Then Leo's room sailed back again, bright and trembling and inviting.

Once, when she glanced up, she thought she saw La Pasionaria parked outside the storefront, but when she looked again the street was bare. The cold, she told herself, must be playing havoc with her mind. Leo hadn't looked her in the eye since New Year's Eve, nor had he said a word about her new vocation. Wasn't he curious to know why she had left a perfectly good job at Universal Tool & Die, what had led her to impersonate an elderly Ukrainian clairvoyant and how on earth she had acquired the extraordinary powers she had displayed at Pavel and Juanita's party? Vera too, she realized, squinting deep into the crystal ball, had been oddly, provocatively, silent. She wished she knew what they were thinking. Were they too stunned to ask? Too upset? Too angry? It wasn't like them to be so nonchalant.

The cold was creeping up her spine at an alarming rate, and my aunt was feeling more like a stalactite than a palm-reader when a gust of arctic air blew through the door, followed by a woman in an enormous broad-brimmed hat with an opaque black veil.

"Don't move," the woman said in a distinct French accent, and my aunt, already frozen, froze some more. The woman reached under her fashionable coat. "I love this place," she said, and when my aunt looked up in mortal fear she saw her own pale cheeks reflected in the dark eye of a vintage Leica. Balancing the camera in a pair of elegant black gloves, the woman spent the next five minutes moving frenziedly around the store, stopping only to advance her film and occasionally telling my aunt to turn this way or that. "Now look at me," she said at last. There was a final click, and when the camera was lowered and the veil was raised, my aunt was staring up into the radiant, mischievous face of—but it was Vera! "Did I scare you?" Vera said, obviously relishing the thought. Beneath two artfully curved eyebrows, her amber eyes were bright with pride. "I'm sorry. The light's been crazy. I didn't have a second to explain. I don't usually work this way."

"Me neither," Natalya, God's Messenger, replied.

*

Today those pictures are collectors' items. They show my aunt at twenty-seven, her eyes dark with a mysterious beauty I never knew in her. In several of the best shots, the shimmer of her turban is echoed by the crystal ball, which is shot through with light, and her fingers, either resting gently on the table or propped under her chin, are a luminous white. They all have the same caption: "Clairvoyant, Lower East Side, 1946." The old plank floorboards are there, along with the curved sink and broken mirror I remember from when I was a child. And in one, a profile taken from the back of the store looking toward the plate glass window, Vera's reflection, pale and dreamy in the shadows, hovers in the background, half lit by the light of her own hand-held flash.

"So," Vera said when she was done, peeling off her gloves and stepping back to take a good look at my aunt, "you weren't kidding." She reached out and rolled the cloth of Rita's sequined turban between her thumb and forefinger. "Terrific material, darling," she began. "Wait a minute," she said, catching herself. "What the hell are you doing here?"

"What the hell are *you* doing here?" my aunt replied.

"I came to see if you were serious," Vera replied matter-of-factly. "I mean, this is you? You really work here?"

"You think I come here to get warm?"

"This has to be some kind of joke," Vera said, shaking her head. "The question is," she added deliberately, as if thinking to herself, "which kind?"

"You seem to have forgotten New Year's Eve," said my Aunt Rita.

"Of course not," Vera said. "You put on quite a show. A real entertainment, yes?"

"Entertainment no," Rita said emphatically, only now beginning to grasp the point of Vera's visit. "Do you mean to tell me," she continued, sizing up the effort that had gone into her friend's disguise—the fashionable hat, the borrowed coat, the camera (not to mention the French accent), "that you went to all these lengths just to see if I was really here?"

"I do."

"And that on New Year's Eve you thought I was just kidding?"

"Absolutely."

"And since when do you take photographs?"

"And since when do you read hands?"

"I give up," my aunt concluded. "Your move."

Vera held out her ungloved hand with a flourish fit for the silver screen and placed it in the center of the damask-covered table, right beside the crystal ball.

The minute my Aunt Rita saw the upturned palm she gasped. It was narrow and white, with hardly any lines, like a kid glove still in its translucent glassine sleeve. The fingers were long and exquisitely tapered, but it was the hourglass thumb, swanlike as it parted from the palm, that gave the whole away. The pulse, neither slow nor fast, was perfectly calm. My aunt didn't have to consult the Count of St. Germain to know that she was staring at the first philosophical hand ever to be seen in New York City. The unusual thumb endowed its owner with long life and the ability to survive catastrophes and accidents of every kind.

"Is something wrong?" Vera had seen the color drain from Rita's face.

"No—right." It was too late to turn back the clock, so my aunt blinked twice and let the images flood in.

She saw a woman younger than Vera, but with the same Roman nose and incandescent halo of blond hair, stepping out onto a gilded stage to thunderous applause; a handsome doctor, broad-shouldered and bearded, standing in a doorway on a cobbled street somewhere in Europe; Hitler waving from an open car; an enormous, white-haired man and a woman who resembled Vera, but much older, seated on a bench in Central Park; and then—but why in Vera's hand?—she saw herself, Natalya, God's Messenger, many years into the future, staring down into a palm in which an endless multitude, red and black against a fiery horizon, was streaming from a poisoned city in a cloud of smoke. Caravans of buses clogged the roads, children howled, loudspeakers blared and sirens wailed. Like ants pouring from a blazing hole, the horde of people swarmed across the smoldering landscape. Seconds later a man and a woman emerged against the flickering red sky and stood silhouetted, without moving, like figures in a magic lantern. Then, as if aware that they were being watched, they turned and beckoned. The ground beneath them seemed to shift and sigh, and suddenly my aunt was sure the upturned hand in Vera's palm belonged to somebody she knew and that the lovers' faces were familiar; but as she bent to look more closely she felt the colossal roar of an explosion and plumes of fire shot into the air and she was falling, falling, free as Alice tumbling deep into the earth, and someone was calling to her as she floated down down

down away from the known world into a molten core of happiness and silence where Leo awaited her with open arms.

Down into Leo's waiting arms?

"Are you all right?" The voice was Vera's, almost in her ear.

"The dance of chance and necessity begins," said my Aunt Rita, shaking her head. "Not what was; what will be . . . She who shapes the shadows . . . She who shines in the dark."

"My God," a voice beside her said in a half-whisper. "You're the real thing." It was Vera, who had never seen such light as was playing on my Aunt Rita's high cheekbones and who now pulled her to her feet in the dark store.

*

Chaim was practicing the violin, tapping his foot to the rhythm of a melody only he could hear. "Keats and Mama," Abey said, looking through the half-open French doors into the living room, where his white-haired father was playing his mute plywood violin, or rather plying it, his eyes ecstatically closed as the bow coursed back and forth across the strings. "'Heard melodies are sweet . . .'"

"'But those unheard are sweeter,'" the Bedbug smugly finished the quotation. "I know another one," she said. "'I wandered lonely as a cloud . . .'"

"You want to get rich?" Maurice turned to his brother-in-law. "Invent a mute for my daughter."

It was Saturday morning and the family had lingered over breakfast. Gittel was in the kitchen shelling almonds for yet another cake and Esther, her gaze adrift above the lawns of Forest Hills, was washing dishes by the window. Fay had gone upstairs to set her salt-and-pepper hair with a mixture of flat beer and lemon juice that took all day to dry and made her wheeze even harder when it had; but vanity was vanity, and in those days a certain gentle-man caller still figured, albeit with decreasing frequency, in her sparse, unsettled life. Only Abey, Maurice, my Aunt Rita and the Three Mosquitoes, as irrepressible as ever, remained in the dining room.

Abey gave my aunt a gentle kick under the table. From the moment Rita had peered into the hand of a would-be astronomer named Helen to announce that the star-gazing student and her brother would soon wed, there had been a new complicity between them. "These kids don't need mutes," my future father said with a wink at my Aunt Rita. "They need exercise. Come on, girls, let's go!" The Three Mosquitoes piled after him into the hall, pulled on their wool-lined galoshes and overcoats and followed him out onto the street. My aunt, left to fend for herself with Maurice, excused herself and went into the living room. As she sank into the green tweed armchair just inside the door, she heard her sister's bald-headed husband plodding up the stairs in disappointment.

Chaim seemed unaware of Rita's presence. He was leaning amorously into his violin, his eyes still shut, and his face bore the look of distant rapture that should have told Gittel from the start that luck was not her middle name, as she ceaselessly reminded everyone around her, including her own children. "What can I tell you?" she would say with a bitter shrug, palms up to God's un-daunted face. "I fell for it. It shouldn't happen to a dog." She had married a good-for-nothing dreamer, a master cabinetmaker who spent more on sandpaper than he did on wood, and who charged so little for his work that in later years his own son-in-law, who had to feed and clothe forbearing Esther and three redheaded daughters, was often forced to tell their customers that the old man had made a mistake on the bill. Word in the neighborhood, thanks primarily to Gittel's merciless complaints, was that Chaim had left his brains behind when they left Russia.

Their mother's judgment notwithstanding, Rita, Esther and Abey believed their father could do no wrong. Who else had stroked their hair so gently, carried them piggyback around the block until they were ten years old, carved them each a set of marionettes with intense, interesting faces and sung them to sleep with lullabies of sunflowers and sleds? As children they had always come to his defense. When distant relatives on their mother's side whispered that their father was a *luftmensh*, a man with his head in the clouds, they were indignant. "*Luftmenshes* are the real chosen people," nine-year-old Rita told an audience of first and second grown-up cousins two years before the Great Depression. "They live in the air, so they're closer to God." The company laughed, but Gittel was unmoved. "From *luft* you don't eat," she chided her kin.

"Prodigy," she used to say back then, putting on her hat and coat to venture out into the hard *goyishe* world for food, "I need ten dollars." Year after year, Chaim stretched out his empty hands and smiled. Once in a blue moon he handed her a few crumpled dollar bills. "Every village has its idiot," Gittel would say under her breath. "The fool's wife is a fool twice," Chaim would softly reply, his eyes brimming with love, but to her dying day my grandmother never understood.

This was what my aunt was thinking that Saturday morning as she watched, not heard, her father play. About the power of love, and the equal power of those who resist its call. About parents and grandparents and all the far-flung ancestors who had long since turned to dust—generations of Russians in thick waistcoats and skirts, Spaniards in the toques and tunics of Toledo, formless Semites wearing sandals and desert robes, all darkly whirling in receding time—and about whether it made any difference if they had gazed into each other's eyes and drunk the honey from each other's lips before climbing into bed or if they had simply lived and died in blind obedience to nature's pulse. Nature's pulse: hardly one to flicker and go out. Chaim, Gittel, Esther, Maurice, Abey, Helen, herself, Leo—and there her heart stopped. No wonder she hadn't slept the night before. Because of course it mattered; if not for all eternity, then at least to yourself and those around you. While relentless nature, which has no choice, beat on oblivious, you could either give yourself to love or, like her own mother, you could plant your two feet firmly on the ground and press with all your might against love's door.

On the other side of which she knew, because she had just seen it in the first philosophical hand ever to appear in New York City, a momentous force was gathering and would soon spring.

"Poppa," she said. Her father jumped. "Is it really Mama you've been so in love with all these years?"

"I knew you would ask me that some day," he said. There was a long silence as he clasped the practice fiddle to his chest like a soloist awaiting his next cue.

"Well?" My aunt braced herself for the hard truth.

A smile crept across Chaim's face. "Of course not," he said slowly.

"Then who?"

"A girl I left back in Russia . . ." His voice trailed off.

"What was her name?"

"Gittel," her father said at last. "Her name was Gittel, and her hair was so black you could see colors in it."

*

That night, while the city shivered beneath freshly fallen snow, my aunt and Leo sat in the center of the last row of the top balcony of Carnegie Hall. They were so close to the curved ceiling that they could see the dusty top of the chandelier, which hung below them on its velvet rope like a cluster of rock candy, partly blocking their view of the ant-sized orchestra below. Leo was hunched over the seat in front, his head propped on his elbows, in rapt attention to the music. Ants, it seemed, were just as capable of playing Mozart as man-sized violinists, and fleas could play the flute; but despite the flailing arms of the conductor, the sound that reached the last row in the house had lost some of its luster.

While Leo listened, Rita considered what to do. For weeks she had assumed that sooner or later he would make some reference, veiled or otherwise, to her powers. But New Year's Eve had come and gone as if her revelation had fallen on deaf ears. Things could not go on this way. It was time to act. After the concert she would tell him about Vera's visit and explain how much had changed since she took over the storefront on East Seventh Street: how the vast, uncertain future had become visible to her, how everywhere she looked the air was alive with images, how a hypnotic, dreamlike voice swept through her when she looked into the outstretched hands of strangers.

The sooner Leo understood the better. She was not the woman he had asked to marry him but someone absolutely, indisputably, ir- revocably different. Her life was no longer her own; it belonged to her customers, and her first allegiance was to the visions that lay just beneath the surface of their palms.

Under the circumstances, she could hardly be expected to em- brace an ordinary life. Still, if Leo was willing, they could work to- gether side by side, like Pierre and Marie Curie, comrades in the dazzling laboratory of the hand.

My aunt was surprised by her own thoughts. For months she

had done everything she could to keep her powers to herself. Now she was practically asking him to join her in the storefront.

Poor Leo. Palmistry represented everything he hated most: the dark, ancient world of superstition, that pale-to-end-all-pales in which their Russian forebears had dwelled for centuries, prey not just to the whim and cruelty of czars but to the swirling, guilt-filled, dybbuk-ridden chaos of their own imaginations. It was into that bottomless pit, that Kabbalistic realm lit only by the flicker of religious candles, that Rita had unwittingly plunged when she exchanged her machinist's uniform for the crystal ball and turban of Natalya, God's Messenger. To Leo, there could be no greater loss. Goodbye, Marx; goodbye, enlightenment. The woman of his dreams had become a dimestore quack.

My aunt knew what she was up against. "It's not what you think," she would begin, and she would tell him everything, beginning with her own astonishment, and little by little he would come to understand that her clairvoyance was a gift neither of them could refuse. It would be a bitter cup, but he would drink it. She could feel him struggling with the words. "All right, so you're God's Messenger. We all have to make a living. Just don't swindle anybody out of their life savings." Suddenly, strangely, as the music drifted past her on its journey to the roof, she was full of longing. She glanced to the side, where Leo—kind, dependable Leo—still staring straight ahead and lost in Mozart, was oblivious to the conversation taking place inside her head. "I love you too much to put up a fight. I always will." Leo was the noblest person she had ever met. She could almost predict what he would say.

Meanwhile, she tried to concentrate on the musicians. They had worked so hard to perfect their technique and they were probably playing their hearts out down below, all to no avail. Well, to the avail of some. Music, unlike heat, does not rise; only the rich, complacent in their front-row seats, hear it as it really sounds, close up and undoctored by technicians. Was that true? It was the sort of proposition you could never really test. This much she was sure of: if Chaim had been in the orchestra, he would have looked up every now and then to salute the faithful in the distant balconies. He would have tipped his imaginary hat. On the other hand, it occurred to her for the first time, since no one in the family but Gittel had ever heard her father play, and that nearly fifty years ago, it was anybody's guess if he still could; for all she knew, his silent devotions to his art were the only homage he could pay it. But such devotion! Surely, she thought, there must be some law governing these things, some natural balance of endowments; surely his gifts must have been commensurate with his lifelong inability to do virtually anything else . . . So doth distraction lead thought by the arm, and before she knew it my aunt was standing on the perilous edge of the gulf that yawns before us all when we try to imagine our progenitors in different lives: if there had not been anti-Semitism in Russia; if Chaim had not been turned down by the St. Petersburg Conservatory for being Jewish; if instead of being forced to play in small cafés he had found a job as a concert violinist; if, in short, he had left Shtebsk for Moscow or Odessa, he would never have met Gittel, in which case she and Esther and Abey would never have been born and she would not be sitting here staring down into this splendid chandelier, each of whose dangling diamantine facets now refracted back at her—is this really happening?—the image of Vera leaning in the doorway of the storefront on East Seventh Street, a heavy camera bag over her shoulder and cheeks as red as apples beneath an enormous broad-brimmed hat.

"Jesus!" my Aunt Rita said. Leo sat back in his seat. "What's wrong?" he whispered.

"Nothing," she whispered back. "I just saw a friend of mine."

"You have a friend named Jesus?"

"Doesn't everyone?"

"Not me—I'm still waiting for the Messiah . . ."

"Ssshhh!" They were being hissed into silence from all sides. Leo squeezed her hand and kissed her on the cheek. "It's almost over," he whispered, but my aunt was too distraught to wait. Before the last chord reached their ears they had made their way downstairs and out into the glacial night. It had begun to snow.

"Well?" he asked when they were on the street. They were standing directly across from Vim & Vigor, the first and only restaurant in New York City for people whose idea of a good meal would have pleased the most discriminating cow: a plate of alfalfa sprouts, a slice of barley loaf and a drink of pureed beans that had been given the bracing name of tiger's milk.

"There's something I have to tell you."

"That's what you always say."

"This time I really mean it."

"Then this time I'll really listen."

Leo made a mock-serious face as they headed down the block to Horn & Hardart's.

Suddenly it dawned on him: she wasn't kidding. He shuddered. And then, as he so often did at night or in the bitter cold, when his bad leg began to ache, he thought of Spain (but anything could make him think of Spain), a whole country fighting to survive the fascist boot—a fight beside which his struggle to win Rita's heart could only pale; and he thought of the bloody hillside where he'd learned to put mind over matter. Whatever Rita had to say, he was prepared. Vera had already told him the result of her surprise visit to the storefront: Rita's parlor tricks on New Year's Eve had been for real. Rita, she said, actually appeared to have some sort of extrasensory perception, and somewhere along the way she had apparently figured out how to read palms. How Vera could believe such claptrap was beyond him, but she did.

Courage, he whispered to himself as they went through the revolving doors.

The Automat was nearly empty when they arrived; their fellow concertgoers were still clapping. My aunt looked the other way when Leo peeled a dollar from his wallet and the cashier filled his outstretched palm with twenty nickels perfectly dispatched. After all her efforts to avoid his hand, this was hardly the moment for her to learn what lay between his lines of Life, Fate and Heart.

"Well?" he said when they sat down, fishing in his breast pocket for a cigarette.

"It's not what you think," she began.

Leo looked relieved.

"It's something else."

He pressed his lips together silently.

She told him everything, beginning with the advertisement in the *Daily Mirror* and explaining how at first she had felt like an impostor and how she had spent hours trying to memorize the order of the mounts and learn the names of all the lines from an ancient book called *The Practice of Palmistry for Professional Purposes,* until the day she had looked into the hand of Mrs. Harlan Bell III and seen the atom bomb explode in Hiroshima, and all the visions that had followed, and her sense looking back now that destiny itself and nothing else had propelled her to Natalya's door. And as she spoke the words poured from her lips like water so that, instead of a disjointed series of peculiar moments, the improbable became a seamless flow containing all her customers and all the secrets that lay just beneath the surface of their palms, and she was speaking now of the mesmerizing sense she had that if only she could bring together all the separate pieces—the tantalizing images that led her on like fragments of a dream—that then, once and for all, she might truly understand the future. "And then," she said, looking up at Leo and pausing as if to take in her own words, "Who knows? We might finally know what should be done. Or not done."

"Wait a minute," Leo interrupted.

"No," my aunt said gently, reaching for his hand, which she held face down in hers in the center of the marble table. She could feel his heart leaping through his palm, blindly seeking the comfort of her own.

But her heart was far away, pounding like a sea gone wild, and nothing she could say or do would stop the visions that were coursing through her, wave after wave.

"I don't understand . . ." Leo's voice brought her back to earth.

Because time was of the essence, she went on, speaking faster and faster. There was so much to see, so much to learn. Even now there were fleeting images she had only glimpsed, atoms and molecules of truth she must train herself to read, the sands of a vast invisible desert endlessly shifting back and forth, back and forth, like dust drifting through light. Who knew how much lay in the balance? Or whether she might even now be standing on the threshold of a revelation whose significance she could not yet grasp? She had received a gift, and she would do everything she could to carry it to its conclusion. History itself might be at stake.

"I know," she said when she was done. "It's strange for me too. But it's true."

Leo cleared his throat. He could feel my aunt receding from him like a character in a film run backward, still talking but harder and harder to understand, her voice, too, vanishing into a blur, a whisper, a lost terrain. Still, he didn't shout, didn't cry, didn't pound his fists on the hard table.

In the end it wasn't courage that got him through; it was an immense wave of relief that rose up and knocked him almost breathless as it broke between them.

"I love you too much to put up a fight," he said, smiling his gap-toothed smile. "I always will. But this is more than I can take."

My aunt never got over it.

"Not because he left me," she insists, "but because I was so sure he wouldn't. That's when he finally won me over: when he stopped being so predictable. And then it was too late."

"Better late than never," I remind her, and she laughs.

"Vera was right," Leo said as they stood up to leave. "She said you were a different person."

"I was," my aunt replied. All her generosity had drained away.

"I mean it," Leo said. "You believe in things that aren't there . . ."

"No more than you do. At least I believe in what I see."

"Let's not get carried away," Leo said, suddenly sarcastic. "What you see is a figment of your own imagination. I mean, you might as well be living in the Middle Ages. What I believe in is based on history, on facts. On the scientific basis for material change."

"You mean on hope. What you believe in doesn't exist."

"Yet," Leo corrected her.

It was almost midnight and still snowing when they stepped into the brilliant, frozen air. A single horse-drawn carriage lurched up Sixth Avenue, its coachman quilted like a Cossack, two reckless passengers blanketed above their necks. The horse's breath curled like smoke along the edge of the sidewalk. "I'll drive you home," Leo said sadly. My aunt said she would take the train.

"One last trip—for old times' sake . . ."

La Pasionaria was parked around the corner. My aunt hesitated for a moment. Then she broke into a run.

The fountain at Columbus Circle glistened in the moonlight as she neared the subway. Columbus and his entourage of conquering angels looked as if they had been sculpted out of ice instead of marble. Behind them, flat as any tundra, the park was arctic, frozen, still. Except for the occasional passing car and a handful of brave tourists, the city was deserted.

At the corner of Fifty-ninth and Broadway my aunt waited for the light. A snow-covered hulk of a car swept into view above the Mayflower Hotel and glided slowly toward her in the stream of traffic, disappeared behind the fountain, then swung around again, then yet a third time, like a figure skater circling a rink. When the light changed and my aunt stepped from the curb, Leo rolled down the window and waved not once but twice with his bright red handkerchief from Spain.

And then, as a powdery snow continued to fall, La Pasionaria, white as a whale and bathed in moonlight, moved north along the silent park.

Six

"I was just getting my feet wet in the hand trade," my aunt says now when she explains what happened next. "I was good, but not that good. I was off by a whole year."

When she turned onto East Seventh Street the following Monday morning, José Delgado, Jr., was shouting at her from the middle of the block.

Rita could see by his frantic gestures that José Jr. was trying to tell her something, but she had to step into the street to detour Eddie Carney's coal truck, which was backed onto the icy sidewalk, its tilted cargo hurtling into the basement of the Ukrainian dry goods shop next door, before she could make out what he was saying.

"Surprised?" My aunt raises her eyebrows. "Who had time to be surprised? When reality marches right up to your door you don't wait for it to knock. You let it in. Besides, I knew she would be there. I just didn't know when."

From the very first, Vera worked as if there were no tomorrow. She shot my aunt arriving at the store, jaunty in her navy coat and feathered hat; pinning up her Rita Hayworth curls and wrapping the sequined turban tight around her head; centering the adhesive ruby exactly an inch above her eyebrows; straightening the two framed pictures of the Bay of Naples; smoothing the blue damask tablecloth; and reflected in the cracked Venetian mirror above the sink, half clown, half Mona Lisa, now laughing and mugging exactly as she does today, now suddenly pensive, the clouds of inner thought shadowing her face.

By the time my aunt had pulled the spangled curtains to the side and flipped the cardboard sign around to OPEN, Vera was on her seventh roll of film. And when Lucy came down the stoop a few minutes later on her way to mass, Natalya, God's Messenger, and Mrs. Mildred Levy of East Third Street, a redheaded widow with a hand as plump as rye bread and a face to match, were sitting for their portrait as if it were the most natural thing in the whole world.

What was not the most natural thing in the whole world were the legions of tanks my aunt saw rolling through lush fields in Mrs. Levy's palm, the clouds of smoke rising from invisible villages or the helicopters whirring overhead, but for the moment no one was the wiser. In fact, had it not been for Vera, who saw and captured for all time the darkness that had crept into the corners of Mrs. Levy's eyes and the hope that clung like the finest European powder to her cheeks, there would be no trace of what my aunt observed that day. Mrs. Levy is no longer here to tell her side of the story, and Vera was too preoccupied with her camera to hear what my aunt said. Lucy, the only other witness to the session, was already out of earshot. But from out on the sidewalk, where she had stopped to hand José a thermos of hot coffee, she saw my aunt's lips moving faster and faster and the eyes of the widow with the fox around her neck opening wider and wider as she spoke.

"And her?" she asked no one in particular, suddenly noticing the well-dressed woman crouched behind a tripod in the far corner of the store, with a large black camera aimed directly at Natalya, God's Messenger, and Mrs. Mildred Levy.

"I guess she takes them as they are," José Junior replied, leaning on his shovel, "while Natalya tells them where they're going."

"What will they think of next?"

By noon Vera had filled another seven rolls of film with the double portraits that are still among her finest work, and by the end of the week the line outside the store was longer than ever. Word had gotten out.

Sometimes a customer objected and Vera sat in the back pretending to read *The Brothers Karamazov*, but most of them were flattered to have their portrait taken while my aunt was peering deep into their lives. Some even secretly believed they were getting two futures for the price of one. Perhaps they were.

Before the month was out she had taken most of the portraits that hung in her first one-woman show, including the famous one of Lucy (*Superintendent, New York City, 1946*), and the close-up of my aunt that has been so widely reproduced. With the exception of *Delivering Coal,* which Eddie Carney bought with his own money and has steadfastly refused to lend, all Vera's early photographs have been shown around the world, most recently in the retrospective of her work held several years ago in Paris and Berlin. (Even *The Thief of Dreams,* the photograph of Harry Gross that was lent to a reporter and subsequently vanished, survives in archival reprints and is known to connoisseurs as one of the great portraits of its day.)

As the cold let up, Vera began to explore the neighborhood, poking into all the secondhand shops and producing the first of her memorable studies of life on the Lower East Side, including the shots of the storefront that enjoyed such fame as postcards in the Sixties: the customers on line outside taken from inside the store, with the bowed letters on the plate glass window in reverse,

ЯОƧIVⓄA ЯƎⓄАƎЯ; and the view from outside in, the same letters left to right, sometimes perfectly in focus and sometimes blurred to let the faces in the store show through.

Anyone who knew Natalya in her heyday will recognize Al Diamond from the garage and his wife Sylvia; Lucy and José Delgado; José Jr.; Nat Sarnoff and his newly rescued son; Anthony Caputo from the corner store and his wife Mary; Mrs. Levy; Mrs. Sullivan; Eddie Carney; Blanche DelBianco; and Mrs. Harlan Bell III, whose fragile hand concealed much more than it revealed.

The most striking thing about those early pictures is the way the light falls everywhere at once, so that even professional photographers have been unable to tell where Vera was standing when she took them. My aunt, so young and yet so defiantly mature with the turban tight around her head, has a buoyant, evanescent glow whose source is nowhere to be found within the photograph. The customers too are doubly lit, their faces seen both as they themselves would see them in the mirror, familiar as the kitchen sink, and suddenly strange, as only an unflinching outsider could see them in the moment that precedes compassion.

"A photograph is not a portent," Vera used to say whenever people asked if she saw more in her subjects than was actually there. "It's the statement of a fact that cannot be stated any other way."

Facts that could not be stated any other way filled the storefront all that spring and on into the summer.

Among them, that delicate cracks had begun to appear in the palms of my aunt's customers; that the world, like a huge stone, was rolling toward the edge of a terrible abyss; and that, for the moment, there were certain things best left unsaid. Such as? "Put it this way," says my aunt, averting her eyes, "we had our mind on higher things." For reasons neither she nor Vera understood, humanity in its vast sweep had become their daily guest, deciphering its intimate and varied script their only goal. With each passing day, each scrap of news, their sense of urgency increased. And with good reason. Less than a year after V-J Day, the victors were in a headlong rush to perfect the staggering new tools of mass destruction. The United States had just evicted every man, woman and child from an island called Bikini to test a bomb ten times more powerful than the one that had brought such ruin to Japan the year before, and the Russians were in hot pursuit of hydrogen. The Nuclear Age had catapulted everything into fast forward. Or had it? When five thousand Polish Jews who had survived the Holocaust were killed in a pogrom in mid-July, it almost seemed that history itself, like a used film, was running backward. In either case— whether events were hurtling dangerously forward or plunging back into the horror of the recent past—if there was to be a future, my aunt and Vera realized, their own lives would have to wait. Like scientists bent over microscopes in a mad lab, they were in a race with time.

As if trying to oblige, customers streamed in and out, placing their upturned palms on my aunt's table. Here, the hands seemed to say: take us, read us, use us as evidence or proof; your search is ours, our fate your own. "What a country," Vera said triumphantly, looking through the plate glass window at the scores of people lining up outside. "For everything there are volunteers, yes?"

Not that anyone on line, any of the local residents or, for that matter, any of the nearby shopkeepers could possibly have guessed what a transcendent search was underway inside the storefront with the palm-shaped sign that had been a fixture on East Seventh Street for years.

To her customers, my aunt was still the same Natalya, God's Messenger, to whom they turned for comfort, knowledge, a glimpse of the future, but above all for her scintillating, hopeful speech, which gave them the sense of being freshly arrived in their own lives.

By mid-summer, however, her words were neither as scintillating nor as hopeful as before.

"Even those not called are called," she told a bewildered Blanche DelBianco a year after Hiroshima when jagged cracks appeared between the lines of Life, Heart and Fate in the waitress's frail hand. Blanche, whose mind was not what it had been (and it had never been much, according to my aunt), had painted her long nails a spectral pink that made her otherworldly skin look even paler. Always fearing the worst, she waited patiently each Friday afternoon after picking up her check to ask my aunt what the executives of Schrafft's had up their starched, indifferent sleeves.

"Fear, like mercury, breaks up and slips through cracks," my aunt began. "Appearance becomes the mirror image of reality. Things become shells. The greatest damage is invisible and has the longest recovery . . ."

"But that's not . . ." Blanche interrupted. My Aunt Rita waved her silent as the words spilled on. "Not to be allowed to dream—empire's end. Not who we are—what we pretend. Certainty collides with truth . . . Danger with risk . . . But who will know? Ah, there's the rub . . ."

"Risk? Rub . . . ?" Blanche DelBianco stammered, gliding toward the blinding August light. "All I ask is will I have a job and instead I get a whole rum and raisin about—to tell you the truth, if my life depended on it, I couldn't tell you what she said . . ."

Vera stepped behind the lens and pressed the shutter, immortalizing the aged waitress in the doorway as she looked back one last time and shrugged her skimpy shoulders at my aunt.

Of course, not all Rita's visions were so cryptic. A few days later, when José Delgado, Jr., finally agreed to place his tattooed fore-arm on her damask-covered table, my aunt was more forthcoming. "Ready?" José asked, rolling his sleeve up to the shoulder and casu-ally pumping his artichoke-sized biceps like a prize-fighter granting a rare interview. The muscle shot up and down José's bare arm while my aunt pretended not to look and concentrated on his palm.

My aunt was stunned. Not only did José's broad hand contain exactly the same landscape as his father's, right down to the last swaying palm tree on the beach, but it was laced with the same hair-line cracks she had seen in Blanche DelBianco's hand two weeks be-fore. Though there was much to celebrate in José's future, including a spectacular wedding to a girl he would save from a burning rooftop nine years later, there was also much to fear.

It was in José's hand that my aunt first saw the ice—a vast, po-lar continent of snow that stretched in ghostly silence while hordes of people, trying desperately to flee, were turned to living statues like the trapped citizens of Pompeii.

My aunt did not mince words. She told José about his bride and about the row of coconut trees in his hand, and then her voice dropped to a whisper as she spoke of the spreading cracks and the chill that would soon envelop the country and the world. "Win-ter will descend on us like a shroud. We will be buried alive by cold of our own making. There will be no thaw, but when one day the ice is chipped away, generations not yet born will see the shape of hope."

"*Caramba*," José Jr. said and shook his head. "They told me you were some kind of a shrinx, hooked up to the clouds or God or something, but I never thought . . ." Vera caught him with his sleeve rolled up, his lips still pursed, one fist pressed against his forehead as he stared at his own hand lying face-up on the table. *Veteran,*

Lower East Side, 1946, she called her portrait of José, who remains as proud of it today as when he first beheld it, framed and signed, on the wall of one of New York's finest galleries.

That afternoon, over bowls of sorrel soup at the B & H, Vera asked my aunt about the cracks. Could they be seen with the naked eye? Of course not, my aunt replied. Vera was not convinced. Somewhere in the contours of the palm, she said, there had to be a trace, a residue, a sign—some changed volume or texture—whose hidden light she would eventually capture with her camera. Like character or lust, which wrote itself into people's lips or curled itself into their noses, this latent news must somehow fill or change their flesh.

If only, my aunt sighed. If only the hand held its secrets to the light as resolutely as a page in braille, revealing them at will to touch or sight. But it wasn't like that, she explained; there were no clues on the blank page of the palm. Besides, it wasn't enough to see whatever you were seeing, or to say that you had seen it; you had to tell the customer exactly what it meant. And that, she said, was infinitely harder than it looked.

"Let's face it," Vera said, lowering her voice. "Those cracks have been there all along."

"Yes, but . . ." said my aunt. She knew Vera was right.

"But what?"

"They're spreading," my aunt said. The cracks might be invisible to ordinary eyes, but they were there and they were growing. They were robbing half her customers of sleep. Beneath their sheets, despite the dreams held out to them by *Life* and *Time,* they knew at night with their eyes open what the magazines denied: that life on earth had been irrevocably changed. What, she wondered aloud, would hold everything together?

"Glue," Vera replied.

"Glue?"

They both sighed.

Nat, who always waited on my aunt even though his job was in the kitchen, served them each a slice of strudel. "On the house," he said. "Relax, girls. The wise man eats with his tongue, not with his brain."

My aunt and Vera both looked blank.

"In other words, when you're eating, eat. Life and its eternal mysteries will still be waiting for you when you're done."

But what was waiting for them when they returned to the storefront was a line twice as long as it had been when they closed up for lunch an hour before. At its head was a short, gray-haired woman with the body of a dumpling and the voice of a canary. While my aunt was still turning her key in the front door, the woman introduced herself as Faith Kincaid, chief sandwich maker and part-owner of the Gypsy Tea Room on East Forty-second Street, and explained that she was sick and tired of hearing that her uptown tea-leaf readers couldn't hold a candle to a storefront palmreader on East Seventh Street who read hands the way other people read the morning paper. She had come to see for herself what all the fuss was about.

The fuss, it turned out, was nowhere more evident than in her own small hand, which was literally teeming with the future. "My Rosetta Stone," my aunt still calls it, but in fact Faith's emphatic hand, so often clenched into a fist to make a point, had more in common with a sponge. The triangle between her lines of Life, Heart and Fate contained the essentials not only of her own life but the lives of everyone around her, including people she had never met, as well as the outlines of a larger and more public fate.

It was clear from the start that Faith's would be no ordinary hand. Her thumb, squat as a mushroom and similar in shape, was gnarled beyond her fifty-or-so years, as if someone else's life had somehow been grafted onto hers. The palm itself, no bigger than a child's change purse, was so deeply creased that for a moment my aunt despaired of ever finding the crucial lines of Heart, Life and Fate. Then she felt the pulse. Neither slow nor fast, it was perfectly, metronomically, demonically even.

My aunt ran her fingers down her customer's diminutive wrist onto the velvety surface of her palm. The cracks were there, of course, but they were hardly worth mentioning when there was so much else. There seemed no end to the images that swam into view before her widening eyes. A fact checker's green visor strapped to somebody's bald head. The Secretary of Defense jumping out a window. The Caputos' two squirming sons growing into shiftless men. The Beatles with their mops of straight black hair. Monks on fire. Mrs. Sullivan's false teeth leaping from her open mouth into the jaws of the Atlantic as she saw an old man drown. Eddie Carney's long-awaited namesake, Eddie Jr., growing up to join the Army and have his name engraved in stone. A black man leading multitudes like Moses. And more.

Troops falling out of planes onto small islands; men landing on the moon; a missing brain; an actor waving from the White House steps; and a book in which all this and more would one day be told.

Then she saw Faith's son, who had been sent home from the war wrapped head to foot in bandages that would never be removed. My aunt froze. "A life stolen but not lost," was all she said, but it was enough. Across the table, a gasp and then a flood of tears burst from Faith Kincaid. When she finally stopped shaking, her voice was that of a young girl. "I should have known," she said. "You really have what it takes."

"You mean *you* do," said my Aunt Rita, still reeling from the unexpected beauty and crush of this new palm.

Within the space of one small hour, Faith Kincaid had become not just a loyal customer, but a lifelong friend. And when the tables turned and the scores of customers outside became a trickle, she remained true to her name.

*

Meanwhile, undaunted by the crowd that awaited them from dawn to dusk and encouraged by the possibility that they were drawing nearer to their goal, Vera and my aunt pressed onward with their mission. Day after day, they sat in the closed store after the last customer had gone and tried to distill the cornucopia of images that had crossed the damask-covered tabletop since morning.

Faith Kincaid's palm was a gold mine, but she was not alone. Among the other regulars whose hands supplied my aunt with vital clues were Nat Sarnoff, who was unable to resist her penetrating gaze and who came every Wednesday, his day off, pulling his embarrassed wife behind him and all but pushing his recalcitrant son into the storefront; Anthony and Mary Caputo, who always arrived with bags of groceries, as if they were making a delivery, and departed quickly, so that their employees, half of whom were ardent customers, would not suspect that they had fallen under my aunt's spell; Mrs. Sullivan, who knew no greater rapture than to sit and hear my aunt describe the waves breaking on a distant shore, the moon above, and the smile on the face of an elderly gentleman maneuvering his skiff toward a strange object floating in the sea; Lucy and José Delgado, who had already heard enough to count themselves among the lucky but returned each week to hear again how José Jr. would become a fireman and how, his first night on the job, he would carry a young Puerto Rican actress from a burning rooftop and how then, after breathing life back into her exquisite lips, he would propose to her and how, right then and there, still in his arms, she would accept; Eddie Carney's cousin Jimmy, just over from Ireland, who was so shy that his palm itself seemed tongue-tied but who quickly warmed to my aunt's presence and began to deliver himself of some of the most technically perfect and brilliantly colored images she had ever seen; and Mrs. Mildred Levy, whose hand, second only to Faith's for the quantity of information it contained, flickered like a newsreel in the dark but was also the staging area for an astonishing display of sexual encounters that bordered, my aunt thought, on the pornographic, though Vera disagreed.

"A little love never hurt anybody," she said.

"I beg to differ," said my aunt in a rare burst of self-pity.

"You don't have to beg—just differ," Vera said, coaxing a smile from my aunt and masterfully chasing a familiar shadow back across the street.

Where it was waiting all along?

"Back to the future," my aunt commands, pretending not to hear. I dutifully follow.

My aunt and Vera were determined, but despite their valiant effort, the hidden truth they sought continued to elude them. Still, by summer's end, it was clear to both of them that Rita's powers were growing exponentially. In the months since Vera had joined her in the store, not only had the visions begun to leap more quickly from her customers' expectant palms, but the words that flowed from my aunt's lips had grown purer, more concise. To many who came again and again to have their hands read, her speech seemed almost liquid; whole paragraphs poured into them like an elixir. As Mrs. Levy put it in a conversation with her son, "With her in the neighborhood, who needs medicine? Every time I see her, I feel like a million dollars." From Eddie Carney to Al Diamond to my aunt herself, but above all to Vera, who was unstinting in her praise, everyone could see that Rita's palmistry had reached new heights. The change was mirrored in her whole demeanor. Gone were the apologies about her new profession, the dread of running into people she had known before. No longer did she feel like an impostor. Vera's belief in my aunt's powers had made her more fully believe in them herself.

In fact, with Vera by her side, my aunt became convinced she had been called upon to see the world anew. Like Balboa looking out over the parrot-blue Pacific, like Mozart transcribing the music of the spheres or Marx surmising the immense ecology of human labor, she would discover a whole greater and more beautiful than the sum of its parts: a message that would change the world.

*

"Surely you jest," my father said. He was on the phone with Vera, who had just informed him that his sister Rita, known throughout Lower Manhattan as Natalya, God's Messenger, was no ordinary clairvoyant. After six months in the storefront, Vera could no longer keep the magnitude of Rita's talent to herself. One by one, on a single Saturday in mid-September, she decided it was time to tell her closest friends—first Arthur, whom she summoned to breakfast; then Pavel and Juanita, who came to her for lunch; then her assorted beaux, whom she received one by one at various cafés all afternoon; and finally Abey, whom she called at his new job an hour before closing instead of at his parents' house in Forest Hills where, due to the sheer number of inhabitants and the eternal cu-riosity of the Three Mosquitoes, it was impossible for anyone to hold a private conversation. Like Arthur, who had wept in disbelief, or Pavel and Juanita, who had left speechless and afraid, Abey might not understand. Still, she thought, he ought to know. Not only could my aunt read hands. She had, Vera said into the telephone, a gift of epic proportions.

Abey sank back into his boss's leather recliner. "I thought something terrible had happened," he said. Naturally, his thoughts had rushed to Helen, whom he was about to marry, then to Chaim and Gittel. The last thing he expected on the job was to hear from Vera. Unless, of course, Leo had returned.

He bit his tongue. Good luck. Wherever Leo was, he wasn't telling. And Vera was hardly the one to ask. Along with the rest of their crowd, she had given up on him when he vanished from their midst without so much as a goodbye after ending his relationship with Rita.

So now Vera had followed his sister off the map. Or out into the woods. Or wherever this wild woolly primitive beast of a palm-reading business was leading. It was all well and good for Rita to have found a job, and there was nothing wrong with trying to make people laugh, but things had gotten out of hand if someone as smart as Vera had fallen hook, line and sinker for what his sister had obviously intended as a prank . . . Of course he had gone ahead and proposed to Helen after Rita said she saw their marriage in her palm . . . It was New Year's Eve and the perfect excuse. But now of all times, when people of good will needed more than ever to con-front chaos with knowledge . . . when the Party was preparing for its finest hour . . . Helen would never fall for something like this. She would rather gaze forever at a single star, measuring its life by a light that lay millions of years in the past, than guess the shape of things to come by staring at the empty space in people's hands. Which made him wonder what Helen was doing on this splendid autumn day: sitting in the planetarium, no doubt, craning her beautiful neck at the blue ceiling where, it occurred to him for the first time, she was probably the object of equally devoted attention from the rows of adolescent boys behind her. He wished he could see her right away, hold her, feel her radiant heat against his chest. Two more hours: he had reserved a table at L'Etoile to celebrate her twenty-first birthday. My future father shook his head and picked up the receiver, which was lying on his boss's desk like the fallen horn of a rhinoceros. "I lost my train of thought," he said into the strange black tube. To his amazement, Vera was still there. "You'll find it," she said.

"The hell I will," Abey replied, anger seizing his throat. That train, and everything it represented—peace of mind, shared ideas, belief in a just future—had already left the station. And now his own sister had derailed it. With Vera waving from the caboose.

"Do me one favor," he said before hanging up the phone. "Don't tell Helen. She knows my family is strange, but we don't need any last-minute surprises. Why rock the boat?"

"I wouldn't dream of it, darling," Vera answered. Let Abey rock it in his own good time, when he and Helen were man and wife.

*

It was the domino effect before its day. Leo had bolted, running so far and so fast that none of his close friends knew why he had left or where he was. Arthur had wept, then vowed renewed commitment to the struggle. Pavel and Juanita were too appalled to speak. Abey felt betrayed. Nothing had prepared them for the news that Rita's end-of-year display of chiromantic powers had been more than a mere caper for her friends.

Meanwhile, as word of Vera's supposed defection leaked out, people on both sides of the Atlantic debated what to do. But Vera confounded everyone by calmly turning up at meetings, continuing to lead her weekly study group and refusing to publicly repudiate what had finally—to spare her more serious charges—been termed a bourgeois deviation.

"It's not bourgeois and it's not devious," she told Arthur, who begged her to reconsider.

"Deviation," Arthur said.

"Have it your way. The point is, I know what I'm doing. This kind of talent doesn't come along once a decade, maybe not even once a century. It's bigger than all of us. But you'd rather stay in your little box and point your finger. Why? Revolutionary thought requires revolutionary methods. Look at Marx. Progress is a paradox. I'm disappointed in you, Arthur. You could open your mind one little fraction of an inch and see something new. But you refuse."

"Vera, listen to me," he said finally. "The Party needs you."

"The Party has me," Vera said. "So what's the big deal?"

*

Only the sociologist took Vera's change of heart in stride. And so, three weeks before her fortieth birthday and a month after plunging all her other friends into despair, she married him.

"Hold it," says my aunt. "Don't put words in someone's mouth."

There are times, and this is one of them, when my aunt is cut from the same impossible cloth as Gittel. I don't even have to look at her to know that she's dead-set against whatever I'm about to say. It's as if her whole expansive self has been replaced by a suspicious look-alike from Shtebsk.

We've been through this before. Age before beauty, I tell myself, swallowing my pride.

Far be it from me, I say. Tell it your way. I'll just write.

What's bothering her, it turns out, is the expression "change of heart."

"First of all, Vera didn't have a change of heart. She believed what we all believed, and we still do: that the world could be a better place. And it will be—maybe not in my lifetime . . ."

"Fine," I interrupt her. "The point is—"

"Let me finish. The point is this: Vera didn't change, I didn't change, none of us changed. The only thing that changed with the storefront was our ability to see ahead. We knew more sooner, that's all. And don't make Sasha out to be some great romantic. She married him because he was persistent."

"Fine," I say. "I stand corrected."

"You can sit," says my Aunt Rita, and I know she's back to her old self.

Unlike the other men in Vera's life, Sasha was in love. His abundant size and mournful face—disappointed, round, like an old tire—had propelled her time and again into the arms of more voluptuous men, but it was Sasha who stood by her when everybody else drew back in horror and alarm.

"My mother was like that," he said over a cup of espresso in the Café Dante the day Vera summoned him to hear the truth about my aunt. "She dreamt about Hitler before we ever heard his name. My father made fun of her, but one day she saved his life. He was supposed to go to Antwerp on the night train and Mother saw that something terrible would happen. Father refused to change his plans, so she grabbed his ticket and threw it on the fire. The next day we heard the news: thieves had entered the train just north of Cracow and slit the throats of all the passengers in his compartment. That must have been in 1900, when Father was still selling lumber. Later she told us that when she was young she worked for the police, helping them solve murders. She could lead them straight to where the bodies were."

Sasha handed Vera a dozen blood red roses. His shirt was rumpled, his tie flaccid on the vast slope of his chest, but for the first time in years he felt elated. His battered briefcase was stuffed with plans for a monumental housing complex he was helping to construct above Fourteenth Street, where thousands of modest-income families would dwell in safe, well-lit buildings scattered on a swath of green. Sasha, a pioneer of urban planning, had been called away from teaching for a year to oversee what the builder proudly referred to as "the human factor"—which meant everything from schools to laundry rooms to shrubs. To someone of Sasha's political persuasion, this was an offer he could not refuse: the chance to create a whole equitable world within the implacable confines of capitalism. It was Sasha's job to make sure this instant town became synonymous with the best America could offer in planned communities, and on this radiant October day he felt particularly optimistic. Using a formula he himself had devised, the first three hundred tenants had just been chosen from a waiting list almost as thick as the Manhattan phone book, and he had reached an equally decisive point in his own life.

"Verochka," he said, setting his attaché case down in the vestibule and inhaling the cloud of mint and basil that was wafting toward the door from Vera's stove. "Will you marry me?"

Sasha was lonely; his wife had died fifteen years ago and he had advanced alone, surviving on tunafish and ravioli, into the barren no man's land of middle age. He was nearly old enough to be Vera's father, but the look on his face was that of a small boy who had been left forever in the care of strangers. In fact, he had no living relatives. He longed for quiet evenings like this at home with Vera, and the solace of her apron in the distance as she cooked.

Vera had been expecting Sasha to propose. She knew he loved her, and that he needed to be married. She had seen that at a glance when he joined her study group three years before. She had been aghast when he invited her to dinner; she had never seen a man so large. But curiosity got the better of her, and when they first made love she closed her eyes and imagined she was playing the string bass. Sasha was not so much fat as he was massive, "built," as someone said behind his back, "to last." The next time she saw him as a giant oak, then an armoire, then an ox, larger than life and capable of hauling prodigious loads through fields as big as oceans. Little by little she began to look forward to their weekly rendezvous, which were never the same twice. Besides his size, one thing compelled her: Sasha was ugly. His hooded eyes were small and round and sat as far apart as possible on opposite sides of his broad face. His nose, pressed close to his cheeks with no real shape, looked as if it had been leaned on by a man twice his height, and his mouth was as round and thick-lipped as any fish's. But there was a silver lining. Like an enormous frog, Sasha had the tenderness that sometimes comes with ugliness, and he had it in proportion to his size.

For Vera, Sasha was a complete departure: neither his politics, which were sentimental and groping, nor his appearance, which was strangely forbidding, gave him entry to the world of passionate ideas and easy friendship in which men like Arthur and Abey, Leo and Pavel considered each other brothers under the skin. Sasha was too big and too gentle to fit in.

Vera knew she didn't love him, but she had come to find him lovable—in part because of his immense capacity for love, and also because she knew how painful it would be for him if she said no. Still, only recently had she made up her mind: if Sasha found the courage to ask, she would find the courage to accept.

"I'm ready when you are . . ." she began, handing him a goblet of red wine. ". . . but on one condition: I want Natalya, God's Messenger, to read your hand."

Sasha, whose native language was no closer to English than Vera's, had spent the past two weeks poring over books of etiquette. He swallowed hard.

"Your wish," he said, "is my command."

The following morning, a bear-shaped man with a rumpled shirt and wrinkled tie and a copy of the *New York Times* under his arm was first on line when my aunt pulled the spangled curtain to one side and turned the cardboard sign to OPEN.

Vera was right: he was huge, and endearingly ugly.

Sasha set his briefcase by the door and smiled nervously at Vera. "Don't be shy on my account," Rita said, pointing at her friend, and he kissed Vera on the cheek.

"Now sit," she said, pulling up an extra chair. "Both of you."

Sasha's heavy lids and tangled hair reminded Rita of a Russian actor she had seen once in a Yiddish version of *The Seagull*, a rough-hewn giant of a man with arms like logs and hands like stones. But when she took his upturned hand in hers, all resemblance ended. The palm was soft and warm, like fresh baked bread. And it smelled of honey.

My aunt cupped her hands over the crystal ball and circled it three times before starting to read.

At first all she could see was a deep glow. Then a thread of light from Sasha's palm shot through her like a sigh, and the images poured in.

The cracks were there, of course, along with the usual array of shopworn facts—the depressing results of the upcoming elections, the advent of electric blankets and TV—but so was Vera, reflected deep inside his hand as in a lake: not some imaginary, future Vera, not Vera recollected and retouched, but Vera now, exactly as she sat, radiant and nervous at the table's edge. The portrait was more than faithful; it was astounding. On the threshold of forty, Vera was lovelier and more expressive than ever, as if the blondness of her youth had ripened into a more somber, though still golden, light. Irony as well as suffering had brushed her face, giving a mischievous glint to her eyes and a hint of darkness to her lips. My aunt glanced up, and her suspicion was confirmed: while bending over Sasha's hand she had been staring straight at Vera. His palm was a mirror.

"Yes," my aunt said, looking back into his hand. The face in the lake was still Vera's, untouched by any gaze, yet luminous with love.

Vera had walked into the arms of luck. Though Sasha would take her deep into his heart, he would never change her.

"Yes," she said again, but the image of Vera was already breaking up into a thousand pieces, dissolving to a map of Europe, then to a brilliant sweep of trees and leaves and giving way to a dark shed that met the horizon in a haze of smoke. From the expression on his face, my aunt wasn't sure if Sasha was listening or if he was lost in amorous reverie, but despite herself she kept on talking. The image shifted once again and she saw his childhood home with its gabled roof and double chimneys, the cobbled street with swastikas

scrawled on shop windows and lamp posts and the younger brother who had stayed behind to take care of their aged parents when
Sasha left for the United States. And then she stopped, as if she had
stumbled onto a small grave. She had: there, in a sloping field behind the house, Sasha's parents and brother had been shot to death
by Nazi soldiers in retaliation for the firebombing of a local bar-
racks.

My aunt heard Vera gasp. "It's all right," Sasha said. For the
first time in my aunt's life as a clairvoyant, a customer took her
hand in his. He pushed his palm closer to her on the table, and
something hummed inside her.

When she looked back into the triangle between his lines of
Life, Fate and Heart she understood. Sasha's world was lit from
within by a glow of his own making.

What lay before her was a honeycomb of exquisite proportions.
Bees flew every which way, mixing the honey that had kept him alive
through so much loss and that would light the days of anyone who
ventured deep into his trust. It was this world to which Vera had
unknowingly been drawn.

But now it was Sasha who was speaking and his words were music to her ears.

". . . because before you know it, each and every one of them—
Helen, Abey, Arthur, Pavel, your parents, even maybe Leo—will accept this . . . Verochka, how do you say in English—?"

"—this gift," Vera replied, her voice almost inaudible.

"How do you know?" asked my Aunt Rita.

"Trust me," Sasha said.

After everything she had just seen, it would have been hard not to.

Seven

People say I'm always in a hurry. It's true I eat standing up and that my handwriting shows all the telltale signs of haste gone haywire: dots thrown every which way over i's, t's crossed on the run, the curves of j's and g's and y's flung out like sheets flapping on a line. My mother, who was rushed across the Queensboro Bridge three weeks before her due date, doing her best to hold me back while Manhattan's lights blinked on and off like Cassiopeia in time with her contractions, says I was impatient even in the womb. "You still think if you rush you'll get more done," she says, "but look at physics: if you run in the rain you get just as wet." Is that true? My mother walks, slow and deliberate, holding her umbrella high; her calm is an example.

Even my Aunt Rita, who predicted the exact hour of my birth but not the fact that I'd be born three weeks ahead of time, tells me to slow down.

She's right. I know every moment has to be lived through; I know when you do more you also do less. So, in the interest of respecting time's unerring flow, I hereby plant my two feet squarely in the fall of 1946, restraining myself from leaping forward to the hour of my birth. Either way, as the saying goes, you get where you're going: my birth, once a mere glint in the sky over Manhattan, is now, if nothing else by virtue of having been proclaimed, a fact. Not a full-fledged fact, because it hasn't happened yet; more like a fact-to-be: a factlet covered with the peach fuzz of possibility. A foregone conclusion whose time has not yet come, but will.

Everything is in place. Abey and Helen have already met, and have taken such a shine to each other that their cheeks are permanently polished, red as apples; their wedding, after almost a year of expectation, is now only weeks away. Their eagerness for each other has become the kind of contagious excitement that conjures up familial visions of great dynasties and that makes prospective in-laws chew their fingers with delight.

Chaim and Gittel are nothing if not smitten with the wide-eyed astronomy student their only son has chosen for his wife. They call her "the living cameo," and it's true she bears a startling, if dark-haired, resemblance to the girls in the ads for Breck shampoo. The Three Mosquitoes enthusiastically agree, tiptoeing around her when they wake one Sunday morning in September to find her sleeping on the downstairs sofa, covered with the army blanket Chaim uses for his naps and exhaling the sweet breath of apparition. For once it is Chaim, summoned from the kitchen in his slippers and robe, who gives the slumberer her special name, which leaps from his lips as he bends over her: *Ponim*, he says in Yiddish, harking back to the ancient Greeks, and to this day Helen's name in the family is *Ponim*, the Face. How she escaped the lash of Gittel's tongue is, as my Aunt Rita would say, between herself and God.

Helen's parents, a hard-working couple who run a delicatessen in the Bronx and have no other children besides this red-cheeked beauty, consider Abey the Baby, with his perfect diction, Hollywood crewcut and straight white teeth, as fine a son-in-law as anyone could wish for. They are especially impressed by his ballroom dancing, which is pure Fred Astaire, his ear for French and Russian, which is flawless, and his ability to recite long sections of *Hamlet* and *The Odyssey* by heart. They aren't overjoyed about his politics, but Helen, who enthusiastically shares Abey's views, is proud that she has found a husband who will be her comrade too.

Still, my future mother, the tiny diamond on her finger telegraphing the luminous news of her betrothal to the world with what she hopes is sufficient modesty ("It wasn't a real diamond," she would tell me proudly when I was eight, "it cost five dollars and we each paid half ..."), wonders whether she is doing the right thing.

It's not that she doubts her love for Abey. What worries her, at twenty-one, is her career. Which is to say that her jitters these last weeks before her wedding are more galactic than romantic. Science, not love, has been tugging at her sleeve for years, and she is suddenly afraid that if she adds her name to the honor roll of postwar brides, her dream of following her scientific heroines to stardom—and of naming whole yet-to-be-discovered solar systems after Madame Curie, Gertrude Stein, Sojourner Truth, Amelia Earhart and Rosa Luxemburg—will vanish in thin air.

She's right of course, as any woman looking for a job or flipping through a rack of clothes knows perfectly well. In part to combat any lingering fantasies women might have about leading a more useful—or a more remunerated—life, the ads are daily growing more belligerent. "I dreamt I went shopping in my Maidenform Bra," will be the ultimate statement of woman's postwar place and shape; and, to Madison Avenue's mind (which is fast becoming the mind of the whole country), the expression of her deepest lust. If she ventures from her home it will not be to the factory or office, but as a bra-clad dreamer, to glide through the beckoning aisles of department stores.

It doesn't take much to know that in this brave new world, accolades will be few and far between for a girl in cardigans and dungarees who plans to spend her life behind a giant telescope peering at the stars.

But Abey the Baby, like Chaim a dreamer in another realm, promises his Helen that marriage and science will go hand in hand once the country is back on track. "It's a matter of time," he tells her; change is just around the corner. Besides, when the revolution comes, the "woman question" will be solved. "Presto," he says, his hands sweeping the air like a magician whisking a white rabbit out of his black hat. Like Pavel and Arthur, with whom he has discussed all this, he believes that men and women are one in struggle, and he has found a job that will support them both while Helen continues with her studies. For the past six months he's been selling bedroom sets on Steinway Street, in Queens, helping couples of all ages, newly released from wartime worry and forbearance, choose the mattresses and headboards that will catapult them to domestic bliss.

What he hadn't counted on was Vera's startling claim about his sister, and the ensuing uproar in the Party, which have made this nuptial autumn unexpectedly tense. With each passing week he breathes a sigh of relief: determined to graduate before her December wedding, Helen has been spending all her time in the physics lab at Hunter College, oblivious to the shock waves that have struck their little world. Like Chaim and Gittel, she has yet to hear that Rita, with Vera by her side, has set up shop on the Lower East Side as a bonafide, beturbaned, unrepentant storefront kook.

*

Six weeks before my parents' wedding, Rita broke the news to Chaim and Gittel. "I'm not seeing Leo anymore," she said from just outside the living room, where the two old people, already in their flannel nightgowns, were curled into adjacent armchairs. This was the moment she had dreaded. For months she had supplied them with a vast array of excuses for Leo's absence—he had gone to see his uncle in Chicago, his mother's cataracts had gotten worse, he was collecting signatures for this candidate or that—but with Abey's marriage practically around the corner, her repertoire was wearing thin. In any case, Leo's failure to attend an event of such importance could hardly be explained away. Abey himself, still worried over Leo's disappearance and hoping against hope that his friend would reappear before the wedding, agreed the time had come to spell things out. "We might as well get it over with," he had said between clenched teeth that morning as my aunt was putting on her coat. Chaim and Gittel would have to accept the unpleasant fact that their daughter's long deferred engagement, the promise that had given rosy shape to the future, now belonged, prematurely, to the past.

"But please," Abey said under his breath, "don't tell them what you're doing for a living. I don't want Helen finding out. She's jittery enough as it is."

My aunt assured him she had no such plans. There were certain things Chaim and Gittel didn't need to know. At least not yet.

Now she girded herself for their response.

Chaim shook his head. "Such a nice boy," he said softly. "He should be healthy and live a long life."

Was that all? My aunt held her breath, waiting for the other shoe to drop.

"What?" Gittel obliged with a corrosive blast, cupping her

hand around her one good ear. My aunt's heart sank. Not only would she have to repeat what she had said, but she would have to shout. "I'm not seeing Leo anymore," she said again, louder than before, stepping into the living room. "I heard you the first time," Gittel replied, her voice slicing into the air with razor-sharp precision. Her voice was withering.

Although she would prove a relentless matchmaker over time, for the moment my grandmother had moved on to worries of a more practical kind. If Leo wasn't coming, someone else would have to drive the bride and bridegroom to the Catskills right after the wedding.

"He's not coming?"

"I don't know."

The fact was, no one knew. It had been almost a year since the wintry night my aunt and Leo went their separate ways, almost a year since Leo headed north in La Pasionaria along the snowy park. At first no one realized he was gone. But when he missed three consecutive meetings of his weekly study group, his friends became concerned. Pavel advised them not to worry; Leo was probably just working overtime to keep his mind off Rita. Juanita, who had always considered Leo an enigma, counseled patience: Leo had his own way of doing things, she reminded them, and in due time they would know where he had gone and why. Vera disagreed. It wasn't like him not to call, especially if he was upset. Besides, in all the years she had known him, ever since they met in Spain, he had never missed a meeting. Arthur got in touch with Leo's mother, who hadn't heard from him in weeks, though as she readily confessed, this was not the first time her son had disappeared without a word. The same thing had happened when he volunteered for Spain. He told no one he was leaving, and it was months before a rain-soaked letter had arrived explaining that he had survived the Battle of the Ebro, and that he would be shipped back to New York City as soon as he recovered from his wounds. What could she do? Her son was a grown man. But please, she told Arthur, if you hear from him, tell him to call home. By the end of March, his friends decided it was time to act. Leo might be lying low; he might also be in trouble. So when a small delegation went to see his landlady, they were astonished to learn that his latest rent check had arrived on time, along with a brief note asking her to water his begonias and hold his mail till his return. Abey turned the envelope this way and that; it was Leo's handwriting, no doubt about it, but without a clue to where he was or why he had dropped so precipitously out of sight.

At least they knew he was alive. But with that certainty established, new doubts crept in. Month after month, the rent checks continued to arrive like clockwork, Mrs. Callaghan assured them, always addressed in the same familiar boxy hand and always scrupulously on time. How Leo could maintain his room on Sixty-eighth Street while living elsewhere for so long was only one of the questions that disturbed his friends.

By the end of August even Vera, who loved him like a brother and thought she knew most of his secrets, admitted that her loyalty was shaken. It was one thing for a man to have a broken heart, she said, and another for him to disappear into thin air, leaving everyone distraught. After all, it was Leo who had called things off with Rita, not the other way around.

In the privacy of the storefront, where she and my Aunt Rita continued to survey the world through dozens of assorted hands, Vera ventured the hope that Leo would eventually turn up in someone's palm. "Not if I can help it," said my aunt. My aunt thought Leo was best left to his own devices—"whatever they are," she said whenever Vera mentioned him by name. But with the approach of

Abey's wedding, even she began to hope he might return, if only to clarify the reasons for his strange behavior and put his friends' anxieties to rest.

*

The girl staring at the floor one chilly morning in November is wearing a nondescript blue coat, a navy blue wool scarf and a blue felt hat with a large brim. She is clutching the elbow of a matronly woman whose name is on the tip of my Aunt Rita's tongue.

"Pearl Silverstein," the woman says. "Remember? I was here with my sister." My aunt remembers. Mrs. Silverstein, sparkling from ear to wrist with rhinestones, had sat in silence while my aunt read Mrs. Levy's hand back in July, her mouth so agape that a fly not only could but did fly in and out before Vera, who caught the whole scene with her camera, had a chance to warn her.

"This girl's out on a limb," Mrs. Silverstein explains. "She wants to know if she should marry the man she's engaged to."

"Have a seat," my aunt replies, completely deadpan. "I don't give advice, but I'll tell you what I see."

The ivory hand is narrow and long and curved slightly to the right, like a beautiful object meant to serve some special but mysterious purpose—a tool, my aunt says, musing aloud, perhaps even a ritual serving piece, rather than an ordinary hand. With its elegant wrist and tapered arm, it could almost be displayed in one of the domestic objects corridors of the Metropolitan Museum. At first glance, the palm is smooth and almost without lines. But when my aunt bends forward to examine it more closely, there in the center, at the very point where the lines of Life and Heart sweep toward each other in perpetual embrace, stands Abey the Baby, triumphant and handsome as a statue, his face alive with expectation, his hair ruffled by the wind of his impending marriage.

There is a storm cloud gathering behind him, but it has nothing to do with his engagement. "Yes," says my Aunt Rita without looking up. "She should."

The room is silent, except for the soft hum of my aunt's voice, which continues for a moment, then precipitously stops.

"Helen?" she finally manages to say, the play of a smile crossing her lips.

"You mean you know each other?"

"Abey the Baby is my brother," says my aunt.

Once again, Pearl Silverstein's mouth has fallen open like a trap, but this time there is no one in the store to take her portrait. Today is Election Day, another chance to change the system from within, and Vera has taken her entire study group uptown to canvass for the embattled congressman from Harlem, Vito Marcantonio.

"What can I tell you?" says my aunt. "She didn't say anything, and I didn't ask. Of course I recognized her. Deliberately? I doubt it. She was probably just curious to see what would happen. I was curious myself—so I played along."

Helen's side of the story is that when Mrs. Silverstein, secretary of the physics department at Hunter College and confidante of all the students, first suggested that she take her doubts and lay them on the table of a certain Natalya, God's Messenger, she had politely declined; that eventually it had crossed her mind that the Lower East Side seer Mrs. Silverstein had mentioned might be her future sister-in-law; and that by the time she finally agreed to be taken by the hand and have her palm read she was almost certain she would wind up face to face with Abey's sister. Abey had always been evasive when she asked him about Rita, but she had put two and two together the night she spent on his parents' couch in Forest Hills.

After everyone had gone to bed, she had overheard him on the phone with Arthur saying something about Vera being off her rocker and begging Arthur not to breathe a word to her, Helen, about Rita. "Me? Go down to Seventh Street?" Abey had exclaimed. "Over my dead body. Let the two of them stew in their own juice."

According to my mother, it was shock, not forethought, that kept her from greeting my Aunt Rita. "Of course we recognized each other—we had to. I'm sure I was about to say 'Hello,' or 'So it *is* you,' or something like that, but you have to imagine the impact of it all. I was literally dumbstruck. Just the sight of her through the window was enough to knock you on your ear. She radiated mastery. You could almost see the principles at work inside her brain. Then, on top of everything, her silence threw me off. Once she took my hand I couldn't interrupt her. It would have been like interrupting Einstein. . . ."

There would be times when my aunt would wish she had seen less in Helen's hand, or comprehended more, but the images came rushing out before she had a chance to stop them. Time shot ahead, then back, and before my aunt was done she had seen both the terror that was escalating all around them and the disconcerting glimmer of reunion.

She saw the covers of a book clamped shut, and students not yet born grappling with events that would turn back the clock; then, in a crowd of half a million, she saw Helen and Abey cheering while a prophet spoke.

She saw the storm clouds she had seen before, but this time she saw something else: she saw the storefront empty and an unmarked car across the street, and she saw the lights go on in Mrs. Sullivan's apartment down the block. She saw Vera giving someone wrong directions and Sasha burning papers in the empty lot next door. And then, as if the hand before her were a stage, a curtain opened and the landscape changed.

Partly hidden in the courtyard of a stucco house, beneath a portrait of La Pasionaria—but she would recognize that shadow anywhere!—she saw a man step forward to receive his mail. A little girl, barefoot in a bright pink dress, was jumping rope behind him. My aunt felt Helen's pulse begin to race. Slowly, deliberately, he opened the blue envelope and read his mother's note: "A man brought this yesterday, dear. I said you were out of town." It was odd to see him now, so far from home, unaware that he was being watched. He unfolded the subpoena: "You are hereby summoned to appear in Federal District Court of the State of New York, Southern District, on June 15, 1952." My aunt peered deeper into Helen's hand. There were a thousand questions on her lips. If only she could get a glimpse inside his room—she was so close she could see the second-story window, the pots of red geraniums against the whitewashed wall, the iron grillwork on the balcony . . . but Leo was already a blur on the horizon and dozens of new images were streaming across Helen's hand.

"Relieved? Well, I suppose," my Aunt Rita says today. "Of course I hadn't seen the half of it. Ignorance is bliss."

But her astonishment was swept aside by what swam into focus next: a dark-haired couple in their thirties, their portraits exactly as they would appear in newspapers around the world; the waves of protest in which hundreds of thousands would demonstrate in cities everywhere to save them; and the harrowing final hour when they would be strapped into the electric chair to die. This would be in 1953, she said, the same year in which Helen would finally give birth to the daughter who would one day write the life of Natalya, God's Messenger.

"The child will be born out of a wound," she said, and then fell silent.

Once again my aunt felt the quicksand pull of fear that had gripped her when she first became clairvoyant. Then she remembered: she held her breath, and the translucent screen before her on the table flickered and went out.

When she looked back a moment later, all signs of time and place had vanished, and Helen's pulse had slowed.

What she saw next was a loose image, written on the air. She saw doubt fluttering overhead like a great bird and Abey wringing his hands. Before him stood Helen, dressed in a white robe. "Do you still want to marry me?" she asked. There was no hesitation in Abey's voice when he replied, "Of course."

Helen was ecstatic. "And to think you'll be my sister-in-law!" she said, jumping up and throwing her arms around my aunt.

Across the room, Pearl Silverstein sat with her mouth still open, rhinestone glasses sparkling in the cold November light, blue glints dancing in her hair.

With the wedding only six weeks off, Abey had to know. Helen told him everything, from the moment Mrs. Silverstein first confessed that she had been to see a woman who read palms the way Horowitz read music, to how she had finally succumbed to curiosity and how all her doubts had flown away as soon as she set foot in Rita's storefront. She took a deep breath. "We saw you saying yes to marriage, but we saw terrible things too. We saw books being burned. We saw an execution. And we saw Leo," she said. "He's back in Spain. Or at least he will be in 1952." When she was done, Abey's face had turned the color of cement, and sweat was running from his forehead.

"If it was anybody else, I might believe it—but you?"

"What can I say? I saw it with my own two eyes. Now I know such things exist."

"In the eye of the beholder."

"In reality. Your sister Rita is a born clairvoyant."

"My sister Rita is a born con artist," Abey said, wiping his brow.

"Your sister happens to be a chiromantic genius."

"You can't be serious. What about science?"

"At her level, it *is* science."

"Helen, please. My sister doesn't know a hypothesis from a hippopotamus."

"She doesn't have to. Believe me, everything she said is going to come true."

"I don't believe in 'going to.' I believe in proof."

"Do you still want to marry me?"

"Of course."

"See? You said exactly what she said you would. That's proof!"

"What is the world coming to?" he said.

"That remains to be seen."

Abey knew he had no choice. He phoned Arthur and told him Helen had followed Vera over the edge. "I give up," he said. "It's like a plague."

"Do you still love her?"

"Unfortunately, yes."

"Well, then," Arthur said, "I guess you're next."

*

Six weeks later, Abey stepped into the living room. "This just came," he said excitedly, still in his bathrobe and waving an envelope from Western Union. He pulled out the sheet of yellow paper and read the message aloud: "REGRET CANNOT MAKE WED-

DING. Stop. OTHERWISE ENGAGED. Stop. STILL YOUR
BEST MAN."

"Jesus," Abey said, looking down at the telegram. "It's from
Madrid. He's either in hot water or he's gone off the deep end."

"Or both," said my Aunt Rita.

"*Nu?*" Gittel said triumphantly, turning to her son. "Maurice
will drive you and Helen to the mountains."

But Abey the Baby, U.S. Army Corporal First Class and rookie
salesman of the year at Astoria Bedding & Carpet, had fainted into
a small heap on his parents' afghan rug.

When he came to, Helen and her bridal retinue were at the
door, and Chaim was holding up the three-piece suit Abey had ordered for the wedding. My future father jumped in.

*

"What can I tell you? My daughter can't see what's right in
front of her own freckled nose," Gittel told Mrs. William
Dougherty during the wedding, in what would be her lifelong
explanation of what she always referred to as my aunt's decision not
to marry Leo.

Dressed in sky blue tulle with matching gloves, Mrs. Dougherty, who lived across the street in Forest Hills, and the only neighbor invited to the wedding, had just made the mistake of asking
Gittel whether Rita's long-awaited marriage to her boyfriend—
"the lad with the taxi," she called him—would be next.

It had been months since La Pasionaria last turned onto Essex
Street and pulled up by the curb, but apparently no one had
noticed. "I'm so—how very thoughtless of me—I'm so sorry, dear,"
Mrs. Dougherty stammered, then rose to the occasion. "A man
proposes, God disposes—isn't that what they say? Oh my—or is it

the other way around? I'm so sorry. The Lord must have someone else in mind for her, God bless her."

"If God wanted us to fly we wouldn't have to take the subway, right, Mrs. Dougherty?" my grandmother replied in a sarcastic whisper, leaning toward her neighbor while the band played "Stardust."

The three-tier cake had been sliced and served and the younger set—Esther and Maurice, Helen and Abey, Helen's roommate Ruth and her boyfriend George, Arthur and a girl named Kay—were dancing an endless stream of rumbas, cha-chas and foxtrots while the rest of the guests lingered over coffee or champagne. Laughter and jokes floated up through the smoke-filled chandeliers of the Henry Hudson Room at the St. James as men and women moved in perfect squares across the parquet floor. The women wore the flared ballerina dresses that were all the rage when hemlines finally descended from their wartime heights, with frothy petticoats that flashed as they kicked their legs up in the tango; and for the first time in years, their nylons, elegantly crisscrossed at the ankle by the straps of their suede shoes, were real, not penciled on.

Vera and Sasha, reveling in the exuberance of a real wedding after their own spartan one the month before at City Hall, raised glass after glass to each other and the bride and groom, jumping up each time there was a slow dance, then holding hands back at their table while sitting out the fast ones. From time to time Vera coaxed Sasha to his feet, convinced him to ask one of the old ladies to a waltz, and set off with her camera to photograph the guests.

"What?" Gittel could barely hear above the music. Mrs. Dougherty wanted to know more. "She says she has her mind on higher things," my grandmother confided. "If you want my opinion, she's up in the clouds flapping around like a lost bird and before you know it her brains are all shook up, a regular milkshake. What can I tell you, Mrs. Dougherty? She called it off. She's my own flesh and blood, but when it comes to the important things in life, she's a sleepwalker in a fog."

The band began to play "Doin' What Comes Natur'lly."

Vera caught them as their glasses met, giddy with surprise. What they are looking at with their mouths open, according to Vera, is my Aunt Rita, who at that very moment was sailing across the dance floor with one of the musicians as flawlessly as if they had both been born in Argentina.

"You see, miracles never cease to happen," Mrs. Dougherty said in earshot of the Three Mosquitoes, who were practicing the fox-trot in their first high heels.

"Here's mud in your eye," my cousin Brenda swears she heard my grandmother reply, still brandishing her glass of seltzer, but nobody believes her.

Moments later Gittel, thick-waisted and stooped in the same navy dress with dime-sized polka-dots she would wear to Brenda's wedding ten years later, was on her feet, and so was Mrs. Dougherty, who had swept her out onto the dance floor to dance the tango *"Nunca Más."* This called for another photograph. How Vera knew to turn around in that split second is further proof of her extraordinary eye, which captured not only a family occasion, but an age. What difference does it make if my grandmother looks like a midget beside her heavily corseted neighbor, whose ample bosom, satin-clad, towers Walkyrie-like above her head?

There are other pictures from that sequence, including one of Sasha dancing with the bride and one of Chaim asleep in his chair with a slice of wedding cake before him and a seraphic smile on his face. But of all the photographs Vera took that day, the one of my grandmother and Mrs. Dougherty was the most widely reproduced. Gittel kept it on her night table until she died. "This is Abey's wedding," she used to say. "But it's really about my Rita."

*

The telegram changed everything and nothing. Everybody had a theory, and no one wanted to be right. If Leo had really returned to Spain, Abey said, then he had probably joined the anti-Franco underground, and it was anybody's guess when they would see him again. "You mean *if*," said Arthur, who shared the depth of Leo's political commitment but not his willingness to risk his life, which he regarded with pure awe. They were seated around Vera's round oak table, where they had gathered a week after the wedding to read the telegram anew. " 'Regret' . . . 'otherwise engaged' . . . 'still your best man' . . ." According to Pavel, who had intercepted Nazi documents during the war, the message was in code. While wishing Abey happiness in marriage, Leo had simultaneously managed to convey in just ten words that he himself was wedded to the struggle—"best man," Pavel felt, meant that Leo was working for the principles they all believed in. Vera agreed that Leo had probably gone back to Spain in order to continue the good fight; she also thought, but didn't say, that he had probably returned to a woman she knew only as Carmen, who had brought him Whitman and Blake after he was wounded and taught him to drink wine like a Spaniard while he was awaiting transfer to a hospital in France. But Sasha's immense hands were trembling when he passed the telegram to Helen. He thought it sounded like a smuggled cry for help.

It was Helen, in whose hand their missing friend had fleetingly appeared, who came up with a plan that they all immediately endorsed. By unanimous acclaim, Abey was chosen for the mission.

Two days later, he was on his way to visit Leo's mother in the

Bronx. "I need to ask you something, Mrs. Kaplan," he had said over the phone, "but I need to ask you in person." He took the subway up to the Grand Concourse and found himself in the mirrored lobby of a miniature Versailles. In fact the building bore a freshly painted sign that said THE PALAIS ROYAL.

The tiny woman behind the door to 7J was so elegantly attired that at first Abey thought he had the wrong apartment. His doubts were instantly dispelled. "Abey," she said, clasping his right hand in both of hers, then ushering him through a set of double doors into a sitting room filled with oriental carpets and antiques. "I'm so glad you've come." Frieda Kaplan was probably the same age as Gittel, but she belonged to another world.

My father tried to focus on the purpose of his visit, but it was difficult to keep his eye from wandering around the room. After six months of selling bedroom sets at ABC, he still didn't know the difference between a sideboard and a credenza; still, he knew enough to tell that everything in sight was of museum quality. It didn't make sense.

He remembered hearing that Leo's father had had a penchant for inventions and that when the first synthetics had appeared, after World War I, he had tried his hand at manufacturing plush animals that growled or roared or barked or squeaked, but that someone else had beat him to it. There had never been the slightest hint that he had been successful. Leo had always made it sound as if his parents' circumstances were pinched at best. When he and Rita were first keeping company, right after Pearl Harbor, there was nearly always a large swatch of polar bear skin draped over the driver's seat of La Pasionaria—from my late father's late menagerie, Leo used to say with a mixture of affection and embarrassment.

"It wasn't like this when my husband was alive," Mrs. Kaplan said gently, reading Abey's mind. "Unfortunately, he didn't live to see the fruits of his labor. Leo took it very hard when I redid the apartment—I think that's partly why he left for Spain. You know how sensitive he is. Of course I don't have to tell you that his politics came first. He's never been back since; we always meet at the Eclair. He feels the money isn't ours—he calls it filthy lucre. You probably feel the same way. I understand—but what are we supposed to do, give it away?"

"What will you have—" Mrs. Kaplan was saying. Abey had heard her vaguely the first time, but now she repeated the question. "Coffee, tea, seltzer, juice?" Seltzer sounded fine. "With a slice of cake?" He nodded, deciding it was time to explain why he had come.

Five minutes later, just as he began to wonder how seltzer and cake could possibly make their way into the sitting room if Leo's refined, well-spoken mother did not uproot herself from her pale velvet couch, a woman appeared before them with a silver tray on which sat a crystal siphon, two matching goblets, two napkins, two forks and two glass plates, each holding a slice of cake. "Thank you, Millie," said the widow in the cashmere sweater and wool skirt, and Millie vanished as silently as she had come.

There was a mystery here, but by now my father had progressed too far in his own speech to stop.

". . . so once the telegram arrived, we knew he was all right. Of course, it also proved my sister Rita really does have some kind of powers." Leo's mother took a sip of seltzer. "Don't mind me—I have high blood pressure," she said, reaching for a tiny pill. "The problem," Abey continued, taken aback by her apparent calm, "is that we still don't know what he's doing there or why he left without telling any of us—myself, Vera, Arthur, you, the people he would normally confide in—that he was going. Or how and why he's kept his room on Sixty-eighth Street. Now, most clairvoyants can see only so far and no further, but my sister is no ordinary clairvoyant. She's willing to give it a try. She says if he's in anybody's hand it's yours. . . . So . . . what we were actually hoping was that . . ."

Leo's mother declined in no uncertain terms. "I have never set foot in such an establishment," she said, pumping a second blast of seltzer into Leo's glass, "and I can assure you I have no intention of doing so in my old age."

Abey pressed forward with his mission. "The point, Mrs. Kaplan," he said as tactfully as he knew how, "is that other people's safety could be involved. We really need to know what Leo's up to, and that whatever he's doing, he's taking the necessary precautions. Now do you see . . . ?"

The following morning, personally escorted by Arthur, who had taken the day off from his family's dry cleaners, Frieda Kaplan emerged from the subway in her silver lambswool coat and walked the two blocks to the storefront.

"My sister, the soothsayer," Abey said as the door swung open, proudly reintroducing Rita to Leo's mother.

"I'm not at all happy about this, dear," said the woman who had once embraced my aunt as her prospective daughter-in-law. "Leo told me you had opened some sort of fortune-telling emporium, and I thought he was right to break off the engagement. But I must say, even with that dreadful turban on your head, you're as pretty as ever."

"Thank you so much for coming, Mrs. Kaplan," Vera interrupted, showing Leo's mother to the metal folding chair across the table from my aunt. "We know it isn't easy to get here from the Bronx."

"This nice young man accompanied me," said Mrs. Kaplan, pointing to Arthur, who, like Abey, though with less enthusiasm, was making his first visit to the storefront.

Vera positioned herself discreetly in the back, where Sasha's girth had been enlisted to conceal her tripod. This was one photograph she didn't want to miss, and she was sure Leo would be as grateful for it later as his mother would be dead-set against it at the moment.

There was an awkward silence. "Well, dear, I'm here. You may as well go ahead and do whatever it is you do," said Mrs. Kaplan, who had peeled off her gray leather gloves and was sitting stiffly in her chair, palms downward on her lap like a pharaoh on his throne.

"I need your hand, Mrs. Kaplan," said my aunt.

A small wrinkled hand rose to the surface.

My aunt turned it face-up on the table and let her fingers play across the wrist. Leo's mother might have high blood pressure; still, this was a fast pulse by any measure.

"And now, Mrs. Kaplan, Natalya, God's Messenger, will attempt to locate your son," said my father, who had suddenly acquired the air of an impresario.

My aunt waved her hands three times over the crystal ball. "Easier said than done," she said, as a high brick wall came into focus. It was the back of a factory, but it might just as well have been the back of Frieda Kaplan's mind. Leo's mother was determined. Her mouth was set in a small line. My aunt had to wait until she saw a fleet of gleaming trucks pull up, freshly painted with the logo KAPCO. Then silence. "No go?" somebody said with a low chuckle, and it was true there was no sign of Leo in his mother's opaque hand.

My aunt glanced around the room. She knew time was on her side. When she looked back, the palm before her on the table was taut as a drum and bright as an empty movie screen before the film comes on. In fact, it could have done with a marquee, because once the images began to flow there was no stopping them.

There was Leo's father running toward a train forever pulling from the station, and Frieda waving back with Leo in her arms; Leo, now a boy of nine or ten, standing all alone in a fierce storm while a man in tattered clothes reached out his hand and begged; Leo's father weeping in a judge's chamber; then Leo's father in his dark oak chair, bent over his desk as he sailed into the waves off Amagansett, and Leo swimming out to save him in a dream that had no end.

The words flowed from her lips faster than my aunt could do them justice, but several of those present can still repeat whole parts of what she said verbatim.

"What things seem and what they are, are eternally apart. His father's claim becomes his shame; his father's throne his own. Loss haunts, gain taunts. To be late is to outwit an early death, but to live is to plunder." Apparently there had been some sort of lawsuit; apparently Leo's father had been overtaken by despair. The money had come later, years after his death. No wonder Leo had tried so hard to break the grip of wealth. Or that his dream had stayed behind, fleeing to his mother's hand while he returned to Spain. From facts like these, there was no escape.

Frieda was impassive as my aunt began to speak, but by the end her face had softened and she looked relieved.

"Where is he now?" Vera asked gently.

"I wish I knew."

"Any idea?" Leo's mother shook her head.

"Where?" Abey was impatient.

"I'm not done yet," said my aunt, staring back into the depths of Frieda's hand, where a set of heavy curtains shimmied open, revealing yet another, which opened to reveal another, then another, until finally, on a streetcar in Madrid, she saw Leo, his arm around a slender waist.

"Spain," she said with a deep sigh. And to her everlasting shock, Leo, his hand a tiny flag in Frieda's palm, waved slowly, unmistakably, back.

Everybody spoke at once. "Why didn't he tell us he was rich?" "Did your husband commit suicide?" "Are you divorced?" "Where's the money from?" "Who's the girl?"

Vera was the hardest hit of all. "Who the hell is he then? Everything he told us was a lie. He made it all up—the room, the taxi, the worn-out shoes: his whole scraped-together life. And while he's off gallivanting on behalf of the oppressed, his inheritance is sitting in some vault on Wall Street, collecting interest the way curtains collect dust."

"All that meant nothing to him," Frieda said, her eyes filling with tears. "That was the lie. What he told you was the truth."

"His room was a lie," said Vera.

"No," said Leo's mother. "That room meant everything to him. It was his truest self. Besides the taxi, it was the only place he felt at home."

"But even the taxi was a lie!" Arthur exploded.

"That taxi was the only way my son could keep his truth and still be in the world. Leo is a tortoise—he has to have a shell."

"What is he, an invalid?" someone asked. Mrs. Kaplan wiped away a tear.

"What is he?" she asked slowly. "A sensitive, sensitive man. Someone who can't bear injustice. You of all people should understand."

"We of all people know when we've been had," said Arthur, fighting back tears of disappointment. "For all we know, he probably never even fought in Spain."

"Believe me, he fought."

That much Vera could vouch for. Anything more would have to wait. A reinforced steel door had just descended over Frieda Kaplan's palm.

There was no arguing with Leo's mother. For now at least, her son's strange life was safely under lock and key.

By the time Pavel agreed to pay a visit to the storefront one Saturday a few months later, the cracks were spreading, and my aunt could no longer hide her sense of doom. The news, both as the *New York Times* saw fit to print it and as it had begun to press its way into the hands of my aunt's customers, was anything but good.

War raged that spring in India and Madagascar, in Indochina, Palestine and Greece. In Europe and the Soviet Union, the silence of the dead had given way to the din of reconstruction. Here at home, a different form of warfare, less lethal and more lasting, had begun. With HUAC's budget steadily climbing and a presidential order requiring loyalty oaths from all federal employees, the committee had extended its reach into the records of two million Americans. Fear was the ultimate weapon. Invisible as nerve gas, but everywhere, like air, in just a few short months it had spread across the country. The unions, unbidden, had started purges of their own, and schools and colleges were falling into step, with Hollywood not far behind.

The coldest wind was yet to blow, but my aunt could see it coming.

"There's going to be a sacrifice," she said, as a clenched fist came into view in Faith Kincaid's small hand. The fist swung forward, then back, as if preparing to land a devastating blow. Then, to my aunt's horror, a microphone appeared before it and the fist, with a broad leer, began to speak. "I have here before me . . ." it proclaimed, waving a small piece of paper before a crowd of several dozen Republican ladies. "McCarthy," my aunt whispered, clapping her hand over her mouth in disbelief, and sure enough, it was the sneering senator, announcing a crusade against subversives. "Harm will come to us by water," my aunt continued, groping for the words as darkness flooded Faith's soft hand. "Lies will drown us and crush the air like birds. But the bones of the truth will jut from us in time, and one day strangers will read what we ignored . . ."

For an hour Pavel sat in silence while the April light poured through the plate glass window. Now he jumped to his feet, set up his easel, raked both hands through his electrified gray hair and began to paint while my aunt, her chalk-blue summer turban bent over the table, continued to read hands.

Mrs. Levy came and went and so did Eddie and Jimmy Carney. Just before noon, Vera arrived with sandwiches and coffee and took up her accustomed post behind her camera. Today there was no time for lunch. There were several customers from out of town, including a French banker whose hand was brimming with long poems, and a friend of his from Argentina, a writer whose peculiar stories would make him a contender for the Nobel Prize. Then Mrs. Sullivan stopped by on her way home from the dentist, who was slowly refitting the teeth she had lost the preceding summer while watching a man drown off Coney Island.

"How you knew . . ." she said again, laying her repentant palm before my aunt, her eyes as wide with wonder as her mouth had been that fateful August day.

And once again, as she did every week, my aunt saw the elderly couple pressed together on their little bench; as always, Mrs. Sullivan sighed and squirmed and blushed.

But suddenly that passionate scene dissolved in a whirl of color and my aunt was staring at the foyer of her parents' house in

Forest Hills. As her eyes adjusted to the light, she saw Chaim's plywood fiddle lying in its long flat box on the bookcase in the living room. On the glistening surface of the dining room table lay a copy of the *New York Times,* whose date she read without the slightest effort. The house was a perfect miniature of itself, and oddly silent. She saw Abey standing on the stairs below the first-floor landing, and she could have sworn she heard a clock, sharp and quiet as a knife, tick-tock, tick-tock.

It was nearly five o'clock when Pavel wiped his hands on his smock and asked for water.

His portrait of God's Messenger was done.

Vera left her tripod and stood beside my aunt. "What's this?" she said, staring at the red velvet turban and opulent robe he had given his painted version of Natalya. Pavel shrugged. "It just came to me," he said, surveying his luminous yet brooding canvas. My aunt still shakes her head. "He did in five hours what most artists don't do in a lifetime: paint not what they see, but what they don't."

All that year, the news was unrelenting. "Pride of the street and curse of his own house . . . Woe of the centuries . . . The man who feeds on his own fury feeds on fear. His tastes untamed will haunt the just. His name will be a lesson in despair . . ." It was the end of November and my aunt looked up at Mrs. Harlan Bell III, whose thin, dry hand lay flat as a beached fish on the blue damask tablecloth.

"But you," she went on, looking into the crystal ball, "will know none of this, neither his rise nor his fall. I see him after you are gone, working late into the night, his reputation assured. Your son, and not your son: a clerk, a zealot. I see terror in his heart as your health fails, but he will be a busy man the day you die."

"What if you're wrong?" Mrs. Harlan Bell III asked when she recovered her composure.

"I wish I were, Mrs. Bell. For your sake and the country's. Forgive me for saying this, but this is what I see: he has the face of a dog and the body of a pig."

"Heaven help us," his mother said, composing her face as she pressed a fifty-dollar bill into my Aunt Rita's hand. "I can't believe he's as dreadful as you say—and yet I must. When have you ever been wrong?"

"I haven't," my aunt said.

"Then we have nothing to look forward to."

"Wrong," my aunt replied. "We have everything to look forward to—more than we need. The problem is knowing what to do with it."

"The problem with you, Natalya," Mrs. Bell said, putting on her high-collared New Look coat, "is that you're getting too smart too fast. I can't keep up with you."

"You don't have to," my aunt said under her breath, watching Mrs. Harlan Bell III step out onto the frosty street and into her waiting Rolls.

As the car left the curb and the next customer sat down, my aunt was still scratching her head. She had yet to catch a glimpse of Harlan Bell IV close up, either in his mother's hand or in her crystal ball, but she had a nagging feeling that they had already met.

*

Bernard Baruch had given it a name—the Cold War—and George Marshall had given it a plan, but when an endless snow began to fall, rising like lava through the corridors of midtown, floating up the avenues and pouring out across the bridges until it had swallowed doors and windows along the streets and boulevards of Brooklyn, Queens and Staten Island, there were some during the winter of 1947 who wondered if Baruch in his vast wisdom had been talking about Russia or, as it now appeared, the weather.

The answer would not be long in coming.

The snow came and went, and winter gave way to spring, but the cold persisted.

At HUAC's request, FBI agents had already fanned out across the country, "always in pairs like nuns," as a British friend of Vera's put it, "with one to cajole and one to threaten." It wasn't long before they were turning up such incriminating information as "employee's convictions concerning equal rights for all races and classes extend slightly beyond the normal feelings of the average individual."

The chill was steady and pervasive. In rapid succession, a film about Henry Wadsworth Longfellow was canceled on the grounds that Hiawatha, an Indian peacemaker, might be viewed as a Communist sympathizer. The Indiana Textbook Commissioner called for the figure of Robin Hood to be struck from school books, since by robbing from the rich to help the poor, Robin Hood gave free publicity to communism. The citizens of Moscow, Idaho, requested the citizens of Moscow in the Soviet Union to change their city's name because, they alleged, Moscow, Idaho, had claimed it first. And a congressman from Detroit launched a personal campaign against painters he accused of polluting the public with their canvases: "red art termites," he called them.

No longer a mere color, red was anything that showed a grain of sympathy with "Negroes" or the citizens of countries less democratic than our own.

One of the experts HUAC had called the preceding fall to prove that a Hollywood film was on the tomato-radish-beet end of the spectrum was the writer Ayn Rand, who had confirmed the congressmen's suspicions: the film was red. Why? Because the Russians it depicted were smiling. Fledgling congressman Richard Nixon didn't bat an eye, but one member of the committee remained incredulous. "They don't smile?"

"Not quite that way," Rand replied. "If they do, it is privately and accidentally. Certainly, it is not social. They don't smile in approval of their system."

Now, with the lid clamped tight on films, there remained one other threat: books. Since a word to the wise was obviously not sufficient—with their endless curiosity, Americans would never voluntarily refrain from reading certain books—serious measures were required. Dangerous books had to be removed from circulation. Along with the usual suspects, works immediately receiving this deferential treatment included *The Grapes of Wrath*, which was believed to induce too great a sympathy for the country's poor, and Howard Fast's *Citizen Tom Paine*, whose firebrand hero, once praised in every schoolbook, had advocated revolution. *Walden* was soon added to the list: conscientious objection was too objectionable for impressionable minds.

With the war barely behind them, Americans were being asked to learn a strange new lesson. Think twice, it said: twice about what you read, twice about what you think and, most importantly, twice about what you say and to whom you say it.

No one was above suspicion. Thomas Mann and Albert Einstein, both recent immigrants, implored the government to halt the hearings. Quoting Franklin Roosevelt's final pleas for peace, Mann suggested that the late lamented President, had he lived, might himself have stood in HUAC's chambers facing charges of subversion.

The message was clear. By the time Senator McCarthy made his infamous speech, the Three Mosquitoes had learned to sing their favorite song indoors so that no one—not even Mrs.

Dougherty across the street or the Levitans next door—could hear them.

"What is America to me?" they crooned in their second-story bedroom, imitating Frank Sinatra, who had brought tears to millions with his wartime hit.

> *The house I live in,*
> *The plot of earth, the street,*
> *The grocer and the butcher,*
> *And the people that I meet . . .*
> *The place I work in,*
> *The worker at my side,*
> *The little town and city*
> *Where my people lived and died . . .*
> *What is America to me?*
> *A name, a place, a flag I see,*
> *A certain word—democracy!*

"Shhh!" Esther would call when she heard Maurice coming up the stoop from work. Maurice, his three redheaded daughters knew all too well, believed that they (and all their mother's family) were Stalin's agents in America. What better proof than the songs they sang or the movie stars, some recently purged, whose autographed pictures adorned every available surface of their room?

You didn't have to be wearing 3-D glasses to know that the Cold War had come home. The fifties had begun, and fear, a silent citizen, had settled in.

*

The first dispatches from Korea showed soldiers climbing up the same mud-covered slopes my aunt had seen the day she first read Mrs. Levy's hand four years before. And though at the outset

Americans would be hard-pressed to explain exactly where those hillsides were or why the younger brothers of men just back from World War II should have to fight another war, their ignorance would be short-lived.

Before the year was out the economy was back on track, and none the worse for the fact that Russia now had the atom bomb. "Government planners figure that they have found the magic formula for almost endless good times . . ." *U.S. News & World Report* exulted as the war moved into full swing. "Cold War is the catalyst. Cold War is an automatic pump-primer. Turn the spigot, and the public clamors for more spending . . . Cold War demands, if fully exploited, are almost limitless."

"You see?" Vera said. "They're filling in the cracks. First comes spackle. Then comes glue."

One month after the start of the hostilities, a thirty-two-year-old machinist was arrested in New York City while putting his young sons to bed. His wife would soon follow him to jail on charges they had smuggled drawings of the atom bomb to Russia. The picture in the morning paper gave my Aunt Rita the chills. This was the doomed couple whose faces had stared up at her from Helen's ivory hand.

During the months and years to come, demonstration would follow demonstration, and arrest would follow arrest. The trial and conviction of the Rosenbergs would bring home the ultimate price of dissent in postwar America, casting a terrifying pall over the last courageous remnants of thought. Yet somehow life, or what passed for life, went on.

Teenagers thrilled to songs like "Come On-a My House" and "Hello, Young Lovers," wore bobby socks and ponytails, and idolized Elizabeth Taylor and Joe DiMaggio. Moviegoers swooned over Clark Gable, Marilyn Monroe, Humphrey Bogart, Katharine

Hepburn and Spencer Tracy, and everybody got a kick out of Silly Putty.

Never mind that hundreds continued to be swept into the net of fear or that soldiers were dying by the thousands. Americans ate and drank their way through the first years of the decade like no other people in the world, consuming 750 million pounds of hot-dogs and 320 million pounds of potato chips in one year alone. It was our American Century, and nothing, not even another war, could stop it.

*

"Take a deep breath," says my Aunt Rita. "You're almost born."

"Thanks," I say, wondering how on earth a person can be almost born. The way I see it, you're either born or not born. Maybe I'm just superstitious, but I never count my chicks before they hatch. Why tempt fate?

*

Abey was on Steinway Street, in Queens, with Harry and Rose Schwartz of Ozone Park and their two children, extolling the virtues of a seven-piece mahogany bedroom set complete with mirror, vanity and upholstered bench. "There's a gentleman here to see you," the boss whispered in his ear, appearing out of nowhere.

Helen was at Hunter College, on her way to the physics lab to check an experiment on light.

Sasha was grading sociology exams in Vera's kitchen.

Arthur was counting shirts at his family's dry cleaners in the Bronx.

Chaim and Gittel were in the basement of their house in Forest Hills, making homemade vodka in a wooden tub.

My aunt was in the storefront staring at her crystal ball, in which a tiny replica of Leo's room in old Madrid had just swum into view. It was the room she had tried so hard to see in Helen's palm six years before, and now it floated effortlessly before her in minute detail, from the billowing lace curtains to the porcelain sink to the engravings of Santander and Salamanca to the elaborately carved bed on which he sat, a dark-haired woman by his side, slowly tearing his subpoena into ever smaller parts.

Two weeks later, as June hummed in the city's ear, Helen, Abey, Sasha, Arthur, Chaim, Gittel, Rita and their lawyer were walking up the steps of the Federal Courthouse at Foley Square.

At the far end of a stuffy room, a side door opened, sending a faint breeze toward the long rows of wooden seats, and three official-looking men strode in. "Your Honor, we are here to investigate . . ." the youngest of the three began, droning on in the familiar sentences of legal and political jargon. Despite his youth he had grown paunchy and dog-jowled, and my aunt shot him a startled look. Wasn't this the same snub-nosed lawyer who had bolted from La Pasionaria in the tumult of V-J Day seven years before? The face that had eluded her so many times in his mother's hand was there before her in the flesh.

"Mr. Bell," their lawyer said, "my clients do not intend to dignify this hearing with their cooperation. I request that their subpoenas be quashed."

"Request denied," the judge snarled.

Harlan Bell IV continued speaking. "I have here a folder that establishes beyond the shadow of a doubt the close ties between the defendants and others presently under investigation." He held up a photograph of my aunt and Vera carrying a suitcase full of chiffon scarves from the Salvation Army on Fourteenth Street three years earlier ("disguises for red infiltrators," he explained). Everybody laughed. "Record that!" he snapped at the stenographer. Next came shots of Chaim and Gittel talking with Sasha at my parents' wedding ("conscripts in Stalin's U.S. army"); Rita and Leo at the Automat on Fifty-seventh Street the night of their last date in 1946 ("exchanging sensitive information"); Arthur, Vera and Sasha at a demonstration for the Hollywood Ten the year before ("supporting the red propaganda machine"); Leo returning from Spain in 1939 ("a foot soldier of world revolution"); and two pictures of La Pasionaria: one of the entire car seen from the side, the other a close-up of the dashboard, complete with castanets and images of Roosevelt, La Pasionaria and Marx ("proof positive of suspect's subversive views").

"By the time they got to people like us," my mother says, "they weren't looking for new information. They knew we were small potatoes. Who were we supposed to name—each other? We took the Fifth Amendment, got our names on Hoover's blacklist and were done in time for lunch."

Vera, the only one not called, was waiting for them at a restaurant in Little Italy with gladiolas for my aunt and roses for my mother. The day is memorable not only for keeping my future parents and Natalya, God's Messenger, out of jail, but because it was the first time they or anyone they knew had pizza. Just as the *Atlantic Monthly* had described it to readers not lucky enough to live in the heart of civilization, they ate it sitting in a booth in a bare, plain restaurant, with a mural of Vesuvio on the wall, a jukebox and a crowded bar. When the waiter asked what they were celebrating, they only laughed and ordered more.

They never did find out who turned them in.

What they did learn was what Leo had been up to all this time, at least according to the FBI. "We have reason to believe that this individual has been providing technical assistance to Communist operatives outside the United States," the prosecuting attorney had declared before the proceedings were adjourned, "and that he is planning to continue said activities upon his return to the United States. Our records show that Mr. Kaplan and his wife Maria del Carmen de la Torre Ogurrez y Zanahoria have established a legal entity that will enable them to channel funds between New York and Spain, and that they intend to utilize said mechanism to advance their nefarious goal of promoting world revolution. Furthermore, Mr. Kaplan's failure to answer this subpoena places him in contempt of this court and shows his flagrant disregard for the laws of the United States of America."

Which is how my aunt, who had seen so much but understood so little, first heard what everybody else already knew—that Leo had a Spanish wife—and how they all found out that he was on his way back to New York.

*

"I have nothing to hide and nothing to tell," Vera declared one week later when the special prosecutor insisted that she tell him everything she knew about an alleged conspiracy to undermine the security of the United States. Before they knew it she was in the Women's House of Detention, which looked out over the heart of Greenwich Village and onto Vera's house across the street, serving a six-month sentence for contempt and fighting deportation.

"At least it's convenient," she joked to her friends. From her fifth-floor cell in the House of D, as it was known, she could see the flowers blooming in her window and her canary swinging on his perch. From time to time she even caught a glimpse of Sasha coming or going with his briefcase full of papers. The judge had forbidden visitors, but nothing could prevent a local couple from calling to each other in accents no one understood.

It was Vera, peering out across the indigo blue sky one brilliant day in late October, who first saw Leo. He was stumbling along Greenwich Avenue with a suitcase bigger than a St. Bernard. Just behind him, bent under the weight of her own bags, a small, dark-haired woman struggled to keep up. Leo owed a lot of people an explanation, Vera thought. After all these years, he could at least have called. Not that anyone he knew was ever home. All his friends were busy day and night in the campaign to save the Rosenbergs.

*

Meanwhile, back in the storefront on East Seventh Street, my aunt carried on alone. It had been months since she had seen or heard from Mrs. Levy, and shy Mrs. Sullivan had long since vanished like a chipmunk down her winter hole. Eddie Carney continued to deliver coal up and down the block, but neither he nor Jimmy stopped to have their hands read; neither did Al from the garage or the waitress Blanche DelBianco. And although Sasha often joined her for lunch at the B & H, Nat no longer left the kitchen to serve them with his special touch. Aside from Lucy and José Delgado, who came to have their hands read every Friday afternoon, and Faith Kincaid, who was unfailingly loyal, business had come to a near standstill. There was little for my aunt to do but comfort Sasha and wait for Vera to get out of jail.

At home in Forest Hills, things were no less bleak. Chaim and Gittel continued to read the classics, Fay continued to wheeze, the Three Mosquitoes, now Three Teens, continued to squabble and, while Esther washed up, my aunt continued to argue politics with Maurice. Helen and Abey had moved to the top half of a house just down the street and had finally heard from Leo, who had returned with a new name in order to avoid arrest. He refused to answer any questions when they met for drinks after Vera was released from jail just before Thanksgiving, but otherwise he was his same old self— self-effacing and hopeful, wry and tense. He said he was living in the Bronx, but the phone number he left them had the same exchange as Helen's parents', who had left the wilds of Bathgate Avenue for the leafy streets and emerald lawns of Riverdale on Hudson.

"Riverdale is still the Bronx," Abey said in Leo's defense.

"In name only," said my mother, who had less of a stake in redeeming their friend.

As the long disheartening winter gave way to hopeful spring, my parents continued to make frequent visits to the house on Essex Street, where Gittel's cooking and sharp tongue still reined supreme. Which is where they were one balmy evening at the end of May, in 1953, when they and the rest of the assembled family heard the news: the Supreme Court had refused for the third and final time to hear an appeal in the case of Julius and Ethel Rosenberg. My mother was seven and a half months pregnant.

*

"No tucks," says my Aunt Rita. "No pleats in time." But there *were* tucks. I came out early.

To the very end my mother insisted I could not be born in June, because I was due in July. Whatever Rita's talents were, she told my father one airless night, science wasn't one of them. "What does she know about gestation?" she said as the curtains stirred

in the dark window. Abey the Baby kissed her goodnight, reached over her looming belly, and turned out the light beside their
bed.

Four hours later he was frantically groping for the phone
and before they knew it Leo had pulled up at their front door.
There was no traffic at four o'clock in the morning and they
had the freshly hard-topped highways to themselves. As La
Pasionaria raced toward the soaring grillwork of the Queensboro
Bridge and the bright promise of Manhattan, Abey kept his
hand on Helen's stomach and Helen concentrated on the stars. Or
tried to.

The contractions were coming faster and she felt the weight of
the baby pressing toward the light. Not yet, she breathed within herself, hoping that the lifelines that pumped her blood to the
child's heart might just this once transmit her thoughts to its small
mind. Orion looking over his shoulder, Sagittarius tensing his bow,
the Pleiades shimmering like ballerinas moving across the vast stage
of the sky: let me count the ways. She looked for Venus, bright eye
of the night and goddess of the very act that had brought her to
this pass, and there she was, swimming into view, and Cassiopeia!
queen of the heavens, virtuous, reliable. All the expectant stars, she
whispered, and felt the words ring in her pulse. Abey squeezed
her hand. They were on the bridge now, and the stars were being
swallowed by the city flickering ahead, a vast spectacle to fill her
eyes while she held the child in its place with the mesmerizing
strings that tied it to her still, a few more minutes, a few more
hours. Not yet, not yet.

Into the city's welcoming arms they shot, down Second Avenue
to Twenty-ninth Street like an arrow loosed by Sagittarius himself,
and straight across Manhattan's middle to the gaping doorway

where, beneath a huge French flag, two rosy nuns were waiting for them in a blaze of light.

The rest was a blur, the crucifix over the bed, the reassuring voices of nuns named Genevieve and Bernadette with gentle hands and thick French accents (because this was the only hospital in New York City, according to my mother, where a woman could keep her newborn baby by her side), not yet, not yet, night becoming day, day almost night again, and Abey with one ear on her belly and the other to the radio, the last desperate news through shots of sedatives, thousands outside Parliament in London, thousands in Red Square, thousands in Rome, Amsterdam and Paris, thousands here in New York City, say it's not true, *mon Dieu*, the nuns are singing now, a prayer for the heretics and here I come, Julius already dead and Ethel waiting, my mother weeping uncontrollably, my father weeping, I'm premature I'm coming out I'm lurching down the long road to my birth in the executioner's rough cart, lub-dub, lub-dub, and for one final moment there is another heartbeat and then we are just two.

A wound, air rushing in, then out: breath held, released, and then the cry—a girl!—my mother's tears, my own first breath thrust through an accordion of joy and grief. The clock on the wall says 8:16. A voice on the radio says Ethel Rosenberg is dead.

Did I rush because I thought I could save her? Did my mother, unbeknownst even to herself, hold me back until that final hour, hoping I would hurl my small unbreathing self against the forces of destruction, win the race between death and birth and push her back from darkness into light as I was born? I tried, I tried.

*

My aunt and my mother were both right. My aunt knew I'd be born in June; my mother that I wasn't due until July. But on the most important count they were both wrong. Neither of them knew that I'd be three weeks premature.

My aunt still wonders how she could have missed such a compelling fact. But she was right about my name. Thanks to Vera, who still drew freelance monograms for Bonwit Teller and Bendel, I came into the world with perfect sets of sheets and towels, all beautifully embroidered with the letter M.

Eight

"And then what?" Gittel said.

My aunt looked down at the large, slightly wilted hand that lay before her on the table, inches from the crystal ball. Decades of dishwashing and wringing out bedraggled mops and armfuls of wet laundry had given the palm an oddly waterlogged appearance, but its lines of Life, Heart and Fate were still intact. It was a Rhine-maiden's hand, and it belonged to Mrs. Dougherty, whose ample breast had come to rest along the edge of the blue damask table-cloth. My grandmother, the Bay of Naples fanning out sedate be-hind her in its dusty frame, leaned forward in her chair. *"Nu?"* she asked again, cupping her hand around her one good ear. Nearing seventy, she still had the impatience of a schoolgirl.

From the half-eaten sandwich on her lap, the glass of seltzer at her feet, and the stockings rolled to a familiar halt just below her knees, no one looking through the plate glass window would have guessed that Gittel was on her maiden voyage to the storefront.

For five unyielding years my grandmother had turned her deaf ear deafer and her good ear deaf to keep all word of Rita's palmistry at bay. "You didn't tell us, and we didn't hear," she had said in 1948, when Rita finally informed the family of her new profession. Git-tel's hand had gone directly to her forehead. "It shouldn't happen to a dog," she said, and left the room. ("It couldn't," the youngest Mosquito said under her breath, and Maurice snickered.)

"'There are more things in heaven and earth, Horatio, than are dreamt of in your philosophy,'" Chaim read to her aloud that night as the rest of the family listened from the stairs. He was trying to console her. "Things happen," he shouted, stroking her white hair. "Who expected the atom bomb? Who expected children cringing under desks in case of nuclear attack? Who expected television?" But Gittel was being eaten alive by shame. For weeks she cried out in her sleep like a child being chased by Cossacks. She turned the curtains inside out and changed the locks on the front door to keep the evil spirits from getting in the house.

"What I don't know can't hurt me," she would say whenever anyone reminded her of Rita's powers. My grandmother preferred to think that poor Professor Freundlich was still hammering away at his seminal work and that Rita was still faithfully transcribing his wild scrawl—like a doctor's writing, she imagined—into beautifully typed pages of distinguished prose.

But when Abey's wife gave birth to a baby girl at eight-sixteen on a warm June night in 1953 just as my Aunt Rita had predicted, the door of absolute denial jumped ajar in Gittel's mind. And in I leapt, three weeks early for my birth but exactly on time for my first rendezvous with fate.

While Chaim carved three wooden M's and strung them like an abacus across my crib, Gittel rocked me in her arms and gazed at the face of her dilemma. I was the long-awaited offspring of Abey the Baby and his Helen, her lastborn's first, the apple of her aging eye. And my Aunt Rita had predicted me. But didn't that make Gittel herself a fortune-teller's mother? The angel of logic hovered overhead, mumbling lost syllogisms of Shtebsk. Yes, no, no, yes; if this, that; if that, this.

If my grandmother was maybe, I was yes. If she was doubt, I was design. In the end, I chased all question marks away.

When the westbound IND pulled out of Forest Hills the morning after I was born, my grandmother was seated next to my Aunt Rita, hands folded in her lap and a beguiling smile on her face. It was her first trip to Manhattan since the day Chaim had led her and the children, wide-eyed and still sea-legged after three weeks on the murderous Atlantic, into the bright noon of New York City, nearly forty years before.

*

"Is this your mother?" Nat asked later the same day when they sat down at the counter of the B & H for lunch. Gittel, who had never eaten in a restaurant before, could scarcely contain her pride. "This," she said, not knowing he had been a customer, "is my daughter, Natalya, God's Messenger."

"Pleased to meet you, Messenger," Nat said, energetically shaking Rita's hand.

"Hypocrite," my aunt replied under her breath. "You mean long time no see. You blacklisted us like everybody else."

"All right, all right," Nat said obligingly. "You win. What'll it be?"

My aunt ordered cold borscht for two and pretended not to see her mother lift her soup plate in both wrinkled hands and relieve it of its contents with a swift and reverential sweep of her sharp tongue.

"My little almond cake," Gittel said when she came to see me in the hospital, pinching my cheeks and my behind; "my little Message." Before I knew anything else, I knew that I was living proof of Rita's powers. And, like everyone else in the family, I had my second name.

By the end of the week, Gittel could no longer keep her secret. Back in Forest Hills, she hitched up her stockings while it was still

light out, straightened the steel hairpins in her bun and, like Moses
crossing the Red Sea, set out across the summer tumult of the
street. "You have to see it to believe it, Mrs. Dougherty," she whispered through the screen door on her neighbor's porch. Which is
how, one week after I was born, Mrs. Dougherty agreed to ride the
subway to Manhattan and see Natalya, God's Messenger, with her
own eyes.

"*Nu?*" Gittel said again.

My aunt turned toward the crystal ball, which was already
warm in the June sun. She cupped her hands around it, circled
it three times, took a long, deep breath and let the images roll toward her.

Deep within, in a room no bigger than a stamp, she saw a man
tossing in his sleep, the endless ocean rocking underneath him, a
moonlit knife glittering in his right hand. She heard the watch ticking in his pocket. She knew that man; she had seen him as a boy, and
she knew that he was Mrs. Dougherty's lost son, Sebastian, who
had run away from home in 1938 after his father disappeared at sea.
Now he was a sailor, my aunt said, and when she checked the palm
before her on the table she saw two sets of footprints leading up to
Mrs. Dougherty's front door. Sebastian, she said, would soon be
following his father home.

Mrs. Dougherty gasped and clapped both hands over her
mouth.

Gittel could not restrain herself. "What did I tell you, Mrs.
Dougherty? She has visions."

"Mama, please."

"I see your husband at your door," my aunt continued, peering
back into the crystal ball. "You're taking him in your arms and
you're telling him that life moves on."

"I am?" Mrs. Dougherty could not contain herself.

"You are."

"And then what?"

"The rest is up to you, Mrs. Dougherty," said my Aunt Rita.

"What did I tell you?" Gittel said again triumphantly, as if she were personally responsible for the tears cascading down her neighbor's cheeks.

*

The following week, at Gittel's insistence, Vera took her shopping on Fourteenth Street while Rita worked. They returned with a perfect strip of flowered fabric, a gaudy rhinestone brooch, and an old wicker hamper for my grandmother to lean on while my aunt read hands. Vera knew all the best places to buy props. My aunt showed Gittel how to wrap the flowered cloth around her head to make a turban, and Vera attached the rhinestone clasp. When they were done, Gittel pulled two tarnished curtain rings from her black handbag and hung them from her thick-lobed ears. "I came prepared," she said, with a mischievous look my aunt had never seen.

My grandmother was good for business. Before either Vera or Rita had a chance to turn around, she was making lemonade in the back sink and serving it to passersby outside. Soon a line began to form in the hot sun. When the line began to grow, she had my aunt paint numbers on small cardboard cards like the ones they used at Sammy's Live and Let Live Kosher Meats in Forest Hills, the only local store she trusted with her life. "You're next," she would tell each customer as she handed out the cards, and everyone believed her.

One by one the old customers began to trickle back, and by the end of the summer even Nat had stuck his head in. Eddie Carney, whistling "Oh! Susanna," appeared with the first snow. "I'm fixing radiators now," he said. "Coal bit the dust."

"So I noticed," my aunt said.

"You haven't changed at all," he said.

"Oh yes I have," said my Aunt Rita, looking at his palm, in which thousands of young men with floating hair and orange knapsacks were fleeing a war they didn't want to fight. "I've gotten better."

Just after the new year, Al and Sylvia Diamond stopped by, and Mrs. Levy, still wearing her fox and panting under a new layer of fat, came to have her hand read for the first time in two years. "It's good to have you back," she said.

"Back?" my aunt replied. "I never left." Gittel beamed and poured my aunt and Mrs. Levy another glass of tea.

Of course, not everyone returned. Rumor had it that Blanche DelBianco had either died or moved to Florida ("Whichever came first," was Vera's response), and Mrs. Sullivan was in a nursing home in Rockland County. Harry Gross had been arrested, making the first of many trips to jail, and Mrs. Harlan Bell III had died in 1952, just as my Aunt Rita had predicted, with no one at her side.

Still, by the time the seasons had come and gone, my aunt had every reason to be pleased. She had read hundreds of hands and had a following of loyal customers from all over the city and as far away as Philadelphia and Hartford. Thanks in large part to Gittel (and without a single backward glance at *The Practice of Palmistry for Professional Purposes*, which lay gathering dust in the tall oak cabinet in the far corner of the store), she had overcome the losses of the years she calls The Inquisition and become a star in the tough, hopeful firmament of the Lower East Side.

*

Of course, there was a price to pay. Every so often, Gittel would remind my aunt that time does not stand still. "Let's face it," my grandmother would say in her inimitable way. "You're not getting any younger."

"Mama, please," my aunt would say. "I'm not looking to get married."

"I'm not talking about looking. I'm talking about you know who."

It made no difference that a customer was seated at the table, or that my aunt was deep in concentration. Gittel was adamant. Time was passing, and soon it would be too late.

"Mama—" my aunt would say, throwing up her hands. "I have my work. I have my friends. I have a whole independent life. What more do I need?"

"What more?" Gittel nearly exploded. "What you need is to set eyes on him again. You'll see him, you'll take one look at him, and after all these years you'll do what has to be done."

Sometimes a month would go by, sometimes three, but there was no escape. Even in the face of insurmountable fact, Gittel was relentless.

"Mama, for Christ's sake, he's married."

"Believe me, he didn't marry for love. He married because you broke his heart."

This was going too far. "Untrue," said Vera, emerging from behind her photographic hood. "When are you going to stop beating a dead horse?"

"Dead what?" There was a look of horror on Gittel's uncomprehending face.

"Horse," Vera shouted while my aunt got up to lock the door. It was pointless to read anybody's hand until the storm had passed.

"Corpse?"

"Horse!" Vera said directly into Gittel's one good ear. My aunt braced herself for what came next. From week to week the conversations varied, but they always ended with Vera and her mother huddled in the far corner of the store.

From the outset, my grandmother had made Vera her ally in the quest to restore Leo to the throne of Rita's heart; with time, my aunt began to suspect that Vera, however reluctant she professed to be, was gradually succumbing to her mother's will. Whatever Gittel said, Vera always managed to take it one step further. Today was no exception. "Rita never loved him anyway, as you may have noticed. But at least no one can say we didn't try."

"They were made for each other," Gittel sighed, as if she and Vera were alone.

"That may be," Vera shouted, "but the fact of the matter is he seems to have been made for Carmen too."

Lately, all Vera's comments about Leo seemed to have a double thrust: one for Gittel, one for Rita. Maybe, my aunt thought, Vera's own sense of betrayal was finally leaking out. Maybe her two-edged sword was really meant for Leo.

After one brief meeting when he first returned from Spain, Leo had refused to speak with her again. Vera asked too many questions. Where he had been and why he had left were none of her business; besides, anybody working as a palm-reader's assistant had plenty to answer for herself. But Helen and Abey had run into him from time to time at demonstrations and had even, in a gesture of conciliation, invited him and Carmen to their house for drinks. Arthur had also seen them once or twice, and the consensus was that they were not just happily married but deeply in love. After months of legal wrangling, Leo had finally cleared his name, and he and Carmen had bought a sumptuous house in Riverdale where, according to Arthur, they did little else but contemplate each other and the view. Their affection was no secret. Leo called her Olive Oyl and she called him Popeye, and even in the company of strangers they behaved as if they were alone.

Gittel had already heard all this, but Vera insisted on reciting the whole tale again. "We may as well face facts," she concluded. "One: Leo is happily married. Two: he's the last thing on Rita's mind."

Gittel was clutching her forehead by the time Vera wound down. "All right," she said. "So he needs time. You never heard of divorce?"

"Mama!" my aunt said. "Don't you ever give up?"

*

By the time another year had come and gone, Gittel was a fixture in the storefront, and more and more of my aunt's prophecies were coming true. Eddie Carney stopped by in early March to report that after bearing him three daughters, Maureen had finally given birth to Eddie Jr.; and the following May, Lucy and José Delgado burst through the door as if they had been struck by lightning. They were both talking twice as fast as usual, and neither let the other speak. As a result, it was almost five minutes before either of them could be understood.

"It's José—" Lucy bawled.

"He saved her!" cried José.

"Who?"

"Rosita Serrano—remember? The actress? You said he would.

She was on the roof when they got everybody out—unconscious. José gave her mouth to mouth."

Now they were both smiling broadly.

"So he carried her downstairs just like you said . . ."

"—and then he asked her . . ."

"The wedding is next Sunday," Lucy whimpered through an avalanche of tears, "at Our Lady of the Transfiguration . . . We wanted you to be the first to know."

"I guess I was," said my Aunt Rita. "Congratulations."

At their request, she agreed to read the actress's right hand the day before the wedding. With a horde of female relatives pressing in from every side, there was no way to deny what was before her: thrice cursed and three times blessed, Rosita would give birth but twice. What? Pandemonium broke out around them. How many children? Three, said my Aunt Rita. How many? Three.

With her powers increasingly in evidence, the line outside continued to grow and dozens of new messages crossed her lips each day. Still, while there was undeniable splendor to the variations, my aunt was more convinced than ever that the separate palms before her on the table concealed a single underlying truth that would eventually reveal its logic. After all these years, Vera too was unwavering in her belief. Although she had long since moved on to other projects—her portraits of New York stevedores and her photographs of Harlem beauty parlors date from this period—she rarely went more than a week without stopping by the storefront. "It was very painstaking work, very lonely," she says of her devotion to my aunt. "First of all, she needed company; secondly, I was hoping to be there when she finally saw the light." In fact, by the start of the new year, both she and my Aunt Rita began to feel that change was in the air.

But neither of them was prepared for what came next.

"It was like swallowing glass," says my Aunt Rita, looking back to the cold spring of 1956. With one emphatic speech, Nikita Khrushchev had pulled the well-trod rug from under them: Stalin, dead three years, had taken millions with him to the grave.

For many, the Twentieth Party Congress confirmed what they already knew. "Another czar," Chaim said, putting down the paper. "So what else is new?"

For others, the revelations came as a bitter shock. They could no longer tell themselves such things were a fabrication of the right. "This was the horse's mouth," my aunt explains. "It opened, and teeth fell out." Helen, Abey, Pavel and Juanita left the Party in disgust, but Vera, still leading her study group, insisted on analyzing where Russia had gone wrong. "Comrades," she said at their first meeting following the speech, "communism remains a noble cause. We owe it to ourselves and history to understand what can be salvaged." Sasha called Stalin "the lesson of two evils." "Lesser," Vera corrected. "What's the other one?" someone shouted. "Chaos," Sasha replied. "Bullshit," the voice rang out. It belonged to Arthur, whose youthful hopes lay broken in the dust.

The following Saturday, braving the March winds and his own sense of defeat, he managed to be first on line when my aunt unlocked the storefront.

"Now what?" he said, laying his dejected palm before her on the table. "Capitalism to the end of time?"

"Your guess is as good as mine," my aunt replied, vainly scanning his hand for word from Moscow.

For the first time in her life, my Aunt Rita lay awake at night. How many upturned palms had stretched before her on the blue damask tablecloth, how many times had she looked into the hands of this customer or that without noticing the slightest hint of trouble? Gittel begged her not to cry over spilled milk. "So you can't see as far as Russia. So what," her mother said. "It's not enough you see America? You want Europe too? You want the world?"

*

"And now a word from our sponsor . . ." Maurice had lugged the old brown radio up to Chaim and Gittel's bedroom to make room for an enormous console which my grandmother grudgingly called progress and my grandfather stubbornly ignored. With his beloved radio one flight up and his fingers too stiff to play his practice fiddle, Chaim increasingly spent the long afternoons and evenings staring into space. "Thing!" Gittel would shout before dinner as she had over the years, but Chaim no longer rose at her first call. "He's lost in thought," my mother would say whenever we were there. "You call that thought?" my grandmother would say. "He's wondering if a flea has a navel."

The image of a well-known actor with a pompadour of glistening black hair flashed across the screen. ". . . today and every Sunday evening," he was saying, "when General Electric, the maker of fine toasters, blenders, fans and other appliances, brings you the best in home entertainment . . ."

". . . and a permanent war economy," Abey the Baby interrupted.

"It's him," my Aunt Rita said, rubbing her eyes.

Everybody turned in her direction.

"Who?" Abey said.

"The actor I keep seeing on the White House steps. He's going to be President some day."

"Oh sure . . ."

"Do you mind?" Maurice said in a loud voice. "I paid a lot of money for this box. I expect to watch in peace in my own house."

"Your own house?" Abey jumped to his feet.

"Look who's talking about peace," Gittel interrupted, to everyone's surprise. "When the head of General Motors becomes the Secretary of Defense and we sit here in a row like chickens pissing, watching what they want us to."

"Better a hometown thief than an out-of-town rabbi," Maurice shouted.

"Look who's erudite," said Gittel.

Chaim asked to be excused. "Better a bad peace than a good war," he said with a deep sigh and went upstairs.

For a week he lay in bed and listened to Tchaikovsky on the radio. The doctor came and shook his head. "It's nothing that a little rest won't fix."

By the third week of May, Chaim was sleeping almost the entire day. "You don't need a calendar to die," he said on the morning of the twenty-fifth. Esther, who had just brought him his tea and toast, dropped her tray and ran downstairs to get her mother.

When Rita came home from work that afternoon with Vera, she found Abey listening on the stairs. The grandfather clock was ticking louder than a heart. Chaim's practice violin lay on the mantel, just as he had left it, and a copy of the *New York Times* lay open on the table.

With the exception of Brenda and the drape dealer, who were on their honeymoon in France, and the two unwed Mosquitoes, who were ensconced in their respective rooms, the rest of the family was already upstairs. Gittel, her hands folded in her lap and her mouth a tight line of control, was sitting at the foot of the bed staring at the wall. Fay, whose cataracts had grown so thick she couldn't see across the room, was sniffling just inside the door. Maurice was reading the latest *Reader's Digest* in a corner. Esther was kneeling by the bed, and Chaim, his eyelids shut, was stroking her dark hair. At a quarter to nine, Abey came up the stairs. Chaim opened his eyes and looked around the room. *"Ponim!"* he called, like a lost child. *"Ponim!"* again, this time more desperate, a dog baying at the moon.

It was Vera who ran the two blocks to our house and pulled my mother to the door, with me, asleep, in tow.

I awoke in Abey's arms in time to see my mother bend toward Chaim.

My grandfather reached up and stroked her face. A look of infinite longing came over him and then he smiled. "Gittel," he said. All eyes were on my grandmother, who bowed her head and turned away.

*

Exactly two months later, the *Andrea Doria* sank off the coast of Massachusetts; the following week, fulfilling yet another prophecy, Rosita Serrano gave birth to a baby girl. She was officially called Lucy, after José's mother, but was instantly renamed Lucita, to avoid confusion.

All that summer, while my aunt pored over the upturned palms that lay like heat-struck mollusks on the table, Gittel busied herself in the back of the store. She arranged and rearranged the dozen or so glasses that were used for lemonade and tea, shuffled and reshuffled the worn cardboard tickets she had copied from Sammy's Live and Let Live Kosher Meats, and sang half-remembered Russian songs in a low mezzo voice, growing daily more at ease in the new life old age had unexpectedly held out to her. By autumn, the combination of widowhood and her job as my aunt's chief ticket-taker, tea-and-lemonade-maker and bustling administrator had so lightened her step and sweetened her tongue as to make her virtually unrecognizable to her immediate family, who were still adjusting to the change.

Maurice, formerly referred to as the Thief—both because he had stolen Esther's witless heart and because of the suspicious flow of cash that gave the edge of his deep pockets a perpetual green tint—had been transformed into the Prince (like it or not, with Chaim gone and the rest of us living several blocks away, the house in Forest Hills was now his castle); and it had been years since my grandmother had called the Three Mosquitoes by the names she had so cruelly bestowed on them in childhood.

An immigrant once again, but this time without tears, my grandmother rode the subway in each day from Queens as if she had done it all her life, proudly clutching the small canvas satchel in which she carried her freshly washed and ironed turban and the checkered apron she wore when she sliced lemons and washed up. Like my aunt, who often sent her out on errands, she had grown accustomed to her daily banter with the local merchants, the waiters at the B & H and the customers who were invariably waiting when she and Rita turned onto East Seventh Street at nine o'clock each morning.

Nat had dubbed her Mrs. Messenger, and the name stuck. "Good morning, Mrs. Messenger," the hatmaker called out to her as she passed his shop on her way to buy fresh lemons, and Gittel would wave with a graciousness befitting the mother of a queen. "A dozen, Mrs. Messenger?" Mr. Caputo, the corner greengrocer, would ask, already counting thirteen lemons while my grandmother smiled benevolently. (It was the perfect name for suggesting what everybody knew but no one wished to say: that my aunt, counter to their earliest belief, was not the niece of the original Natalya, and that her bloodlines, unlike her predecessor's, could not be traced to the Ukraine. It had the added advantage of conveying the respect they nonetheless felt for her chiromantic powers, and of magically uniting mother and daughter with the name Rita had assumed when she took over the lease to become, for all intents and purposes, God's Messenger.)

The Witch was nowhere to be found. At home on Essex Street as well as in the store, Gittel sang from dawn to dusk, sometimes mournfully, like a dove, but most often gaily, as she went about her chores:

> *What we leave behind who will remember,*
> *The salt of our tears who will taste?*
> *What ship large enough to bear our grief*
> *Across the weeping sea?*

> *From your breast torn away forever, Russia!*
> *From your breast!*

and

> *Over the hills, through the snow,*
> *The groom's coach approaches.*
> *Bells in the night, bells in my heart!*

> *All is still, all is slow,*
> *Let no one reproach us.*
> *Bells in the night, bells in my heart . . .*

Mrs. Dougherty was the only neighbor back in Forest Hills who knew about my aunt's profession and my grandmother's new life. Ever since the day her seafaring husband had appeared on her doorstep exactly as my Aunt Rita had predicted, her faith in my aunt's powers had been complete. "Jesus, Mary and Joseph," she had said, falling to her knees, but she was back on her feet in time to clasp the repentant wanderer to her breast. "Life moves on," she had told him, seeing in his misty gaze how much she had aged while he was leading his mysterious and distant life. From that day forward, she had her hand read twice a year, "just to be on the safe side," she told my aunt, "in case Willie is planning any more surprises."

"What did I tell you?" Gittel would say by way of greeting while she bustled about, attending to the other customers and washing dirty glasses as fast as they were left. "Have a seat, Mrs. Dougherty. You're next."

Years later, when she could no longer make the trip into Manhattan, all this would seem a lifetime away. "Those were the days, my friend, we thought they'd never end . . ." my grandmother would sing, staring through the white organza curtains at the house across the street in Forest Hills. But for now, for a few more years, she was in her golden unexpected glory.

*

Meanwhile, though there were rumors of thaws, winter still held the nation in its grip, as Helen and Abey discovered when they took Gittel to the circus to celebrate her seventieth birthday. The drumroll proclaiming the start of P. T. Barnum's latest act nearly knocked them off their seats. While the band played "The Star-Spangled Banner," sixteen flag-draped elephants careened around the ring, followed by an equal number of curvaceous girls twirling star-spangled batons who proceeded to fling off their satin tutus and strip to red, white and blue bras and panties while the audience went wild. The ringmaster raised his white-gloved hands, acknowledged the applause and announced that Barnum's was dedicating its entire production to "the struggle to maintain our way of life against the menacing horde of aggressors." The drums thundered again, the majorettes did splits and the sixteen elephants saluted with their trunks. Gittel was disgusted. "For this I survived to old age?" she whispered to my parents. They left before the acrobats appeared.

A few weeks later, at a demonstration in support of school integration in the South, Helen and Abey ran into Leo, who was on his way to Mexico. After many furious arguments, he and Carmen had split up. The last straw, he said, had come when she called him a crypto-fascist for suggesting that Khrushchev's revelations about Stalin were only the tip of the iceberg. "What's in Mexico?" my father asked. "What's here?" Leo replied.

He needed a country where the revolution was alive, where hope had not been strangled, where a man who had fought in Spain could bare his soul to strangers without risking his neck.

"Send us a postcard," Abey said sarcastically. Not everyone could just get up and leave when things got tough. But then, as Helen pointed out, not everyone was as sensitive as Leo. "Or as unpredictable," said my father.

By this point, Senator McCarthy had gone too far: to heaven in some people's book, to hell in almost everybody else's. But HUAC, like the circus, continued on its merry way. Having failed to corner Charlie Chaplin, the committee summoned Zero Mostel, who stood accused of appearing at a benefit for *Mainstream*, a Communist magazine. "But all I did," the actor said that fall, "was an imitation of a butterfly at rest . . ."

"If your interpretation of a butterfly at rest brought any money into the coffers of the Communist Party," his interrogators said, "you contributed directly to the propaganda effort of the Communist Party."

Mostel was shocked. "But suppose I had the urge to imitate a butterfly somewhere?" he asked the august body, whose answer may well stand as its crowning achievement.

"When you have the urge, don't have such an urge to put the butterfly at rest by putting some money in the Communist Party coffers as a result of that urge to put a butterfly at rest . . ."

Soon afterward, with a smile as forced and predatory as an Edsel's, the Fifties came to a screeching halt. The Russians had sent a satellite into orbit around the earth in hopes of proving, according to the *New York Times*, that "the new socialist society could turn the boldest dreams of mankind into reality." A wave of panic swept the United States. We were behind. But not for long. From now on our lives would depend not on keeping up with the Joneses but on getting ahead of the Russians. We would add, subtract, multiply and divide and teach our children calculus and trigonometry and topic sentences before they knew which side their bread was buttered on or why it mattered. They would lay down their Hula Hoops, their comic books, their Frisbees. They would eat Wheaties, the breakfast of champions, and they would fan out to the four corners of the earth to make it safe again.

No, said my Aunt Rita, staring into Eddie Carney's weathered palm. The children of the Fifties would refuse to go.

My aunt was speaking now of a huge green lawn and stately buildings with capitals and colonnades. Like ancient Rome, she said, but not in ruins. She watched in fascination as hundreds of young men and women surged toward her. From a distance they appeared more beautiful than the youth of any other age, but as they drew closer, their raised fists and angry voices told her they were not the beatific angels they so resembled.

There were thousands of them now, then millions, and they were surging out over a vast terrain, claiming the earth itself as their own mother, begging the heads of nations to return to their senses and calling for an end to greed, to murder, to the rise of the few and the abject survival of the many. They were everywhere, a tribe that had sprung up overnight and was still growing, blocking entrances and barricading buildings, walking gauntlets of police clubs and defying oncoming tanks with fists and flowers. They were the children of soldiers and they were prepared to die for their beliefs but not to fight.

HELL-O, HELL-O, they were shouting in a strange, hallucinatory rhythm that made no sense at all until my aunt took Eddie Carney's startled hand and pressed it to her ear. That was when she heard the music:

HELL NO: make love not war give peace a chance where does it say the greatest nation in the world HELL NO devouring its young its wretched HELL NO relax and float downstream REFUSE send in the cops REFUSE send the Marines HELL NO the actor in the wings has volunteered REFUSE to bayonet the enemy is us HELL NO if troops won't do try splitting the ranks MY LAI it is not dying the American way of life that sends us ranting and raving WE WON'T GO into the waiting arms of the apocalypse—

Was it her customer's volcanic palm, bursting with paternal pride, or would the Sixties really be this burning river, this crazed magmatic flow shooting forward like hot lava all our wild lavish wonderful ideas propelling us upward and onward, rocket to the moon sock it to us soon the latest news the bravest world hot molten liquid mama maybe the last news we'll ever hear the last hurrah all the promise of a moving hot springs hope springs eternal toil and trouble what manner of mix is this whose witch is brewing what for whom and when and is it just her imagination boiling over or is it really Gittel floating down this fiery Styx, this red-hot river of the damned, and is she waving or drowning, coming or going, because this is the Sixties after all, the earth turned inside out, a fireworks of blood exploding spurting upward all the money in the world our footprints on the moon napalm on earth: Vietnam.

"So what if you can't see as far as Russia," Gittel had said the year before. "It's not enough you see America? You want the world?"

Now, like a fuse going off inside her, the world exploded. Palm after palm held the unwritten history of Africa throwing off its chains, the peoples of Asia shooting to the surface of the news like the near-drowned, Latin America rising against her torturers and tyrants, the Negro people struggling for equality in the United States, students and women and homosexuals demanding life liberty and justice for all, Mexico Paris Czechoslovakia Chicago, everywhere she looked great celebrations and the long story of the damned, both those whose blood was yet to flow and those ranked against them, who would devote their lives to standing in the way of change.

"Hold it," says my aunt, catching me red-handed in the act of rushing ahead just when I should be slowing down. "If you're going to talk about the Sixties, don't forget that for most people in this country the Sixties began as a dream of what the Fifties should have been and weren't: a man and a woman with two beautiful children, a beautiful dog, a White House and enough money for everyone to live happily ever after."

"You're right," I say, taking a deep breath and spreading my accordion as wide as my two arms can stretch.

Nine

"**L**ike an actor," my grandmother would say whenever Kennedy appeared on the evening news, his teeth flashing like real pearls. "But so intelligent! He should live to be a hundred and twenty. And his wife—that's some princess. I wish her all the luck in the world." With her cataracts growing thicker by the day, it was anybody's guess how she could tell the two of them apart. "Jack, Jackie—only in America," she liked to say, rattling off the names of all the Russian czars and their czarinas. But by the middle of the new President's first year in office, her mind had started on its steep decline. Day after day she would ask repeatedly why the Three Mosquitoes, already married and living far away in places like Omaha and Salt Lake City, had not come home from school. And for a whole hour before dinner she would shout for Chaim to wake up from his nap. "Thing!" she would cry again and again, just as she had all the years he was alive.

In the storefront too she was increasingly forgetful, leaving the stove lit after she had finished making tea, shuffling and reshuffling the numbered cardboard tickets until my aunt noticed they were all the same, and flipping the cardboard OPEN sign around to CLOSED. There was no way to avoid the obvious: Gittel, who had just turned seventy-five, was rapidly becoming what my Aunt Esther called "seline." If Maurice had his way, she would soon follow gasping Fay to the large, cheerful building on the water's edge. "That bourne," Abey called it, because it was a one-way trip.

For now, however, with a little help from Mrs. Dougherty, who rode the subway in with her each morning and picked her up at five for the ride home, my grandmother continued to travel back and forth from Forest Hills, which meant that on a chilly Thursday afternoon in late October she was leaning forward in her chair—head turbaned, earrings dangling—while Natalya, God's Messenger, pored over the outstretched hand of Lucy's seventeen-year-old cousin, Filomena Cruz. As luck would have it, Vera was there too.

Filomena wore her black hair parted down the middle, like her idol, Joan Baez. She had finished high school and was packing Chiclets on the night shift in a Brooklyn factory, hoping to save enough money to move out of her parents' cramped apartment and rent a place of her own downtown. She had a boyfriend on East Tenth Street and spent most of her free time hunched over Lucy's kitchen table, lamenting her fate and counting the days until she turned eighteen: old enough to marry Luisito, Lucy warned her, but too young to vote. "So what?" Filomena didn't see why everyone made such a fuss about standing all alone in a little booth and pulling a green curtain shut behind you. Why not just take a shower?

Filomena's mouth was never still: an endless supply of gleaming Chiclets was always moving from her pocket to her tongue, from where, in equally daunting number, its chewed counterparts emerged for an instant and then, conveyed along as if by magic, disappeared from sight.

For months Lucy had been trying to convince her to stop by the storefront and pay a visit to my aunt. "Don't bug me," Filomena would complain, "or I'll never go."

"What do you have to lose?"

Filomena rolled her eyes and let the gum in her mouth go slack before drawing it back into a final snap. "Not my virginity."

Everyone could see that there was something eating Filomena. "I already told you," she said one day in late October when Lucy begged her one more time, "if you don't get off my case I'll never go." Then in she strode, thrusting her palm at my Aunt Rita with a practiced scowl. "Lucy sent me," she said, pointing to a series of small creases between her lines of Life and Fate. "She says this is some kind of sign."

"Have a seat," said my Aunt Rita, stalling for time as Vera moved her tripod from one side of the storefront to the other to catch the changing light. Gittel bent forward in her chair.

"What a beautiful girl," she said, pressing even closer to stare at Filomena. "What grade are you in?"

"Mama, please. I have to concentrate."

At first glance, Filomena's was a hand of secrets. My aunt saw doors opening and closing, and smoke-filled hallways dense with agitation. There was something that could not be said. She heard voices in another room, and the sound of paper tearing. Then she heard footsteps, the heavy beat of several pair of men's expensive leather shoes receding down a narrow hall. But with no hint of time or place, it was impossible to know where they were going.

"What made you come?" she asked, puzzling at the cross-hatched space between Filomena's lines of Life and Fate.

Filomena was determined to reveal nothing. "Curiosity," she said with false bravado, but suddenly her palm spread like a fan, and a galaxy of hidden images shook from its folds. My aunt had to hold her breath to keep from seeing everything at once.

She saw a dance hall in the tropics, and dozens of girls in

turquoise gowns beneath an orange moon, and she saw Filomena's grandmother throw her corset in the sea and do the cancan on the beach after all the other girls had gone to sleep. She saw danger winking from behind the trees and the long snake of a twisted life begin to curl itself around the grandmother's dancing feet. A man appeared from the shadows and led her to a room of red brocade. My aunt turned the reluctant fan this way and that. No matter which way she looked, the story was the same: unbeknownst to Filomena, her mother was the child of a rape. And unbeknownst to anyone, her mother's father was the handsome devil on East Tenth Street to whose son she was engaged.

"What? You're saying Luisito's father raped my grandmother? Is my mother's father? That . . . wait a minute . . . you mean . . . Luisito . . . is my mother's brother . . . ? My uncle—?"

As the world fell in on Filomena, my aunt continued speaking. "Yes," she said, "Luisito is your uncle—something like that. But remember, once you know the hand you're dealt, you can begin to understand the height and width of your desire. Then you can shape your life to your own measure. All these little lines between your lines of Life and Fate are the ways you've been running back and forth between what was done to you and what you need. From now on you won't have to run so much, Filomena."

"What is this, a pep talk?" Filomena said, chewing furiously. "You sound like a counselor I had at Fresh Air Camp when I was nine. I threw up in her lap."

Girl with Gum, Vera mused, standing up to change her film, and Filomena burst out laughing. Her laugh was deep, like a ship's horn in the fog, but brighter, with a glint of saxophone or glass. "That's great," she said, clearly relishing her shift of mood. "Does that mean I get to hang in a museum like José? All these rich people will think it's a mistake—they'll be bending over backward looking for my gun."

Thanks to Vera, Filomena's frozen tears dissolved in laughter, and her stubborn hand became a canvas of the future.

"Look at this," my aunt continued, stroking Filomena's palm as if it were a magic lamp. The doors were there again, opening and shutting, but this time she could see into a dim-lit room of gentlemen and thugs. Then, before she understood where it was leading, she saw what she repeated to the rest of us two years before anyone had heard of Dealey Plaza or Lee Oswald or Jack Ruby. A path of red-hot fire shot across the span of Filomena's hand, in its wake the grassy knoll, the motorcade, the presidential brain exploding in slow motion. It was all over in a flash. When she looked up, Filomena was still laughing, and Vera was washing her hands in the back sink.

But from her ringside seat Gittel heard a rush of words as soft and gentle as the rain outside: ". . . the height and width of your desire . . ." and Filomena laughing, and Rita speaking again about a grassy knoll a man with gum or was it gun. And Gittel could see the worry on her daughter's face, shadows crossing the room, a place called Dallas, the one in the red velvet gown with the familiar face, like a painting of the Virgin Mary, maybe after all a painting but if Rita was speaking how could she be on the wall unless of course there were two of them *the President of the United States* one real one painted someone named Pavel and was her daughter Natalya, God's Messenger, *gravely wounded in an apparent attempt on his life* the one with a red velvet turban on her head the other one right hand face-up on the table—but of course, it was her daughter the real one giving the other one the one with her hand out a manicure: or else the real one was her daughter and the other one was Lucy's cousin but then was Rita Natalya and if she was and if Natalya was God's Messenger then maybe Rita *was* the Messiah when she walked on water—"the hand you're dealt," the one who was giving the manicure was saying—but then she would be the Virgin Mary and she wasn't, she was Gittel, *ladies and gentlemen,* and the only way she could have given birth to God was if she was a virgin and a Catholic like *the President,* John Fitzgerald Kennedy, *is dead,* which she wasn't, God forbid, she said to herself remembering Chaim's exact words as she climbed under the quilt in Shtebsk the night Rita was conceived . . . "Let's make music," he had said and nine months later she had given birth to Rita and nine months after that they had left Russia for America; a whirlwind: Chaim with his violin flying over the Café Centrale, her mother framed forever in the doorway of the house in Shtebsk, satyrs dancing on her father's grave, all memory, all lost.

Who was bending over her; do you know what day it is today, Mrs. Messenger, can you tell me what month, what year, the name of the President of the United States, how many fingers am I holding up, Mrs. Messenger, shining a flashlight in her eyes, your daughter thinks, Lucy Delgado, you may have fainted, Vera thinks, your daughter says, Mrs. Dougherty, your daughter Natalya, God's Messenger.

Who was saying: You'll be fine, Mama, Abey's coming with his car to take you home.

So many faces. So many names.

One month later, over Thanksgiving dinner, my aunt told the assembled family what she had seen in Filomena's palm while Gittel's mind unraveled like a ball of wool. "Time's worldly twin . . ." ". . . assassin . . ." ". . . scribe." I played like a kitten with the tangled threads.

According to my parents, it was less the idea of the assassination than it was the force of Rita's language that took them by surprise.

"It went beyond anything we'd heard her say before."

"Like a searchlight," said my mother.

"Sweeping history," said Fay, furloughed for the day from her riverside abode. Even Esther was forced to admit there was something there. "Let's face it," she told Maurice as we were putting on our coats. "My sister Rita has a gift."

"Yeah," he snapped back. "For comedy."

A vocation is a vocation, and a vacation is a vacation. Helen is emphatic. At bedtime, I ask a lot of questions. A table is a table, and a vegetable is a vegetable, I say, imitating her. A turnip is a turnip and a turban is a turban. Fashion is fashion and fascism is fascism. But what *is* fascism? She tells me to cut it out and I make little scissors in the air. You, my mother says, are a vexation. But what's a vocation, I want to know. Following your bent, my mother says, holding my pajamas in mid-air like a toreador brandishing red. I lean to one side and touch my toe. Not bend—bent, my mother sighs. It means your Aunt Rita has a calling. I imagine an enormous telephone, shiny and giddy with importance like the roller coaster on the beach at Coney Island, and my Aunt Rita, dark-haired and majestic, rising from the waves to answer its mysterious ring. Hello? she says into the invisible receiver. The world is a mouth and she is its ear.

I know this and I don't, because I'm only eight years old and life is a puzzle full of odd-shaped pieces. *'Twas brillig*, Abey says, lighting up a Marlboro and blowing smoke rings through the room, *and the slithy toves did gyre and gimble in the wabe . . . All mimsy were the borogoves, and the mome raths outgrabe.* Now do you understand?

It's time for bed, he adds, and shakes me till I laugh.

Now, of course, I know that the conch shell we hold to history is passed from one generation to the next, and that in each generation there are some who fall under its spell and some who know it can also be a trumpet for telling what we hear. I know that if you have a calling you have no choice but to stare into the crystal ball or press your ear to the ground or raise the trumpet to your lips; and I know why my Aunt Rita worked so hard to hone her sight.

In the weeks and months that followed, my aunt continued to tell us what she had read in people's palms. Long before we had heard of places like Tonkin or Da Nang or Hue, she told us about the war in Vietnam, a twist on the American dream that would tie a knot around our throat, and she told us how it would burn like phosphorus inside us through the long years afterward when we would deny what we had done and wish we had fought better or longer or more wisely or not at all. She talked about the grief that would accumulate like debt within the rich, whose easy sleep would sour with the dreams of strangers. She spoke of young men murdered while they slept, and of hope passed like a bribe under the table where only a few would ever eat. She talked about the gaps that would harden into scars over the highest crimes, and of what would happen to the generations that came of age in a scarred time. She used the language that we knew to tell us things we'd never heard before. And all of it, her news, came from the hands of strangers.

I heard it all.

*

So, temporarily abandoning her other work, did Vera, who returned to the storefront, convinced that my aunt would soon deliver herself of the message that had been so long in the making.

With bits and pieces of the assassination beginning to show up in nearly every hand, the inner life of people's palms was apparently converging. To both Vera and my aunt, it was clear that the years of painstaking effort, the hours they had spent together sifting through the endless avalanche of visions, were finally on the verge of yielding up their secret.

When the images from Filomena's palm turned up a few days later in the hand of Frank Loscandalo, the head of Empire Shipping and Storage down on Mott Street, my aunt rubbed her eyes and shook her head.

But by the time spring rolled around, she had almost—but not quite—become blasé.

From Mrs. Dougherty to Mrs. Levy, from the Caputos to the waiters at the B & H, from Lucy and José Delgado to Faith Kincaid, there was not a palm in which some part of the assassination, like scattered shrapnel, hadn't lodged. In some my aunt saw blueprints, notebooks, even maps; in others she saw broken windows, buzzards, and more death.

When José Jr. and Rosita came to see her with their newborn twins in the fall of 1962, my aunt could not resist temptation. Would the proud couple let her read the babies' hands? "Let you?" José was already pulling them from his wife's arms. "This is José III," he said, beaming at his son. "But we call him Joey. And this is his kid sister Zoë."

It was cold comfort, but even those two tiny palms, still pink as tongues and barely used, contained their own microscopic images of the assassination.

The oldest hands were just as fertile. They belonged to Flora and Jacob Bloom, an elderly couple who had sold their nearby bookstore when their eyes began to fail and had bought the florist's at the far end of the block. "We can still smell," Flora told my aunt in late December when she came to have her hand read. "And Jacob was a botanist before the war. Ach—we had such flowers then. Were you ever in Vienna?"

It was in Flora's gentle hand that my aunt first saw the trail of the assassins. "I see a sizzling streak of light," she said, "a flare that cauterizes its own path while scorching everything in sight."

". . . a mangled newsreel," she said when the familiar sequence turned up reversed in Jimmy Carney's hand a few days later: brain, knoll, motorcade.

But this was more than a worn newsreel snaking back over itself. In Jimmy's palm, searing its way past the jumbled detail of his life, there was the same bright path; and if my aunt moved closer, there was the unmistakable scent of smoke. What was on fire?

While my aunt stared ever more brazenly into the space that lay between their lines of Life, Heart and Fate, Vera would document each session, sometimes following her subjects out onto the street and back to their apartments, where she photographed them alone and with any and all family members willing to subject themselves to her inexorable gaze.

More often than not she was accompanied by Sasha, who had finally retired from teaching and was putting the finishing touches on his memoirs. In old age Sasha had blossomed: his cheeks were rosy, his hair white, and the loneliness inside him had been replaced by a pervasive warmth. After sixteen years of marriage, Vera had abandoned all attempts to get him to lose weight. Perhaps because of his colossal size, my aunt thought, when Sasha stepped into a room people felt immediately at ease. He was like a portable fireplace, an instant, reassuring, one-man glow.

It was Sasha who insisted that Vera take the portrait of Mildred Levy and Pearl Silverstein that caused such a sensation when it was first shown and that soon became an early icon of the women's movement. *Sisters, 1962*, the first of Vera's many photographs of siblings, was shot at Mrs. Silverstein's apartment in the housing complex Sasha had helped build, where the two elderly sisters had moved in recent years. Soon after their arrival, they had joined other tenants in a campaign to integrate the project, which had been found to have systematically excluded everyone but whites. At a public forum Sasha had attended incognito, both Mrs. Levy and her sister had taken the floor and, with shaking fists, eloquently accused the original builders of using public money to protect a private fief.

Sasha said nothing, but Vera knew he was consumed by guilt. He had spared no effort to ensure that the complex would reflect the city's diversity; but after returning to his teaching job he had failed to check on how his ingenious formula was being applied. Like so many academics, he had naively believed that others would practice what he preached. This was the essential truth he hoped to impart to future generations in his memoir: if you want to change the world, you must leave no stone unturned, but even that is not enough—you must turn each stone again and again.

"Put your arms around each other," Vera said, squinting from behind her camera.

"Show to the future!" Sasha cried enthusiastically.

"You mean 'Look,' Vera laughed, and the two aged sisters stared determinedly into the camera, straight into the gaze of those who would take up the struggle after them.

"Any luck?" my aunt asked one week later, as she and Vera huddled in the curtained storefront, peering through a magnifying glass at strips of negatives.

Pearl and Mildred had four hands between them. In frame after frame, their palms were raised, and from them, to my aunt's amazement, smoke was rising.

By the fall of 1963, the country was dry brush, and flames were licking at the edges. In Vietnam, a Buddhist monk had doused himself with kerosene and become a human torch to protest U.S. intervention; at home, the American South was exploding with new terror: the violent summer had reached its peak when four little girls were burned to death in Alabama after white supremacists firebombed a church. "We Shall Overcome," people sang, but my aunt was not so sure.

If Kennedy was shot, more than a president would die. His death would ignite a fuse of disbelief that would sabotage all hope of change. Like a series of explosions, murder would erupt from one end of the country to the other, and the dream of equality would disappear like a Roman candle sizzling across the sky.

Once again she was explaining why it mattered. "Because," she said, "this isn't what you think it is. Call it a play in two acts: the death, and then its aftermath." Hoping to recruit support for a last-ditch effort to deter the assassination, Vera and Sasha had invited a small group of friends to Sunday brunch. Someone my aunt didn't know asked why anybody on the left should care. "I still don't get it," he said. "If something happens to the President, the Vice President—whatsisname—takes over. It's a well-oiled machine. So what's the big deal?"

"I already told you," my aunt said. "This is not about Kennedy the man. It's about the wound he will become. Kennedy is not the target. We are—the American people.

"The plan is brilliant. The so-called assassin gets killed in front of the whole country, the President's brain disappears, the autopsy notes go up in flame, anyone who knows anything turns up dead. And we all know it. So it's not his death they're after, but the effect of getting everyone to swallow an enormous lie. The effect— if we don't stop it—is amnesia, and the way it will be reinforced is by repetition. Like any history lesson. By drumming it in."

"In other words?"

"More of the same. Until it all seems like one big item on the evening news. Each new assassination will make the ones before it seem more normal. Eventually people will get numb. In the end, they won't know the difference between the real death and the re-run. That's the whole point. People will be in a kind of trance—the country will sleepwalk through its darkest hour. The actor will live in the White House and the lie beneath our feet will spread like an abyss, or debt . . ."

"I still don't see why we should get involved." Now Arthur was speaking. "If Kennedy gets shot it's not as if some revolutionary program's been derailed."

Rita's voice was barely audible. "Don't you see? It's an incision, a cut designed to leave a terrible scar: memory with a hole. Believe me, if they pull it off, this will be the perfect crime. Because the real death will remain invisible: the death of hope."

"What if you're wrong?"

"Forgive me," Sasha said, "but in case you didn't notice, every-thing Rita has so far predicted, it came true."

"All right," Vera said, getting up to brew another pot of coffee. "For the sake of argument, suppose we all agree the assassination has to be prevented. Then what?"

The room became a flurry of suggestions. Phone calls to the FBI, the CIA, the White House. Letters to members of Congress and Kennedy himself. If all else failed, last minute calls to newspa-pers and radio stations. There was only one reason to hold off: it was almost Halloween, and their warnings might be seen as pranks. After a brief discussion, it was agreed that they would not begin until November 1, exactly three weeks before the scheduled date of the assassination, if my aunt was right.

A few days later, as Rita was staring down at the palm of Frank Loscandalo, there was a knock on the plate glass window. When she looked up she saw a tall, thin-lipped man in a pale Hanover coat. He had pushed his way past the crowd outside and was clearly determined to keep going. The man pointed at his watch, then at his hand. He was in a hurry; he wanted her to read his palm. My Aunt Rita shook her head. The man insisted with a silent snarl, mouthing the words the way one might speak to the deaf: "READ MY PALM!" "No!" my aunt mouthed back, shaking her fist and turning back to the hand before her on the table. "I couldn't place him," she says now, "but I knew I didn't want him in my store."

He appears only as a footnote in the catalogue of Vera's complete work, because the photographs she took that afternoon were unaccountably flawed. Frank Loscandalo's gentle, poet's face is magnificently sculpted in the dusk, but the stranger in the mohair coat is just a blur beyond the plate glass window.

*

Despite a concerted telephone campaign that made Vera, Sasha, Helen, Abey, Arthur and my aunt all hoarse, their final warnings yielded only silence. Either so-and-so was at a meeting, or messages were not returned, or they were asked a hundred questions by someone who appeared to be important and then promised that the case would be referred to "the first available agent."

The first available agent, says my aunt, was probably someone we knew.

What?

You heard me, says my aunt, waving any further questions out the door.

On the third Saturday in November, with less than a week left to go, Vera sent copies of their press release to all the major papers.

That afternoon, Filomena Cruz returned to have her hand read. "I met someone," she said. "I want to know if this one's safe." My aunt took Filomena's outstretched hand and turned it face up on the table. She stroked the narrow wrist with its three horizontal lines and let her fingers wander up toward the girl's pulse. It was slower than she remembered, but faster than a genuinely slow one. Then she placed her hands above the crystal ball and circled it three times. She studied Filomena's thumb: not a true hourglass, but unusually proportioned, with the lower joint distinctly shorter than the top one. Distractedly, with a glance toward the tall oak cabinet that still held the old Natalya's copy of *The Practice of Palmistry for Practical Purposes,* she wondered what the Count of St. Germain might have seen in such a thumb: murderer, genius, woman of letters?

Now my aunt turned to the task at hand. One thing in his favor: the new boyfriend wasn't playing hard to get. He was standing right inside the triangle between Filomena's lines of Life, Heart and Fate, moping like Romeo outside Juliet's window. "Ardent but penitent," my Aunt Rita said aloud. "Fear only his fear, love only his love." Filomena's face was bathed in light. "You mean he's all right?"

But the question went unanswered. Just as my Aunt Rita was about to speak, someone tapped the young man on the shoulder and he took off like a burglar in retreat. "*Dosvidanya,*" my aunt said. "That's Russian for good riddance," she added quickly, while she stared in disbelief. The features were a blur, but in the depths of Filomena's palm, someone had reached into his pocket, withdrawn a miniature set of keys and opened the door to a tiny, grease-stained garage. There, glowing like a tropical fish inside its tank, La Pasionaria winked in the dark, headlights blinking on and off.

"*Mais voilà!*" Vera jumped up from her chair. "Leo will drive you to Texas. He's our last hope—if I can find him." It had been seven years since anyone they knew had seen hide or hair of their old friend, though she remembered hearing that he had returned from Mexico.

"Shit," said Filomena, shaking her head. "You left me right on the edge. Just like a goddamn man."

According to Vera, you're never more than three phone calls away from anyone in the world. No matter who it is—the Pope, Picasso, the president of IBM—you know someone who knows someone who knows that person. And so it went. Within the hour, she was talking to Leo from the pay phone at the corner drugstore, and at six o'clock she was sitting in the last booth of the Village Diner, where he had agreed to meet her.

At ten after six, Leo walked in the door. "I had to change at Fifty-ninth Street," he said, as if he were the first person in history to ride the subway from the Bronx to the Lower East Side.

Vera got right to the point. "Listen," she said, dropping her voice to a near whisper. "I'm not going to ask you where you've been, or why. I didn't ask you here to talk about the past. We need you to do something. Something unbelievably important. There's a plan to kill the President next week in Dallas. We've been trying for weeks to get through to Washington, but all our telegrams and calls have fallen on deaf ears."

"You don't expect . . ."

"Look, this could be the most important thing you ever do."

"What's that?"

"Someone has to drive Natalaya, God's Messenger, to Texas."

"What?"

"You heard me."

"Why?"

"To stop it from happening."

"Please. I didn't believe in this crap twenty years ago. I'm not about to start believing it today."

"We have incontrovertible proof. Rita's seen it again and again."

"So what's she going to do, throw herself in front of him and give them two for the price of one?"

"She's going to warn him."

"Thanks for thinking of me. I'm not interested."

"Maybe you're just not interested in seeing Rita again." Vera had moved into high gear.

The waitress slapped their check on the table and sped off again before they had a chance to pay.

Leo reached for his wallet.

Vera headed him off. "This is on me."

But the check was the farthest thing from Leo's mind.

"Rita—" he said slowly, as if he were hearing my aunt's name for the first time. "When have I not wanted to see Rita?"

"Seriously?"

"Seriously," Leo replied, pushing his open billfold to Vera's side of the table. The photograph of my aunt, with the night sky of Manhattan in the background, was from the observation deck on the Empire State Building, where he and my Aunt Rita had shocked each other into silence nearly twenty years before, in a sudden up-sweep of red snow.

"She's been everywhere with me," Leo said, sliding the picture from its plastic sleeve. After all these years, Rita was still the woman of his dreams.

"Do you have a car?"

"La Pasionaria's in storage."

"How fast can you get her out?"

"I'm not going anywhere, especially not Texas."

Leo was as mystified as Arthur. "Look," he said. "For the sake of argument, let's say Rita's right: Kennedy's on someone's hit list. Give me one good reason—I mean one *rational* reason, from our point of view—why we should try to stop it."

"Because," Vera explained, "if this succeeds, all our dreams go up in smoke."

Rita had already seen the outcome: the civil rights movement destroyed; the atrophy of cities; galloping poverty—the death of hope, the loss of life. "It's that whole chain reaction we have to stop. That's why we need you. Rita has to get to Dallas by the twenty-second."

"And do what?"

"Stand along his route and shout. Our only hope is that the President will turn away at the last minute. You have to do it, Leo. There's no one else but you who . . ."

Leo was staring at his wallet. It had been seventeen years since the night he offered my Aunt Rita one last ride after calling it quits with her at Horn & Hardart; seventeen years since she fled into the frozen tundra of the city. He thought about how strange it would be to see her now, middle-aged and thoroughly eccentric, how strange his life had been since the night he drove away from her forever—the relief of exile and then its pain, the years with Carmen, exile again and the affair with Margarita, his mother's death,

Ritita—and how strange it was that he was even thinking about saying yes to Vera's inane request.

He rummaged in his jacket and pulled out a pack of Lucky Strikes. He stuck a cigarette between his lips and let it dangle. It would be Monday before he could get anyone to check La Pasionaria. The earliest they could leave was Tuesday morning. "All right," he said at last, cupping his hand around a match. "I'll do it. Not for you. Not for JFK. For Rita. And for my country. We'll have to drive like hell to get there."

Ten

Leo had been to Spain and France; my aunt had spent three summers in Poughkeepsie. Between them, they had never crossed the Hudson.

Now, as rosy-fingered dawn caressed the sleepy pavement of East Seventh Street, glancing off the granite stoops and bathing a small crowd of well-wishers in light, they were about to.

Lucy and José Delgado, rubbing their hands together in the cold, had been up since five to welcome everyone with coffee and hot rolls. Vera and Sasha were there, and so was Arthur, along with a cluster of loyal customers, several of them in pajamas beneath their ski parkas and coats. Some of them were neighbors, but most had never met. Faith Kincaid had arrived early and Filomena Cruz had arrived late; Frank Loscandalo, who had only had his hand read twice, surprised my aunt and Vera by turning up at all. Eddie Carney, revered from Houston to Fourteenth Street for both his sweetness and his skill, showed up with Mildred Levy on one arm and her sister Pearl on the other. There were José Jr., of course, and Rosa, with Lucita in her uniform from Our Lady of the Transfiguration and Joey and Zoë in their stroller. Even the Caputos, who rarely took a moment off, had left their crates of fresh zucchini and were standing with my aunt while Vera bent toward Leo with a few last instructions for the trip.

This ragtag group, united only by its faith in my aunt's talent, knew how much lay in the balance. Again and again, in their own hands and in others, she had seen the President's upcoming death and the poison it would spew into the air for years to come. They had watched the furrows deepen in her forehead as she described the country coming undone, unraveling in chaos, in blood, losing itself, gorging itself, then curling back onto itself bloated with emptiness and fat. They knew she had seen the trail of the assassins and that she had tried for months to get the authorities to stop them. They had come to see her off and wish her luck, although they knew the odds were stacked against her.

My aunt had hoped they could leave quietly, under cover of darkness and from a less conspicuous location, but Vera insisted on a proper send-off. "It's not as if this is some secret mission," she had said; "everybody knows what you've foreseen. Besides, this is where the visions flow from, yes?"

There were practical considerations too. Abey thought it might be too confusing if Gittel saw La Pasionaria pull up on Essex Street after all these years. "She won't know which way is up," my father said. "She doesn't anyway," my aunt reminded him. "You know what I mean—she'll think she's seeing things," Abey explained. "She will be," said my mother.

At Vera's urging and Sasha's behest, my aunt had agreed to sleep at their West Village apartment the night before she left. Leo would drive directly to East Seventh Street, and they would meet in front of the storefront at exactly six o'clock on Tuesday morning.

Everything had gone according to plan. When Vera, Sasha and my aunt, each carrying a shopping bag full of provisions, stepped off the crosstown bus, the bells of St. Vassilikos were striking six; and when they turned onto East Seventh Street, La Pasionaria, yellow as an ear of corn in the first light, was sitting by the palm-shaped sign halfway down the block, her trunk and all four doors open to the sky.

Leo was leaning up against the stoop, a mug of coffee in his hand. Even without his black beret, my aunt would have recognized him anywhere. He still wore the same baggy pants and khaki jacket as before, and he still had the same casual way of falling back against the nearest wall to keep the weight off his bad leg. Of course he had aged: seventeen years was a long time. She had prepared herself for that, and in Filomena's hand she had glimpsed the steely gray that had overtaken his dark curls. But as she drew closer, she almost dropped her small valise. It had never occurred to her that he would be so handsome.

"God's Messenger," he said, flashing his gap-toothed smile.

"Leo," she said, suddenly as shy as a young girl.

People were already beginning to arrive. Leo reached for her valise and put it in the trunk. "Take your time," he said as my aunt greeted her supporters and Vera organized the troops.

It was nearly an hour before everyone had gathered and before my aunt, who was chatting animatedly with the Caputos, glanced back. When she did, she saw Vera whispering into her hands, which were cupped directly around Leo's ear.

"It's time to get this show on the road," Vera announced as soon as she felt Rita's gaze.

The crowd swung into action. In the space of a few seconds, La Pasionaria, like a ship setting sail from Spain or Portugal during the Age of Exploration, had been outfitted with everything that might be needed on an extended journey into the unknown. Vera and Sasha had prepared a dozen peanut butter and jelly sandwiches (because they kept, Vera said apologetically), a dozen hard-boiled eggs (which wouldn't, she reminded them), and three mayonnaise jars filled with dried apricots and figs. Arthur had brought a gallon of cider from Vermont. The Caputos contributed a bushel of apples, thirteen oranges, a loaf of bread, three boxes of imported macaroons, a thermos of hot coffee and two cans of powdered milk. Faith Kincaid had supplied the most luxurious gift of all, though as she cheerfully admitted, "I'm in the business." She arrived with a steamer basket piled high with cheeses, fruits, crackers and an assortment of small crocks of jam, as well as a dozen of her famous lettuce sandwiches, each individually wrapped in colored cellophane. Frank Loscandalo had brought a whole Genoa salami and a dish of his wife's homemade lasagna, and Filomena Cruz proudly handed my Aunt Rita a bag containing an entire gross of spearmint Chiclets.

When everything was safely stowed away, Lucy ran upstairs and returned with a large rectangular pan covered with aluminum foil. "I made you flan," she said, beaming from ear to ear; not the easiest dish to take on a cross-country trip, but never mind. Lucy helped my aunt slide the tray of custard under the front seat, hugged her goodbye and rejoined the crowd, leaning back against José, who wrapped his arms around her in the cold.

Sasha stepped up to the car. "Ladies and gentlemen, I don't have to tell you this woman is a national treasure," he said in his odd, accented English. Then he folded my Aunt Rita into his enormous arms. "I don't know about God," he said, "but she's a messenger from somewhere. I consider it the privilege to know her."

Before my aunt had a chance to wonder what had prompted this unlikely paroxysm of speech, a car pulled up across the street and a cub reporter from *The Star* jumped out with a camera in his hand. "I'm sorry," Vera said. "This is a private occasion."

"That's strange," the reporter said. He had a terrible lisp and his words created a great frothy hiss. "Aren't you the lady that sent us all those press releases?"

"All right, all right. Just one picture of the two of them."

My aunt sat down in the front seat and took off her gloves. Before her on the dashboard, Roosevelt, Marx and La Pasionaria greeted her like long-lost friends.

"Ready?" Leo asked, adjusting his beret.

"Ready," said my aunt, too dazed to think.

As Leo turned the key in the ignition and La Pasionaria roared like a tiger, Lucy pulled free of José. "Wait!" she shouted. It was nearly eight o'clock and East Seventh Street had come alive with people on their way to work. The crowd outside the storefront had doubled in the past half hour. Before the gaping eyes of her husband, her son, her neighbors, the fledgling reporter and La Pasionaria's two startled occupants, Lucy waved her arms over the yellow cab and made the sign of the cross. "God bless you," she said. "And drive safely."

"*Mami!*" José Jr. scolded from the sidewalk. "They're Jewish!"

"*Sí*, but the President is Catholic—he's the one we have to save!"

Leo shook his head.

"Now what," he said, glancing at his watch.

My aunt looked toward Second Avenue and saw Nat Sarnoff coming up the street in a half-run, trying to wave beneath the weight of an enormous package. "From me and the boys," he said when he reached the car, panting in the frosted air. "Four loaves challah, six quarts borscht, ten pounds vegetarian chopped liver, fifteen pickles—good luck!"

"Goodbye! Goodbye! Drive carefully! Goodbye!" The chorus

of farewells was anything but solemn, though everyone had the assassination on their minds. Vera leaned through the window. "Break a leg," she whispered.

Leo revved the motor one last time and La Pasionaria shot west toward Second Avenue, toward Texas. They passed the Ukrainian National Home, the Hebrew Actors Union, McSorley's Ale House and the Great Hall of Cooper Union, where Emma Goldman and Leon Trotsky had stirred huge crowds to action, and where thousands of immigrants had learned to write their names and say thank you very much in English. Before they knew it they were at the water's edge, staring at New Jersey and everything beyond it. The Grand Canyon, my aunt thought in admiration; slot machines and cactus; sequoias—the whole sparkling USA. Soon, as soon as they had crossed the salty Hudson, Manhattan with its weight of stone and grit and hope would be behind them.

*

Which of them spoke first is hard to say, since neither one remembers.

"This is really very generous of you," my aunt is sure she said as they were swallowed by the Holland Tunnel.

"Not at all," Leo swears he replied.

It was finally beginning to sink in. He was in La Pasionaria with Rita, and they were on their way to Texas. They were in a race with time, because they were trying to save the President of the United States. He stole another glance at my Aunt Rita. He had girded himself for the worst: she was bound to be eccentric, and she was seventeen years older than the last time he had seen her. Vera had warned him that she wore a sequined turban on her head and an imitation ruby fastened to the center of her forehead. But the woman by his side had jet-black hair and ivory skin unblemished by fake jewelry or time. There was no turban on her head. She was the living image of the girl who had traveled back and forth across the ocean clasped between his driver's license and his library card. At the tollbooth to the Jersey Turnpike he extracted the photo from his wallet.

Since Saturday he had held his breath. Now, he let it out.

"Worse things have happened," he said.

"Than what?"

"Than not seeing you for all these years."

"You didn't want to, remember?"

"Of course I did." He handed her the photograph. "See? You've been everywhere with me."

They were heading south through the flat, sulphurous wastelands of New Jersey.

"Well?"

My aunt was still too stunned to speak.

"You haven't changed a bit."

Age cut both ways. Leo must have cataracts, she thought. No one else could possibly have looked her in the eye and seen the dark-haired girl of twenty-seven who had posed so nonchalantly for the camera that long-ago December night. What distance lay between herself and that young self, whose face stared back at her with a beauty that shocked her all the more when she realized how transparent it had been, though not to her, and how ephemeral.

"Remember that red snow?" Leo asked.

They had left New Jersey behind and crossed the border into Pennsylvania. "How could I forget?" my aunt replied. Blood-red, she had said to herself as they shuddered on the building's edge, the city lights spread out beneath them.

She realized now, as she had then, that if she looked, Leo's hand would be an open book. But that, she told herself again, would be the last thing she would do.

My aunt peeled an orange and they ate it slice by slice. She peeled another, then another, and then she reached into the steamer basket, which was wedged between the bag of groceries from the Caputos and the package from the B & H on the backseat. They each ate two of Faith's celebrated lettuce sandwiches, a macaroon, an apple and a piece of cheese. They shot past Bethlehem, past Reading, past Lebanon and Lancaster, and Leo began to whistle "Where Have All the Flowers Gone?" They had a swig of cider. By the time they stopped for gas in Harrisburg, it was like old times again.

"Maybe you should change your tune," said my Aunt Rita.

"I already have," Leo replied. "Didn't you notice?"

My aunt hadn't noticed anything. All her thoughts were on their mission. "I'm serious," she said. "You never know who might be listening."

"Come on—"

"You never know. As a matter of fact, it might not be a bad idea to put our icons in the glove compartment. They could get us into trouble."

"Trouble?" Leo was indignant. "These are my beliefs! People can take them or leave them, but I'm not taking them down."

When she returned from the ladies' room, Leo was humming "Deep in the Heart of Texas," and there was a familiar object propped on the backseat. "This Machine Kills Fascists," it said.

"Wait a minute," said my aunt. "That wasn't there before."

"Of course it was."

"No it wasn't."

"You just didn't see it."

Leo had brought his guitar.

*

No one told me anything until it was too late: they had already left. Over dinner Tuesday night, Helen and Abey explained that Rita had been reunited with Leo, that they were on their way to Dallas in hopes of saving the President and that, depending on the way events unfolded, I should be prepared to see my aunt, Natalya, God's Messenger, on the evening news. If I wanted to stay home from school I could; it was going to be a very difficult week.

"Does Grandma know?"

"Does Grandma know anything?"

My father had a point.

There were things I understood and things I didn't. I was ten years old, and I had known for two whole years what fate had in store for JFK.

"If Rita already saw it, what makes her think she can undo it?"

"She doesn't *think* she can, she only hopes so," my mother explained, serving me another layer of her meat loaf, inedible except to members of the immediate family and those with an interest in the properties of rocks and minerals. "Remember when we talked about cause and effect? How the tides rise and fall because the moon draws them like a magnet? How grasshoppers are green because their bodies are transparent? Well, in a way that's what your aunt's been working on. She can't stop the shots from being fired, but she hopes she can stop the President from being shot."

"But if she already *knows* he's going to be shot, then how can she make it *not* happen? Wouldn't she first have to see herself stopping it in someone's hand?"

"Good question," said my father. "She might and she might not. The problem with clairvoyance is that you can't choose what you see—you see what comes your way. A possibility might be there, but you might miss it. The person whose hand it's in might walk right by you on the street, but if you didn't see their palm you'd never know. It's all a matter of chance. Sometimes your Aunt Rita wants to know something and she has to wait for it to turn up in someone's hand. Sometimes it does, and sometimes it doesn't."

"Like what?"

"Oh, I don't know. Maybe things about her own life . . ."

"Like whether Leo would come back?"

"From the mouths of babes," my mother said.

I was no babe. I was overwhelmed with pride. Now I understood what patriotism was. Like Judith in the Bible, like Joan of Arc or Rosa Parks, my Aunt Rita had a mission. She was on her way to Texas to try to save our President. At the very last, when everyone had given up, she would ride into battle on her trusty steed, grab the upraised sword and smite the enemy—in this case, death. Was death the enemy?

All day Wednesday and Thursday I sat in the library and read: Amelia Earhart, Marian Anderson, Catherine the Great; Eleanor Roosevelt, St. Teresa, Madame Curie; Pocahontas, Gertrude Stein, Rosa Bonheur. I read about women who defied the odds. Women like my aunt.

I thought about cause and effect, and I secretly made up a theory of my own: if Leo could return to my Aunt Rita, which no one had predicted, then maybe Kennedy could turn his head at the last minute, or else the killers could sneeze or cough or hiccup, or just miss him, which also hadn't been predicted. But if that wasn't possible, then at least maybe the whole assassination could come later—when Kennedy was old enough to die, and after the Sixties had come and gone without a hitch.

Then I had another thought: maybe Leo's return could be a cause, and President Kennedy not getting shot could be its effect.

I was only ten years old, and I didn't know yet what connected and what didn't.

*

La Pasionaria hurtled toward the Smoky Mountains, a streak of yellow against the darkening blue hills. Inside the cab, wide-eyed at the scenery before them, Leo and my aunt sat still as rabbits, castanets clicking faster and faster as the highway loped across the tobacco fields of Virginia into Tennessee. Mostly, they rode in silence, hypnotized by the last glints of sun, but as their eyes adjusted to the first dark folds of night, they began, however slowly, to set the record straight.

"I suppose you've had your share of men over the years . . ." Leo ventured. "A beautiful woman like yourself . . ."

"You suppose wrong."

"Then what have you done for company all this time?"

"What anyone in my position would have done," my aunt said dryly.

"Which is?"

"Not a damn thing."

"Surely you don't expect me to believe that you spent nearly twenty years sitting in your little shop all by your lonesome."

"Who says I was lonesome?"

"All right, alone—"

"Don't be ridiculous. I had my work. I had my friends. I had a whole independent life. What more did I need?"

"What more?" Leo could hardly believe his ears. "I had . . . I mean . . . the night I left you standing in the snow I dreamt I was curled up inside your heart."

217

"That's nice. You ran away from me, remember?"

"I didn't run—I drove."

"Very funny. The point is, you weren't interested in me."

"I was passionately interested in you. But when you suddenly changed from one day to the next like something out of Kafka, I was bereft. In any case, I wasn't running from you; I was running from myself."

"So where did you end up?"

There was an edge to my aunt's voice that took him by surprise.

"All right," Leo said gently. "Let's not talk about where we've been; let's talk about where we're going."

"We know where we're going: we're going to Dallas."

Was my aunt running rings around him, Leo wondered, or was she really off in her own world? Something told him it was better not to ask.

They slept by the side of the road just west of Knoxville and continued on at dawn, with Leo's eyes on U.S. 40 and my aunt's eyes on the future: everywhere she looked, behind the hills and underneath the twisted vines that held the landscape in a noose, lines of smoke were rising from invisible fires.

As they moved south, billboards from the Fifties greeted them in every town: "America: Love It or Leave It"; "The Only Good Commie is a Dead Commie"; "Better Dead Than Red." They drove all day, stopping only for gas and a quick bite to eat. On the outskirts of Nashville, they ate the last of Vera's eggs and drank a whole container of borscht. In Memphis, staring at the muddy Mississippi, they finished off the vegetarian chopped liver and started in on Anna Loscandalo's lasagna.

They reached Little Rock by midnight and parked beside a clapboard church to sleep. When the sun came up on Thursday morning, my aunt handed Leo a cup of the Caputos' still warm coffee and a slice of challah from the B & H. It was a glorious Arkansas morning—blue sky, red barns—and roosters were crowing in the distance. Once again Leo turned the key in the ignition and La Pasionaria leapt toward Dallas, toward the wound in time and space that no one else had glimpsed but my Aunt Rita.

The parade of billboards continued without mercy: "The Family That Prays Together Stays Together," "Jesus Loves You" and one that seemed to have been posted just for them: "Remember the Tortoise and the Hare: Plan Ahead, Drive Slowly."

"Better luck next time," said Leo, who had started humming "Hit the Road, Jack" when they turned onto Route 30. He stole a glance at my Aunt Rita, who was looking straight ahead, her face suffused with morning sun. She had told him about the thousands of loose images that thronged the air, and he imagined that, like someone with a short-wave radio, she was scanning them for last minute news of the assassination. Maybe the assassins were somehow broadcasting their final plans; maybe the two of them really would save Kennedy. If they succeeded, he realized with a shudder, the woman of his dreams would go down in history.

A hundred miles out of Little Rock they stopped in Hope for gas. "A hundred ninety-seven miles from here to Dallas," Leo said, looking at the map. "That's four hours if we take it easy—we can probably make it in less. We should be there by one o'clock." His voice grew soft. "We'll take a room in the first house that has a sign out. I want you to get a good night's sleep."

My aunt was watching the attendant, whose name was stitched in script across the pocket of his navy jumpsuit: *Lefty*. "Do your windshield?" he said with a broad smile, already moving a pale rag across the glass. Leo fished for a cigarette and pressed the lighter on the dashboard. There was a sharp crackle, like the sound of an old wireless starting up, and a gravelly voice sputtered toward them from the front of the car: *$50,000 a day it costs to keep them nine little Negroes in that white school in Little Rock. Good money we could have spent for defense. I'm telling you people . . . if it weren't for them nine little Negroes it would be our Sputnik up there tonight and not the Communists'.*

"What the hell was that?" Leo asked.

"Static," said my aunt, who had seen the ghost of an old Dixie congressman stalking the broad flats of Lefty's hand. "The sound of hatred scratching like a rat. A broken record that . . . "

"You mean to tell me you can *hear* things too?"

"So can you, apparently," my aunt replied. "Let's get out of here."

Leo was a champion driver. He had driven tanks in Spain and taxis in New York. He could change a tire with his eyes closed and he knew the inside of a car like the back of his own hand. So when a terrible clanging started up half an hour after they crossed into Texas, he knew they were in trouble. It sounded like a prisoner in chains throwing himself against the iron crossbars of a dungeon. "Shit," he said, letting up on the accelerator and easing the car off to the side of the road. "It sounds like the head's about to blow." It was. They were in the middle of nowhere, with nothing but pale scrub grass all around them.

Leo had often thought of selling his old cab. A friend had used it for a while when he left for Spain, and eventually someone had arranged to store it in a house upstate. He had reclaimed it briefly after he and Carmen first moved to New York; then he sent it back upstate. After he returned to take over the family business, he had the car shipped back to Riverdale and put in storage a block from where he lived. Eventually, he thought, he would get around to selling it. But the one time he actually hung a FOR SALE sign in the window he was overcome by guilt and ran back to pull it off. By now convenience had given way to nostalgia. He didn't need the money, and it was easier to let the years go by than find a buyer for a twenty-year-old Checker with jump seats in the back and a pair of castanets and portraits of Karl Marx and FDR up front. Besides, the car ran beautifully.

They were in luck. A dark blue pickup truck rolled to a stop. "Yew'all stuck?" The driver was a beer-bellied hulk of a man with a face full of freckles and a crewcut that all but assured him the name Red. He was no longer a kid, but he wasn't thirty either. "What seems to be the trouble?"

"Head's cracked," Leo said.

"Mind if I take a look?"

Their new friend was already on the ground. "Sure is," he said, peering up from under the hood. "Darn near fried right up on you, looks like. Where yew'all off to today?"

"Dallas," said my aunt.

"Ma'am?"

"We have to be there by nightfall."

"Uh-uh."

"We have to."

"Ma'am, the Lord giveth and the Lord taketh away. He's taken one hell of a bite out of your engine. No way you're gonna be in Dallas today. Nearest place'll touch a car like this is down in Longview. I can tow yew'all down there if it's any help . . ."

"Myself, I always take the long view," Leo said under his breath.

"How's that, sir?" Red had already pulled a length of chain from the back of his pickup and was threading it around La Pasionaria's front fender.

"Oh, nothing—it's just that everything was fine when we left New York."

"When was that, sir?"

"Tuesday morning."

"You don't say," said Red, looking at his watch. "You certainly made tracks. Must be in quite a hurry."

"We are, Mr. . . ." Leo said.

"You can call me Slim. Everybody does."

"Slim?" The name was incongruous.

"Yeah, it started out serious but it got to be a joke." He grinned. "Like yew'all trying to get to Dallas."

My aunt grabbed Leo's wrist.

Slim looked at his watch again. A car approached in the opposite lane, slowed to a near stop and made a leisurely U-turn, pulling up behind them. "Nice work, pal," one of the state troopers greeted Slim, stepping up to the taxi with the New York plates. "They ready?"

"They don't come much dumber," Slim assented, pointing to the chain.

"Mr. Kaplan, you're under arrest. And so is your companion."

"Under a what?"

"You heard me: under arrest."

"But that's impossible."

"It's entirely possible, Mr. Kaplan, with the level and quality of law enforcement we have in these U-nited States of America."

"But we haven't done anything, officer."

"The hell you haven't. The two of you've been crossing state lines right and left with the intent of threatening the duly elected President of the USA."

Leo looked at my Aunt Rita. It was too late for second thoughts. With Vera's help, the woman of his dreams had led him all the way across the country and dropped him smack in the middle of shit creek. Now what? he asked her silently.

To this day my aunt doesn't know where they were held. "What difference does it make?" she says. "The point is, they had us. We were dead meat, and so was the President."

Was it a jail?

According to my aunt, it was a frontier-style lockup, the kind you see in the movies. While Slim hitched up La Pasionaria and disappeared around the bend, the troopers handcuffed Leo and my aunt and drove them through the hills. They were blindfolded, but they could feel the road head south. When they arrived, the blindfolds were pulled off and they found themselves in a small sheriff's office of adobe with two adjoining cells. "You're in the clink, my friends," said the sheriff, a dead ringer for John Wayne, with bulging holsters, high cheekbones and a ten-gallon hat.

Now it was my aunt's turn to be questioned.

"Do you answer to the name Natalya, God's Messenger?"

"That depends on the question."

"Sarcasm will get you nowhere, young lady."

At forty-five, his words were music to her ears.

"Do you claim to read the hands of strangers?"

"I don't claim to — I do."

"And have you been telling your so-called customers that the President was going to be shot to death in Texas?"

"I tell them everything I see. I'm worried sick about what's going to happen."

"And did you ever attempt to so inform the FBI, the CIA and other high government bodies?"

"I tried, but no one listened."

"And was it not your intention to disrupt the motorcade tomorrow by shouting at the President of the United States?"

"Look," said my Aunt Rita. "I know exactly what's going to happen and exactly what has to be done. I know exactly where to stand so that the President will hear me. There's still time to save him. We haven't done anything wrong. We're trying to prevent a crime of state."

"And I'm here to see to it that you don't. You're both being charged with crossing state lines with intent to incite a riot. That's punishable by five years in jail and a $2,500 fine. I'm also charging you with threatening the President of the United States: punishable by ten years in jail, and a $100,000 fine."

"Officer," Leo said as calmly as he could, "we came down here to try to keep this country from falling into a terrible abyss. It's not just the President we want to save, it's America. It's the future of this country."

"We don't need no knights in shining armor to come save us, Mr. Kaplan. And we don't need no Trojan horse full of Commie propaganda. As soon as this blows over you all can go straight back where you came from."

Blows over? Leo could no longer contain himself. "We need to speak to a lawyer," he said.

"Well you're plum out of luck, pal," said the sheriff, "because we need a phone. We need one real bad, but they haven't gotten to us yet."

My aunt and Leo exchanged a single glance that told them each what they both knew: they could count on one another to withstand whatever lay ahead.

"Your personal effects'll be arriving shortly," the sheriff continued. "Soon as they get that car of yours repaired. Meantime, we got some clothes we want you to wear and some Texas grub you'll probably be glad to eat. Shorty?" He waved toward a small room off to the side.

Shorty was a carbon copy of the sheriff, only smaller. "Shorty here's my second in command," the sheriff said, stating the obvious. "He'll show you to your rooms."

Am I sure? What are you talking about? My aunt can hardly believe her ears.

It's not that I doubt her memory: far from it. I just can't bring myself to think that anyone would go to such elaborate lengths to keep Natalya, God's Messenger, from reaching Dallas.

Well, start bringing yourself, says my Aunt Rita. Because you don't get a car to fall apart like that out of thin air, and you don't get a quaint little sheriff's office to just happen to be sitting on a nearby hillside. Believe me, they knew what they were doing.

The thump in my aunt's heart began when she saw Leo clench his fists and continued that whole endless Thursday afternoon and on past midnight into the terrible new dawn.

Shorty brought them bacon and toast at 6 A.M. "We need our car back," Leo said.

Shorty shook his head.

"We need to see the sheriff."

A few minutes later the sheriff came in. "Morning," he said. "What can I do you for today?" He was in a jovial mood.

"We'd like to be released on our own recognizance," said Leo.

"Not a snowball's chance in hell, Mr. Kaplan. I intend to keep my eye on you till this thing's done. And any reconnaissance gets done around here is sure as hell gonna be done by me. Adeeyose."

My aunt saw the horses as soon as he held up his hand. There were hundreds of them in formation, draped in black. Their hooves were soundless as they pawed the ground, but there were drums pounding in the distance. A dark rain began to fall and a path of red-hot fire raced toward the heart of Texas. The open car turned onto Elm Street, the gunmen stiffened in their posts and before she knew it my aunt had seen the grassy knoll, the couple waving, the brain erupting in slow motion, the whole country slipping through the cracks. There was still time to save the President, but in the sheriff's upraised hand his death was a done deed.

At twelve twenty-five they heard the screech of brakes outside the jail. "Honk if you believe in Jesus," yelled the sheriff, and whoever was behind the wheel leaned on the horn. "Fucking bastards," Leo said. He would have recognized that sweet cornet sound anywhere. La Pasionaria was back.

The news came over the radio at 12:35. "We interrupt this program to inform you . . ." The announcer's voice was choked. ". . . that the President of the United States has been . . ." Another voice took over. "This just in: President John Fitzgerald Kennedy has been gravely wounded in an apparent attempt on his life. . . . Texas Governor John Connolly, who was also traveling in the presidential motorcade, was also wounded. . . . First reports from the scene . . ."

At 1:39 Shorty unlocked the two adjoining cells and led my aunt and Leo into the main room, where Walter Cronkite's voice was announcing the President's death. The sheriff and Slim were already halfway through a six-pack.

"Heads we win, tails you lose," the sheriff said, flipping a mint 1960 silver dollar.

"Car's fine." Slim handed Leo his keys. "She runs like a dream."

The sheriff personally removed their handcuffs. "You've got exactly an hour to clear the hell out of the state of Texas. It's forty miles to the Louisiana border. Now scram."

Leo's castanets were hanging from the rearview mirror. There was nothing left of all their food, but Roosevelt, Marx and La Pasionaria were exactly where he had left them on the dashboard.

*

Half a continent away, on the island of Manhattan, Lucy and José Delgado were sitting at their kitchen table with Vera and Sasha, José Jr. and Filomena Cruz.

When the news came over the radio, Filomena jumped up. "A coup," she said, looking around wildly.

As Filomena bolted toward the door, Lucy stepped in front of her. "*Cálmate*," she said in Spanish, wrapping her arms around the trembling girl and stroking her hair. "This is the United States, not one of those bananas republics you read about in the *periódico*. Everything is under control. You heard: the new *presidente* has already been sworn in."

Vera slammed her fist down on the table. "That's exactly the point," she said. "Filomena's right. It's a coup. The question is, will they get away with it?"

"Of course they will," said José Jr. "Like my mother says, this is the United States, not some little country dozing face-up in the sun. They do things right here."

"You can say that again," said Vera.

"We have to change the sign," she added, and Lucy ran downstairs to get the cardboard sign my aunt had hung on the door the night before she left. "CLOSED DUE TO POSSIBLE EMERGENCY," it said in large black letters. "Now what?" Vera asked. "CLOSED DUE TO COUP?" "Just cross out 'possible,'" said Filomena, and Vera took a Magic Marker like a sword and ran it through the word that had become a fact.

*

With their windows up, my aunt and Leo beheld a country as mute and dazed as they were.

227

From Longview to Shreveport, the roads were lined with people weeping. It had been less than an hour since the President was shot, but the news had swept across East Texas like a terrible hot wind.

By the time they crossed into Louisiana, there were flags everywhere, all flying at half-staff. Crowds gathered at bus stops, at diners, at churches, and hundreds of people wandered through the intersections. Businesses and restaurants were closing, and factories were shutting down production; at elementary schools, parents were calling for their children. For everyone, the day had ended early.

As La Pasionaria rolled slowly north, through Tallulah, Vicksburg and Meridian, past Tuscaloosa and on up toward Birmingham and Chattanooga, there were more formal signs of grief: the President's likeness, torn from magazines and books, appeared in shop windows and homes; and libraries and railway stations and hotels were hung with garlands of black bunting. "A lonesome train . . . on a lonesome track," Leo began to hum. The entire South was draped in black.

It was evening when they pulled into the outskirts of Birmingham, and almost nine o'clock by the time they found a small white house with a sign that sounded too good to be true: CORA'S GUEST HOUSE—FAMOUS SOUTHERN HOSPITALITY. The whole way from Longview, they hadn't breathed a word. Now, when the door was opened by a mirthful woman with a face round as a bun, they both began to speak at once.

"Two," they both replied when she asked if they would like two beds or one.

"If you can agree on that, you can agree on anything," their hostess said with a broad smile.

It would be ten dollars for the night, including supper if they wanted it and breakfast the next morning.

"You can eat in front of the TV," their hostess offered. "Y'all know about the President?"

They nodded.

"They got the man who did it," she said as she led them upstairs to their room, a small space with flowered wallpaper and sloping ceilings, two wooden beds, a dresser, a looking glass and a picture of the Mississippi on the closet door.

"One thing you can say for this country—"

"Hold it. You mean . . . ?" Leo had just understood.

". . . I mean they don't leave no stone unturned," Cora Vetters finished proudly, pointing down the hall. "Bathroom's that way," she said.

Cora Vetters's palm was wide as an apron, and dusted with flour. My aunt's heart sank. Before she had a chance to turn away, images came flying at her unrestrained.

There were men on horseback, young, with beards, and men on foot, and they were dancing, dueling, dressed in gray and blue, and through the trees she saw them tripping, falling, littering the warm brown of the forest floor, their boots jutting like raised swords, or nails. Deer licked the salt from their eyes and there was silence; the years rolled over them like stones. But now a distant drum began to pound and the voices she had heard from far away broke through the ceiling and the walls became hot coals raining down on four brown girls as the suspect was led out to his death.

It was a fraction of a second, but it was enough. My aunt heard Leo say, "She'll have the same," and Cora Vetters promised to have dinner on the table faster than it takes to skin a possum; then they were alone in the room and she lay down on the bed and cried.

"You're exhausted," Leo said, stroking her dark hair.

"I'm scared," my aunt whispered. "What if they're following us?"

"Sweetheart, it's all over," Leo whispered back.

"What makes you so sure?"

"Because they won. We lost. We're ancient history to them."

"What if I know too much?"

"Do you?" Now Leo sounded worried.

"Maybe not. I don't know names."

"Do you know faces?"

"I know the guy they arrested—and I know who's going to kill him. I just saw him."

"Who?"

"The guy who was set up to kill the guy who was set up to kill the President."

"What are you talking about?"

"I saw it in her palm when she showed us where the bathroom was. He's going to be shot to death on Sunday morning in the basement of the Dallas city jail."

"But no one knows you know that."

"Who knows who knows what? What if they had us bugged all the way down?"

"I think they did."

"I think so too."

"Obviously, we can't talk in the car."

"Obviously, we can't talk, period."

"We can talk—just not about this."

They nodded their agreement. My aunt got up and splashed cold water in her face and they went downstairs to eat.

Their hostess had pulled out all the stops. There was fried chicken and glazed ham and platters full of fritters and vegetables and beans. Cora Vetters was crestfallen when her guests excused themselves after barely sampling her fare. "But I've got pecan pie and apple cobbler in the oven."

"We're too tired to be hungry," Leo apologized.

"What about the eleven o'clock news?"

"We've seen it," said my aunt.

"Ma'am?"

"She's still in shock," Leo replied, leading my Aunt Rita back upstairs.

"Here's what I don't get," Leo said as they resumed their trip the following morning.

"I thought we weren't going to talk."

"We didn't say we wouldn't talk—just not about the assassination."

My Aunt Rita shook her head.

"All right," Leo said with a deep sigh. "I understand."

They shot past signs to Scottsboro and Chattanooga, past towns with names like Soddy Daisy, Chickamauga and Reliance, bought sandwiches in Knoxville, and didn't stop for gas until they were almost out of Tennessee.

It was my aunt who finally broke the silence. "We have to find a place to stay." It was nearly five o'clock and the sun was going down over the hills. "I don't mind driving," Leo said. "We could grab a bite to eat and keep on going if you'd rather sleep in your own bed tonight."

"Tonight? What about the funeral?"

"The funeral?" Leo stammered. It had never crossed his mind that there was anything else for him to do but convey the woman of his dreams safely back across the Hudson.

"I need to see it," my aunt said. "I'm sorry."

"Nothing to be sorry about—except the usual," Leo replied.

"Meaning?"

"Villains run history," he said, parking beside a clapboard house with a sign that said THE WELCOME INN. "Will this do?"

"Anything will do," my aunt replied. They had crossed into Virginia, still too far south for comfort, but far enough from Texas for her to feel the first stirrings of relief. Maybe now, for the first time all week, she would get a real night's sleep.

Maybe yes, maybe no. The room smelled of mothballs and ammonia and a single yellow bulb hung overhead; there were two beds with tight, clean sheets and extra blankets by the door. Downstairs, the voices grew louder in the dining room they had just left, and the drone of a television set came through the floorboards. My aunt closed her eyes, but Leo was wound up like a clock. "Look," he said. "I know it's late . . . we've been through hell . . . I appreciate the state you must be in. But I need to get this off my chest. Before she died, my mother told me that you read her hand. At the time, I didn't quite believe her; now, of course, I understand. So I know you know my father drowned. There were a lot of things I couldn't tell you. That was one. When he died, a part of me died too—but that's another story.

"And you know about the lawsuit," he continued. "The case was settled out of court and we were honor-bound to start production. That's how KAPCO came about—you've seen the trucks. Overnight, the company made millions. I didn't help, because I couldn't stand the thought of all those animals coming to life while my father was lying on the ocean floor. My mother did it alone. In 1959 she had her first big stroke. I was already in Mexico, but I flew home. What else could I do? Now I'm running the damn show and I can't seem to get it off my back."

At midnight, Leo was still talking. "So you see, I didn't set out to create a whole persona. It happened gradually, over a period of years. Everything real made me feel doomed. The grief never let up. I had to focus on what lay ahead if I wanted to stay sane. The only place I felt alive was Spain—and after Spain, my car. Then my room—then books."

My aunt looked up. "What ever happened to that room?"

"Believe it or not, I still have it. I never sleep there, but every once in a while I go up to sniff the air."

"No, really—what happened to it?"

"I just told you; I still have it."

"Come on. You have a whole mansion up in Riverdale. Arthur says you live like a mogul. Why keep an extra room?"

"Why not?"

"Isn't that a little strange?"

"Isn't everything a little strange?"

He reached up to turn out the light. "Wait a second," my aunt said. "Wouldn't keeping it have gotten you in trouble?"

"Not really. When I returned to the States I put the lease in someone else's name." He paused.

"And who paid the rent checks all those years?"

"My mother."

"You mean she knew you were in Spain?"

"She didn't have to. She just followed my instructions. I set it all up in advance."

"She never told us a thing."

"My mother loved me very much—she did whatever I asked. She knew my life—and possibly yours—depended on it."

"Mine?"

"My mother was very fond of you, you know."

He looked across the space between their beds. "Why am I telling you all this?"

"I'll be damned if I know." My aunt turned out the light.

The sky was slate-colored and the streets were luminous and cold when La Pasionaria rolled into Washington, D.C. On the narrow side streets, along the broad diagonals that swept straight toward the city's heart, men and women by the thousands waited in their Sunday best. It was early Monday morning, and they were waiting for the President.

As the sky turned blue above the Capitol, words no one knew flew up like blackbirds and hovered overhead: caisson, cortege, catafalque. The President was dead. Suddenly, all Washington looked like a mausoleum, its chalk-white buildings colossal as the tombs of kings. Leo parked La Pasionaria in a garage and he and my Aunt Rita joined the multitude. At the corner of Pennsylvania Avenue and Fourteenth Street, where people were packed ten abreast, a muffled sound moved through the crowd when the funeral horses came into view. A thousand mourners moaning from a single coat. The sky went black.

Leo heard my aunt cry out and turned to see her cowering beneath her own raised arms. Her face was a mask of horror and her voice careened from word to word—

Rubyoswaldrubyoswaldrubyoswald

—until a terrifying buzz shook her whole mouth. All hell had broken out, a thousand palms had loosed their images like rooftops flung from their rafters in a storm, and the world she had struggled to contain would no longer be contained.

"... and Kennedy again ... and King ..." she sobbed as Leo led her back to the garage. "So many dead ... so many lives ..." She had held her right palm to her face, breathed only through her mouth, but nothing worked. The buzzards were everywhere. Loose images had blackened the air.

"You need to rest," Leo said, wrapping his arms around her.

"I'll be all right." My aunt, still trembling, glanced up.

Her sight had already begun to clear. In a far region of the sky, past the burning trail of the assassins, a jumble of domestic objects whirled and spun. There were eyeglasses and lamps, books and alarm clocks and mugs, the simple objects everyone kept close at hand. In the explosion of loose images, these ordinary things had also broken from their owners' palms and been hurled upward in the air to float above the city.

My aunt remembers nothing of that strange debris except what she saw last: buffeted to and fro by the high winds, a cache of photographs was drifting slowly back to earth. Like pages from a nameless book, the pictures rose and fell in the bright light, sparkling with the lives of strangers. Amid so many unknown faces, there was no mistaking the portrait of herself and Leo, the White House etched behind them as they held each other tight beneath the cold November sky of Washington, D.C.

Eleven

Sometimes, says my aunt, it takes a stranger to show you what's right before your nose. Sometimes, she says, the truth is stranger than fiction.

There were things I saw and things I didn't, things I looked at but I didn't see. When you have a talent, darling, you have to train yourself to be suspicious. You have to second-guess your own mistakes, because no one else will. Hindsight gives you the illusion that you understood things right away, but the first time through it's not so simple. You'll see.

My aunt won't say it in so many words, but if she's talking about Leo, this is probably the closest she has come to admitting she was wrong.

Not once, but twice, she says, eliminating any doubt. Wrong to dismiss him out of hand, and wrong to keep him waiting for so long.

Was Gittel right?

Put it this way, says my aunt, casting an uneasy glance over her shoulder: now I see him, then I didn't. He didn't register with me.

Even after the assassination?

What can I tell you? The important things in life don't happen overnight. The important things can take a lifetime, darling. Even longer.

*

The skyline of Manhattan was a glittering torch against the winter dusk when La Pasionaria emerged from the Jersey Turnpike onto the George Washington Bridge. It was a postcard view of New York City, its beauty distilled and separated from the torment of its streets, but no less true for being contemplated from afar. Though first-time visitors might gasp at the sheer majesty of such a sight, it was New Yorkers themselves, so often at a loss to explain what kept them on this hostile, dirt-choked, asphalt-smothered island, who, more frequently than anybody else, drove their cars into the bridge's edge, mesmerized by the vision of their grimy rock transformed into a celestial metropolis of light. This was the city of their dreams, the one that shone inside them like a beacon while its raucous twin blared on outside. They knew now why they called it home.

It was this vision of New York that welcomed my aunt and Leo back. The sun—the West—their valiant effort—the President's spilled blood—were all behind them. Before them lay the future; or, as my aunt says, the wild blue yonder.

For the moment, there was nothing blue for miles around except the blue-black sky above Manhattan, and nothing wilder than the fleecy clouds racing like mad buffalo across it. The windows along Riverside Drive were tinged with purple and the trees were dark and leafless as La Pasionaria wound south, then east on Seventy-second Street, then south again down Broadway. In the aftermath of the funeral, the sidewalks were deserted, the stores shuttered, as if the entire world had gone indoors. Even Eddie's Luncheonette, the pride of the neighborhood because it never closed, was dark and empty when the taxi with the castanets crossed

Columbus Avenue at Sixty-eighth Street and continued on toward Central Park, where there was a parking space halfway down the block.

Leo had waited all the way from Texas to New York to ask his question. "Now will you read my hand?" he said, turning off the engine. "I don't mean tonight—but soon?"

My aunt nearly said yes. After the thousands of palms she had examined, after the crushing defeat of her attempt to save the President, after the sky itself had blackened with loose images, what did she have to lose? But then she stopped. Leo's hand might be a trap. What if, for good or ill, it held more news than she could stand? Or if, once she looked down, she was unable to look up? There was too much at stake. "I can't," she said. "I really can't. At least not yet."

"You see?" said Leo. "You haven't changed a bit."

"Have *you?*"

They took the stairs one at a time and my aunt held her breath and stared at her right hand while Leo fumbled with his keys. She had said no and she meant it; still, she had to keep her wits about her or his palm might catch her unawares.

They threw their coats on the faded armchair by the door and he switched on the light. The poster of La Pasionaria still hung on the far wall, and the same blue candle, still riding its ancient bottle, stood on the same little table in the corner. My aunt felt the room begin to spin.

"It's late," she said.

"It's six o'clock."

"Well then it feels late," said my aunt.

Leo had promised to drive her home to Forest Hills, but it was anybody's guess how they would get from here to there.

"Come," he said, pointing toward the bed, and she sat stiffly on the edge.

Leo drew the curtains and poured them each a glass of bourbon. "Here's to our safe return," he said, "and many more." Then, taking a deep breath, he sat down across from my Aunt Rita and began to speak. "Last night I had the strangest dream . . . I dreamt I had forgotten my own name. I was in a foreign city and I felt completely lost. My mother was dead, and there was no one I could ask. Then I realized everyone I knew was dead. I was filled with dread. Almost by instinct, I took out a map and began to walk. Suddenly I found myself on Seventh Street—there was a different feeling in the air. I still didn't know my name but I knew that you did. And in the dream, that was enough. When I woke up you were saying 'Leo, Leo,' like a little bird."

"Then you were still dreaming."

"You were talking in your sleep," he said, pouring himself another glass.

"It's true I ran away from you," he continued without giving her a chance to speak. "I was afraid you would drown me in a tangle of unreal beliefs. I needed certainty back then. I thought evil was evil and good was good and never the twain would meet. But all week I've breathed the air you breathe and I understand now that the world lives and moves inside you the way the rest of us live in the world. I'm not afraid of you anymore; I'm just afraid I'll never be the man you're looking for."

"I already told you: I'm not looking."

Already, my aunt was sorry that she had agreed to see his room—"for old times' sake," as he had put it when they hit the last stretch of the Jersey Turnpike. She was exhausted; besides, their mission was done, if not accomplished. There was no reason to spend any further time with Leo. She had let her curiosity get the better of her. "At my age," she chided herself with silent disapproval.

"In that case," he said gently, "you might be surprised by what you find." There was an awkward pause and she realized he was crying.

"I believe in you, Rita," he started up again. "I've seen your gift with my own eyes, and I've seen the price you pay day after day. You've dazzled me with your courage. I want to dazzle you back. I have nothing to hide. Thanks to you, all my ghosts are laid to rest. What can I say? Years ago I wasn't ready; now I am. I want to join you in the laboratory of the hand. If there's a way to lighten your burden, I promise you, I'll do whatever it takes."

His voice was honey, gravel, burnished gold, a gentle ribbon of sound that pushed her to the edge of the precipice into which she was already falling, and someone was calling to her as she tumbled free as Alice down down down away from the known world into a molten core of happiness and silence where Leo awaited her with open arms.

" . . . will be what?" she said.

"I said things will be different this time around," Leo murmured, looking up into the flushed alabaster of her face, the Russian jet of her hair, the cat-green of her eyes, the picaresque contours of her mouth.

"How do you know?"

He moved toward her on the bed. "Because they already are."

*

Like everyone else in the family, I waited my turn. Like my grandmother Gittel, who sat staring out the window at the hydrant across the street, like my father Abey and my mother Helen, I needed proof. When the President was shot, I knew that my Aunt Rita was no ordinary dreamer. What she had seen in Filomena's hand two years before came charging toward us like a horse across a plain and crashed straight through the television screen into our living room. What she had told us had come true.

When the President was shot I didn't cry. First, because I didn't love him. Second, because thanks to my Aunt Rita, I wasn't taken by surprise.

"I expected it," I told my fifth-grade teacher, whose hand froze in mid-air when she finished writing the word "assassination" on the blackboard. "Why aren't you crying?" she had thundered, singling me out from my grief-stricken classmates with the fury of a Puritan accuser. "My aunt predicted it," I said in as straightforward a voice as I could muster.

But beneath my outward calm I was shaking like a leaf. In the tumult of the moment, I had barely noticed that my aunt and Leo had failed to stop the assassins or that the President was dead. All I knew was that my father's sister, my Aunt Rita, had predicted something catastrophic, and that everything had taken place exactly as she said it would. I had always known she had a calling; now I knew that when she put her ear to history, history spoke back.

Not that Kennedy's assassination left me indifferent. Like everyone old enough to remember, I know exactly where I was when I first heard. For me, as for all of us, his death marked a divide. But in my case it meant something else. Beforehand, I thought of my aunt's powers as a kind of magic. If pressed, I would probably have likened her clairvoyance to the ability to juggle or speak Spanish or do cartwheels on a tightrope high above the street. Because of her, our Sunday visits to my grandmother's, which could have been excruciating after Gittel lost her mind, were irresistible and detailed, like a movie or a book. But after the assassination, I understood that while the rest of us were living in the noisy tangle of the present, my aunt was gliding in and out of time itself. This was more than entertainment. It was like having Shakespeare in your family, or Joan of Arc.

It was then, at ten, that I began to think about the future. When I grew up, I would be clairvoyant too. My aunt and I would work together in the storefront, and people would come from far and wide to see us; they would watch while we stared into our crystal balls, and listen while we told them the story of their lives. "Is that your daughter?" the customers would ask when they saw me in my spangled turban with a cut-glass jewel on my forehead like my aunt's. "My niece," she'd reply with that slight accent she's always had. And the two of us would smile. Because it would be true.

But there was a frightening side too. If this could happen, anything could. We were in the gaping hole now, the wound my aunt had said would open up if the assassins had their way. I realized there was little to celebrate, even if events had proved her right. And I began to worry. Would things really come unstuck? Would there really be more deaths? *Now* what would they use for glue? I wondered what it felt like to be the person who saw so much before it happened.

To my amazement, Helen and Abey seemed to take it all in stride. From their point of view, my Aunt Rita was neither to be pitied nor understood: her ability to read between the lines on people's hands, proven to their satisfaction by my birth and re-proven to their horror by the President's unnatural death, was a fact like any other. Scientifically speaking, as my mother put it, Rita's talent was no more deserving of attention than the density of diamonds or the solubility of sugar.

It just *is*, she says.

Is what?

Is what it is.

My mother and I are walking in the rain. *Left, left, I had a good job and I left*, we say under our breath, our rain boots slapping the sidewalk at exactly the same time. *I left my wife and forty-eight children to die of starvation without any gingerbread left* . . . For years this has been our private walking song. When I was little, it made me laugh; now, I barely notice it. *Left, I had a good job and I left* . . .

I understand why diamonds are hard and sugar dissolves in water. What I don't understand is how my parents can be so casual about what lies ahead.

First of all, my mother says, because we can't be absolutely sure how things will be until they happen.

(Having recently dissected a frog, I recognize this as the scientific method.)

Second, because time is long and life is short. As a species, she explains, mankind is in its infancy. Not even—we're more like a tadpole than a frog. There will be good times and bad, times of oppression and times of relief. Eventually, *Homo sapiens* may overcome its innate flaws. Not in our lifetimes, of course. Not even mine? Not even yours, my mother says, shaking her head.

Then what was the point of being three steps ahead of everybody else? What was the point of ringing the bell, of flying through the streets with your nightgown on, if nobody would listen?

Because, my mother says, matter is neither created nor destroyed. Sooner or later everything we know will be of use to someone, somewhere.

Was that true? It was the sort of proposition you could never really test.

Left, left . . . My mother walks, holding her umbrella high. Her calm is her example.

By day we go about our business as if everything has stayed the same. By night we know how much has changed. Galloping, galloping, the heart pounds on, Abey says, and who can say when the truth will out, whether in our lifetime or yours, or the one after. Time, he says, bears the age away, and time—my father is always quoting someone I have never heard of—waits for no man.

What will happen? I want to know.

Great plays will be written, he says, and plays within plays. One day people will wake to the sound of their own applause. It will be dark, they will wonder where they are, and when the lights go on they'll weep for joy.

Why?

Because light after darkness is always a relief. You'll see.

My father and I are standing still but the line we are on is moving. We've come to see the *Pietà*, which has been sent to us by the good people of Europe and, like Chiclets moving one by one, we're on a conveyor belt designed, my father says, to expose the greatest number of Americans to art and ecstasy in the least time. Fair is fair, he says as we drift by, and I have no choice but to believe him, and to smile. Many years ago, somewhere beneath the Virgin's marble grief, when this was still a meadow, my father buried a tin box, a whole time capsule filled with a boy's treasure: wooden nickels, string, a pocketknife, a pouch of agates, a roll of dimes. The World's Fair bulldozers have churned the earth here inside out so many times that we will never find it.

My father tells me not to worry. It will be for generations hence. Someday, he says, a boy digging in the future will strike pay dirt.

*

At the storefront, business remained brisk. Within hours of the assassination, word of my Aunt Rita's terrible success began to spread, and by the time she opened up for work on Tuesday morning, the line outside was wrapped around the block. Even those who had been skeptical before came to see for themselves the woman who had driven all the way to Texas to save the President's life. Never mind that she had failed. She had foreseen his death, and the fact that she had risked her life for him was part of history. Some, merely curious, peered through the window, but others, newly impatient, decided it was time to put their own hands on the table and were elbowing their way up to the door. Vera stayed on, working every day but Saturdays, in part to help my aunt control the crowd outside, but mostly because she couldn't tear herself away. "The excitement was this thick," she says, drawing her thumb and middle finger together in mid-air. "Kennedy got killed, but your aunt came back transformed."

"Definitely," Lucy says, pressing her lips together with awe. The first to welcome my aunt back and to place her upturned hand on the blue damask tablecloth, Lucy swears that my aunt not only looked different when she returned from Texas but that her gaze now felt "like X-ray vision."

"Her eyes were bigger. Right, José?"

"Absolutely," says José Jr., never one to contradict his mother.

Those first days back, Leo drove downtown each afternoon to meet my aunt, rapping on the plate glass window while La Pasionaria idled at the curb; as soon as she caught sight of him, my aunt drew the spangled curtain, turned the cardboard OPEN sign to CLOSED and appeared at the front door. She was glad to see him, but she didn't want him in the store. Vera was indignant. "What are you waiting for?" she said at the end of the first week.

The answer was self-evident, at least to my Aunt Rita. With events continuing to prove her right, this was hardly the moment to jeopardize her sight. Sooner or later, she would produce a message that was clear and clarion and final. Then, and only then, would she read Leo's palm. It was a matter of time.

"You're playing with fire," Vera said. "First you lead him on a wild goose chase that lands you both in jail, and then, when he wants to have his hand read—after all those years—you refuse. I'm warning you, Rita. If you keep this up this you're going to lose him."

But Leo understood. "Of course she's nervous," he told Helen and Abey over lunch at the Eclair. "All these years she's lived with a tremendous strain—shouldering the burden all alone—and suddenly I reappear and offer to help out. Of course she's suspicious; of course she's unsure. How could it be otherwise? She's staked her whole life on this gift. She's probably afraid that if she lets her guard down she'll lose her capacity to work . . . or that she'll lose sight of her goal. I don't blame her."

Abey told Vera and Vera told my aunt: Leo says that he can wait.

Which, like so much else in my aunt's life, was both true and not true.

*

The first note arrived inside a box of long-stemmed roses that was delivered to the storefront by Flora Bloom herself; the second, one week later, was tucked inside a pair of cashmere gloves that came directly through the mail. "I still take the long view," said the first. "To warm your hands while you make up your mind," read the second. By the middle of December, Leo's messages were turning up at the rate of two or three a week. By the start of the New Year they had become a torrent, and by the end of January they were a flood. They arrived in baskets, in boxes, in flower pots and jars, always hidden just enough so that my aunt would come upon them in surprise.

"What's this?" she would say, holding up the latest gift for Vera to examine.

"Open it," Vera would say. And sure enough, if she parted the leaves of an exotic plant or unfolded a silk scarf or lifted the top of a small painted box there would be another note from Leo.

"A bird in the hand is worth two in the bush."

"My happiness is in your hands."

"He's gone off the deep end," she sighed when the seventh pair of gloves arrived. "May your future and mine go hand in glove . . ."

"No he hasn't," Vera said. "He's in love."

*

By this point I was spending all my free time at the storefront. I rode the subway in each Saturday with my Aunt Rita, clutching my plaid overnight bag in case we spent the night at Vera's. Sometimes we did, but mostly we were back in Forest Hills in time for dinner.

My parents were resigned. "At least you'll be learning about current events," said Abey.

The events I learned about were hardly current, but I kept my mouth shut.

"So long as you do your homework," Helen sighed.

I did it in the storefront, with the bathroom door slightly ajar. I used to sit, feet dangling, a notebook open in my lap, pretending to be deep in thought, but in fact I was listening to everything that my aunt said.

My very first day there, my aunt received a visit from Filomena Cruz. She was nineteen years old, with long black hair and dangling earrings. Her voice was dark and husky and she smelled of smoke.

"I have to hand it to you," Filomena said. "Remember that guy I asked you about? A friend of mine went on a date with him and he stole twenty dollars from her while they were at the movies. But I met somebody else—an artist. Look—"

My aunt waved her hands over the crystal ball and circled it three times. "Handsome," she said, peering into Filomena's outstretched palm, where a brooding older man was hard at work before his easel. "He looks like Van Gogh."

"Who?"

"Van Gogh—the great Dutch painter."

"Never heard of him," said Filomena, popping a piece of gum into her mouth. "But I heard of that other guy."

"Rembrandt?"

"No, the other one—the one with the piano."

"Van Cliburn."

"Yeah, him."

"Look at this," my aunt continued, her voice dropping to a whisper. "Haldencranz and Ehrlichstern are dead. No, wait—it's the other way around. Ehrlichcranz and Haldenstern."

"Erlichwho? Haldenwhat?" said Filomena.

"Loyal courtiers," my aunt replied, mystified herself. "The place is crawling with them."

"What place?"

My aunt doesn't know yet; all she knows is that once again the wood-paneled office is there with its huge desk and that this time men in suits are scurrying back and forth like well-meaning valets stuffing whatever they can find into envelopes and boxes; in another room, shredders are humming. Suddenly my aunt's clear voice has vanished and a man is speaking in her place. "Just destroy all the tapes," he says. We hear a click, a whir, and then another click.

"Naturally, the President knows nothing about it," my aunt continues without looking up. "A few more years and he'll be passing himself off as a sage. They all will. Look: there's the actor waiting for his cue. He must be telling himself a joke, because he's laughing . . ."

"What actor?" Filomena wants to know.

"It's on the tip of my tongue. Dark hair with a kind of slicked back look, small eyes, high cheekbones. You know: the guy that did all those commercials for GE. He did a lot of Westerns in the forties."

"Never heard of him," says Filomena.

Who *had* Filomena heard of, my aunt wondered.

Still, there was something to be said, she told me over lunch, for reading the hands of the next generation, in which the past seemed somehow shorter and the future rode the present like a rider hurtling ahead of his dark horse.

I didn't need to be convinced. I was already hooked.

I was there the afternoon in March when a crew from German television came to film her work. My aunt wore her original crimson turban and, at Vera's urging, did her nails. She was not the least bit fazed by all the cameras and bright lights. "We will see ourselves from the moon," she said in her most dreamlike voice, reading from the narrow hand of Frank Loscandalo's son John. "But we refuse to learn what we need most to know. What we don't want to be: seen from afar. What we don't want to see: who we really are." The faces in the room were frozen as my aunt went on. "They killed the wolf in sheep's clothing, yes. The one they bought the costume for. But what is written in blood is not erased. It penetrates. Who wears the masks of state? Other wolves are on the loose."

Then there was Nat Sarnoff with his white apron and sad eyes, who stopped by one Saturday a few weeks later on his way home from the B & H. "Look," my aunt exclaimed, describing a group of men in three-piece suits who were huddled underneath a bridge in Nat's pale hand. "They're thinning the cement. But they do it at night, when no one's watching. Why? Thin blood makes thin hope." She paused, and I could hear Nat breathing.

"Do me a favor," he said. "Speak to me in English."

"I'm trying," my aunt replied. "I have to see what else is in here. Ah—"

I leaned forward in my seat.

"Would you believe this country would accept an appointed president?"

Nat looked dubious.

"I'm staring him straight in the face," my aunt continued, pointing to an open space in Nat's large palm. "He's part of the advance team for the actor."

"What actor?"

"The one that's going to be President some day. Or pretend to."

"That's a hot one," he said. "Then what?"

"In the short run, prolonged self-congratulation. More surveillance. More lies. One will escalate the bombing. Two will pardon him for something else. A generation will be born with its fist raised, and everyone will be amazed. Before the century's out we'll all be hostages."

"To what?" Nat asked.

"To our own guile."

Nat waved her on. "All right, all right," he said. "Torture me with the truth. How do you know these things?" he asked.

"Listen," said my aunt, "I'm forty-five years old. If I didn't know a thing or two, I wouldn't be here, would I?"

Week after week this was my bliss, my private radio show. I heard words I didn't understand—words like gerrymander, Russophobe and filibuster—and words I did—words like equality and justice and conspiracy. But most of all I heard what I had never heard before: the hidden music of events. Like a magic flute, luminous and silver as the moon, it seemed to play for me and no one else.

*

Leo, whose love has been an example to us all, took me to the Museum of Natural History over spring vacation to see the dinosaurs and totem poles and visit the Eskimo fishing through a hole in his slab of artificial ice. I rode up front under the castanets while Roosevelt, Marx and La Pasionaria peered out at us, benevolent and winking. On the way he tested me on long division and told me stories about Spain.

When we arrived we talked about kinship and tribes and the different ways the different peoples of the world live and marry and ship their dead off to eternity in boats or boxes. Afterward we went to the Eclair for ice cream. I knew he wanted more than anything to marry my Aunt Rita and that she wasn't sure. I also knew that they had been engaged before, but that when Leo saw her with a turban on her head he left for Spain.

"If you were so in love with her," I asked, "how come you didn't stay?"

"I was blind," he said. "My mind was made up sight unseen."

"No, really."

"Sweetheart," he said. "The heart of another is a dark forest."

*

Indeed it was. While we were sipping our parfaits, my aunt, unbeknownst to anyone, was at the ophthalmologist's.

For weeks she had been looking up from people's palms with a strange feeling in her eyes, a heaviness, at times a blur. Sometimes parts of objects weren't there; sometimes things came sailing toward her out of nowhere. Sometimes she could barely see the letters on the plate glass window. At first she had assumed she was just suffering from jangled nerves; now she feared it must be something else: her symptoms were getting worse, not better.

The doctor asked her to focus on a bright red dot while he shone a flashlight in her eyes. Tell me when it disappears.

It didn't. Now he placed a wooden paddle over one eye, then the other. This time the light ahead of her began to bounce.

Clean as a whistle, he pronounced. Her optic nerve was paper white.

Paper thin?

Paper white.

Was that good?

Of course it was. Her eyes were fine.

Then why did these strange symptoms come and go?

Come and go? She hadn't said that before.

Was that bad?

Of course it was. He would have to rule out diabetes, intermittent idiopathic asymptomatic optic neuropathy, multiple sclerosis . . .

My aunt's heart sank.

Any trouble walking?

She shook her head.

Any numbness?

Just cold feet.

Any other strange sensations?

Many.

Profession?

Reader.

Ah—librarian?

My Aunt Rita shook her head.

Editor?

She shook it again.

Okay, I give up. You read—?

—palms.

The ophthalmologist stepped back and peered once more through his machine.

It's time, he said, to give those beautiful green eyes of yours a rest.

*

But according to my aunt, there was no rest in sight.

If anything, she pushed herself harder than ever. With customers lined up at dawn and some still waiting at day's end, she decided to work seven days a week. Vera offered to letter a new sign. "By Popular Demand: Now Open Sundays," it proclaimed.

On her good days, the visions were as sharp as if they had been cut with diamonds.

But on the days when her eyes decided to play tricks on her, she had to fight the terrifying sense that the hands before her on the table were tilting at strange angles toward the floor.

The old Natalya's advice came back to her across the years. Although she had long ago stopped checking people's pulse, she found that holding onto a customer's wrist for a few seconds was sometimes enough to steady her increasingly unsteady gaze. And while she rarely looked into the crystal ball, she noticed that it too steadied her sight if she grasped it tightly in both hands when the images in people's palms began to slip and slide.

Once, in a moment of panic, she even reached for *The Practice of Palmistry for Professional Purposes,* which had lain undusted and unseen for all these years in the tall oak cabinet in the far corner of the store. The book fell open to a passage that had escaped her eye when she first read it: ". . . and if ever your eyes shall tire, as they must, and the palms before you seem to swim and glide, do not neglect the restorative properties of water. A single glass of ordinary tap water placed between your crystal ball and the customer's extended hand will straighten any lines that appear crooked and sharpen any images that have gone slack. A small cut flower will suffice to draw attention away from the use of this useful but slightly dishonorable device."

The recommendation was a godsend.

To Lucy and José, to her vast repertoire of customers, the fresh rose that now appeared each morning on my aunt's table was a touch of class.

To Leo, it was a sign of things to come. A woman who likes flowers, he whispered to me one day over lunch, is a woman in love.

To me a rose was just a rose. But what did I know?

In retrospect, it seems astonishing that my aunt was able to keep up appearances as long as she did. To everyone, including me, she appeared firmly in control. There was not the slightest change in her demeanor to make anyone think otherwise. She told no one that without her glass of water she could barely see what lay before her. Why should she, when thanks to its refractive prowess, her wobbly sight was once again a concentrated beam of light?

In retrospect, one person must have guessed.

The first Saturday in April, after the last customer had left and we were getting ready to close up, Vera burst into the store, locked the door behind her and asked my aunt to pull the curtain.

"What's going on?"

Vera almost never came to the storefront without Sasha. He was seventy-five and strong as an ox, but he didn't like to be alone. Recently, after a string of nightmares, he had told her that he felt like an orphan when she wasn't home.

Vera covered her face with her hands. "I just decided it was time."

"Time?"

"There's a couple of things I'd like to know before . . ." Her voice trailed off.

"Vera—" my aunt implored her.

Ashes and honey, Vera's hair, shimmered in the light.

"You want me to read your hand?"

Without taking off her dark wool coat, Vera sat down across from my Aunt Rita.

"You're sure?" I saw her nod.

For the first time in years, my aunt took Vera's palm and placed it face-up on the table. Once again she was struck by the creamy, elongated whiteness of a hand that resembled no other hand on earth.

But when she peered inside, she jumped. There were ladders everywhere, and people trying to escape. Hundreds of small figures charged up the ladders and fell back, then started up again. Still others, wielding hammers, were building an elaborate structure that seemed to have no beginning and no end. They were all trapped. Overhead was a taut dome, perhaps a tent, because it seemed to be of cloth. Or skin.

My aunt looked again in horror. She was staring at the inside of a scar.

For years it had lain quietly while Vera went about her life. Now something had disturbed it, and the truth, like suture, came spiraling loose.

I heard my aunt take a deep breath. I missed what she said next, but I understood the rest. It had all been so long ago. There had been four of them—Vera, her fiancé, two friends of his, both chemists. The men had packed the briefcase; Vera had left it by a chair inside an office of the Nazi command. Everything had gone according to plan. The building exploded like a furnace; everyone inside was blown to bits, including twelve top officers. What they hadn't counted on was the reprisals. Within six hours the Nazis had rounded up every man, woman and child with anything resembling a Jewish surname and led them to a nearby town. Franz and Werner had escaped across the border but, along with a hundred others, Karl and his whole family were shot at dawn behind the house of an elderly couple and their son. Vera, the only non-Jew in the group, learned of the massacre entirely by chance, in a streetcar the next day, when she overheard two women whispering behind their hands. Two days later, without saying a word, she fled to England and from there to Spain—the only place she could imagine laying down her grief. When she reached Madrid, she hadn't spoken in six months.

Now the scar was almost open and light was streaming in. My aunt saw Vera and Sasha sitting side by side on a bench in Central Park.

"Have you told him?" she said.

"I think he knows."

It was then, in Vera's palm, that she first glimpsed what she now calls the trace: the slender lines that were slowly being drawn from left to right, as if a single silken thread, invisible to the naked eye, were being spun across the vast uncharted silence of our lives.

The screen between Vera's lines of Life, Heart and Fate grew larger and more luminous as my aunt watched, and images she had never seen before flickered across it: millions on horseback, galloping across an immense plain; millions on foot, vanishing like footsteps in the sand; millions in chains, herded onto slave ships, into ovens.

Vera, who had studied logic, understood before my aunt did. "Nothing vanishes without a trace," she said. "It's like a law of physics."

"Meaning?"

"Not all stories have been told, but all stories leave a trace. The same as ancestors. The ones we never knew, the ones who left us their space."

"In other words," my aunt was saying now, "nothing turns to naught. Everything makes way for something else. Things connect, but we're taught they don't. Madmen, fools, become kings' tools. Power loves to make things appear random. But in the dust, doubt gathers and abides. And in the end, the truth cuts a diamantine path through lies."

The strange part was the look on Vera's face as my aunt spoke: a look of rapture, as if she were staring at a work of art.

That look, with all it bespoke of memory and hope, delivered me forever to my aunt. Before the month was out, I too, I thought, had seen the trace, a jeweled line that glinted like a lasso when I pressed my eyes closed in the dark.

What fate had written large in Vera's hand was just as evident in others now that my aunt knew what to look for. In palm after palm she saw the luminous connections, the gossamer threads that led from one seemingly random occurrence to another, slowly teasing out the hidden logic of the trace and turning the bright bits and pieces into the whole cloth that would make the separate tales make sense.

Dozens of stories came together in the next few weeks, including those of Mrs. Levy, whose palm contained the incandescent map of vanished streets, Eddie Carney and his wife, whose hands held the glowing husk of tribal thought, and Faith Kincaid, in whose hand my aunt saw the smoldering logic of deceit.

"Look," I heard her say. "People don't just get assassinated. Presidents' brains don't just vanish from a shelf. Tapes don't get erased by sheer unadulterated chance. People don't just happen to be poor. There are reasons why things happen—exact, specific reasons, even if they're hidden. Wars don't just break out. I mean, it's not as if they were some kind of epidemic—besides, even epidemics have a logic. The problem is, we each arrive in the middle of the story, and it takes us a long time—longer than we have—to figure out where we came in. That's the irony: we don't live long enough to understand the very things we need to most. Sometimes we know more and sometimes less, but in either case, we have to act. For better or worse, we add our own twists to the plot. From the moment of our birth, we alter what we find. We move through life as best we can, making choices, taking risks, tripping over our own feet. And so the trace moves through us all and through all living things, like history or weather—not randomly, but in ways that surpass our daily understanding. We think history towers over us, dwarfing us with the immensity of its achievements and its crimes. But we're mistaken. Because history isn't carved in stone. It's made of flesh. And blood. Of billions of overlapping causes and effects that accumulate to form events."

I tried to listen, but I was thinking about cause and effect and wondering how I would find a way to tell all this some day. I remembered how at first I thought they were a team, like Hansel and Gretel, but how then I realized they were more like Pyramus and Thisbe, my favorite characters from Greek mythology, whispering through the wall, or Narcissus and Echo, shadows of each other who also had Greek names. If Vera hadn't planted the bomb, or the bomb hadn't gone off; if she hadn't had to escape, or hadn't made her way to Spain; if Leo hadn't been so haunted by his father's death; if he hadn't volunteered for Spain; if Vera hadn't been a nurse in the same hospital—then my aunt might never have met Leo, because it was Vera who had introduced them; and Vera might never have met Sasha, because it was Leo who had brought her to New York. And so it went.

Had Vera planted the bomb so that my aunt would one day have a driver for the race to Texas? Had Leo's father drowned himself so that his son would go to Spain? Of course not. The path from one point to another was never so direct. But if the living scar in Vera's hand hadn't pressed so hard between the lines, my aunt might never have discovered the existence of the trace. That led me to a new idea: maybe every cause was the effect of something else, and every effect in turn became a cause. In this way, everything that happened would be linked in a great chain of being, like DNA, and all of us, not just the living but the dead, would be connected like chromosomes spiraling along their double thread: cause and effect, cause and effect. But how could anything evolve, how could we hope for change, if everything was prearranged? Ah—by stepping in; you had to give the helix a small twist, maybe even a sharp one, as Vera had, and Leo, and my aunt, if you wanted to change the course of history. Maybe that was what my aunt had meant: that instead of something set in stone, a monument to what had been, history could be the story of those twists, the path traced by living people stepping in.

I didn't hear what she said next, because I was staring at Faith's transfixed expression.

*

My Aunt Rita pulls my sleeve. Snail, she says. How about a couple of tucks?

I can't believe my ears. When I was coming to the birth scene she told me to slow down. No tucks, she said. No pleats in time. What's all this?

To every time there is a season, my aunt explains. Trust me, she says. The heart has its reasons. Besides, let's face it—I'm not getting any younger.

*

By the end of May, my aunt had received sixteen pairs of gloves, eleven rings, three canaries, two Swiss watches, and more jars of hand cream than she's been able to use since.

Leo still desperately wanted her to read his palm. He was still willing to wait. But not forever.

*

Tell them, says my aunt. Tell them what I saw.

She's back, measuring my every step. My scanning, canny, perfectly metered Rita of an aunt.

She doesn't have to tell me. I know it's time for the last tuck, the one that brings us to the gates of hell and heaven.

And so, spreading my accordion wide, I take a deep breath, brace myself for the oncoming cadenza and begin to play for all I'm worth.

Twelve

"**D**arling, enough is enough. For my sake, for your own, for the world's—please. Read my hand."

Leo's final message was delivered on the first Saturday in June by Lucy and José Delgado's seven-year-old granddaughter. Lucita Delgado was playing hopscotch on the sidewalk with her cousin when the taxi with the castanets pulled up along the curb. The man who had driven all the way to Texas waved at her and she waved back, skipping toward him with a piece of melon-colored chalk.

Leo leaned across the passenger seat. "Hi, beautiful," he called through the open window. "Do me a favor? Take this to Natalya."

Lucita nodded and scampered off faster than La Pasionaria could pull away.

"Here," she said, bursting through the storefront door. My aunt looked up from the long hand before her on the table, which belonged to Danforth James, a violinist from Detroit, who was paying his first visit to Manhattan. On a walking tour the day before, the palm-shaped sign had caught his eye, but no one in his group agreed to stop; today he had ventured out alone, determined to learn why his fiancée had just rejected him for a bassoonist with two children from a previous marriage.

"Open it," Lucita ordered, holding out a long, flat box.

"I'm with a customer, sweetheart. Put it down and I'll open it later."

The child was indignant. "Open it now," she said.

My aunt apologized to Mr. James, who sat stiffly while Lucita stood on tiptoe at the table.

The box contained a single rose and yet another pair of gloves. No—her eyes were playing tricks on her again: there were two roses and one glove. It was gray and wide and warm and worn—with soft leather on the palm and fingers. Suddenly, despite herself, she smiled. It was hard not to be impressed. Leo had sent her his own glove, the woolly simulacrum of his own right hand, the hand that was aching to be read.

The message was inside, on a slip of paper tucked carefully into the thumb.

My aunt unfolded the note and stared at Leo's words.

"Read it," said Lucita.

"I will," my aunt replied.

"What does it say?"

"I don't know yet," my aunt said slowly, and Lucita, shaking her head at the strange woman her grandma called a saint, ran back outside to play.

That evening, after we had closed up shop and pulled the spangled curtain straight across the plate glass window, my aunt looked me in the eye.

"Can you keep a secret?"

I nodded. Of course I could. I had been keeping secrets for the past six months, telling no one what was said during my weekly excursions to the storefront and, more recently, lying awake long after Helen and Abey were asleep, staring at the silvery trace lines in the dark. It was probably just wishful thinking, but I could have sworn there were more of them each time I looked.

"I'm going to read Leo's hand," she began.

That hardly struck me as a secret.

"That isn't it." My aunt had read my mind. She paused. "I probably shouldn't even be telling you this—you're just a child . . ."

"I'm almost eleven," I reminded her.

"Still . . ."

"I won't tell anyone. Promise."

"This is just between the two of us," she said, and blurted it all out at once. "Something's happening to me. My eyes aren't what they used to be. I can't focus."

"Maybe you need glasses," I suggested hopefully.

That wasn't what she meant. "There's nothing wrong with my eyesight. I'm just not seeing things the way I used to. Every day now there are gaps. Sometimes things are sharper than ever, but sometimes the light in people's palms begins to flicker and everything goes dim.

"I can be right in the middle of a reading, and all of a sudden— pow. I'm at the height of my powers, darling, but every day images are slipping away from me forever. The worst part is not knowing when the light will come back on. Or whether . . ." Her voice trailed off. "I don't know why I'm telling you all this."

"I do," I said, as a mixture of relief and incredulity spread across her face. "So I'll never forget."

*

As luck would have it, Danforth James was scheduled to perform at the Toscanini mansion in Riverdale on Hudson the next day. Having witnessed the arrival of Leo's glove, and still massaging his own wounded heart, he was not only willing but eager when my aunt, drawing him aside, asked if he would drop a package off at

Mr. Kaplan's house after the concert, since it was just a block away. Which is how, to Leo's amazement, Natalya, God's Messenger, returned his glove on Sunday afternoon with a message of her own: "I'm ready when you are."

Vera was jubilant when she arrived at the storefront Monday morning. "So you finally came to your senses!" she said, throwing her arms around my aunt. News traveled fast.

"I wouldn't be so sure," my aunt replied. "I don't know what I've gotten myself into . . ."

"What are you talking about?" Vera looked her up and down. "Of course you know. You're nervous, that's all. Would you mind telling me what you have against a little earthly happiness? Because believe me, if you change your mind, the world is full of women who would give their own right arm for a man like Leo."

"Just what he needs," my aunt replied. "A bunch of surplus arms."

Vera had never seen my aunt so touchy. Maybe Rita really did know what awaited her in Leo's hand; maybe, it occurred to her on the way home, despite all the bouquets, not everything would come up roses.

According to Vera, it was Sasha's idea that a small contingent should gather at the storefront to witness the historic moment. After waiting for so long, Leo needed to be sure no detail of the promised reading would escape him; and my aunt, whose words often fled her lips before she could recall them, would certainly be grateful for the presence of a few close friends who could be trusted to remember everything she said.

The only question was when.

The sooner the better, said my aunt.

So when Vera mentioned June 19, the Friday of the following week, my aunt said fine. The fact that it would also be my birthday passed her by, but who can blame her? She had bigger fish to fry.

"Of course," my father said over dinner after Vera called him with the news, sounding the note of caution that was part of his inheritance from Chaim, "this could all be much ado about nothing. What's that expression?—all smoke and no fire. For all we know, Leo's palm could be an empty shell."

"Granted," said my mother, "but the opposite could just as easily be true. Leo's hand could be a gold mine. We have to be prepared for anything. Remember, your sister doesn't have an ordinary bone in her whole body."

"Neither does Leo," said my father.

I let them ramble on. If I knew more than I could say, I also knew enough to keep my mouth closed while I chewed.

*

Even now, after everything that's come to pass, Leo remains curiously modest. "Someone had to bring her to her senses," he maintains. "I figured it might as well be me." But to most observers, there can be little doubt that by persuading my aunt to read his palm while her powers were still intact, he singlehandedly preserved them for the future.

"All I wanted," he says now, "was to be standing there before her when she finally opened her eyes."

In fact, he got more than he bargained for.

We all did, says my aunt.

*

My aunt insisted on putting in a regular day. My parents insisted that I go to school. And Leo—kind, sensitive Leo—insisted on driving out to Forest Hills to pick us up because it was my birthday.

I sat up front with Roosevelt, Marx and La Pasionaria staring at me from the dashboard and the castanets clicking as we drove. Helen and Abey rode in back, excited as two children going to the country. It had been eleven years since their last trip in La Pasionaria, and nearly as long since they had been below Fourteenth Street.

I knew that they would be amazed. Beatniks had sprung up everywhere in the East Village. Here, as elsewhere, they lived, ate, sunbathed and slept right on the street; and, seated cross-legged for hours on end, smoked the stuff of dreams from labyrinthine hookahs; when the spirit moved them, which was often, they made love. Now that summer had arrived, they sat barefoot on the steps, peeling oranges like monkeys and spitting out the seeds.

The storefront was in the heart of this new liberated zone, which was home not only to the long-haired beatniks but to a group of bald-headed mendicants my aunt called Hairy Krishnas, who had renounced the world and had a storefront of their own on Second Avenue. The Hairy Krishnas (also known in the neighborhood as Hairy Christians, Harry Krishner or Hurry Christmas, depending on the speaker) spent hours jumping up and down in orange sheets, jangling small bells and chanting in a language that was neither English nor Ukrainian nor Spanish. Tonight they were out in force, an orange cloud billowing on the corner as we drove past.

When we pulled up at the storefront, the fare read $5.65, but Leo pushed the metal flag down and it was gone. Presto, Abey said. I was the first one out. My feet were already on the sidewalk when I stopped, spellbound by the sight of my Aunt Rita through the plate glass window.

Leo had dressed nattily enough for the occasion; God's Messenger deserves the best, he had said when we exclaimed over his gray mesh shirt, his light twill pants, the matching gray suede shoes.

But my Aunt Rita had outdone him.

She was draped from head to toe in snowy, startling, shimmering white.

Not only was she wearing a white satin turban, she had stuck a rhinestone-studded feather in it at a rakish angle; and the jewel on her forehead was neither her accustomed ruby nor the emerald she occasionally favored, but an enormous, blinding, cut-glass diamond, whose light refracted the glow of her ivory moiré dress. From her ears hung two elaborate earrings I had never seen: clusters of artificial pearls the size of mothballs and the color of ice.

Like Copenhagen, I thought, conjuring up calendar photos of the mermaid forever basking in her Nordic froth; like Rome, like Paris, like every fountain everywhere in which a nymph or heroine stands bathing: so I saw my aunt, suspended behind glass through the translucent spray of the open hydrant on East Seventh Street that summer evening, the evening of my eleventh birthday.

Beside me, Lucy put her hands on her hips and stared up at the diamond sky.

"Your aunt should get paid overtime," she said. "She works like there's no tomorrow."

I feel as if I am slowly putting together the pieces of a puzzle.

Inside the storefront, everything is ready. Lucy and José have brought down five more chairs and set up a small table on the side. In the heightened atmosphere, no one knows what to say. We take our seats. My aunt gets up and draws the bright red curtain across the plate glass window where her cardboard CLOSED sign is already on display. At seven-thirty, Vera and Sasha arrive with two shopping bags, which Vera unloads with her usual bravado: a paper tablecloth and napkins with the word CONGRATULATIONS etched in silver; matching plates; two long candles; plastic forks; and an enormous birthday cake. Five minutes later, José Delgado appears at the door with a tray of flan, and Lucy comes in from the street.

Leo himself has brought a bottle of the best champagne. As the bells of St. Vassilikos strike the quarter hour, he releases the cork, deftly capturing it with a flick of his wrist and handing it to me.

"Cheers, everyone!" he says, beginning to pour.

Soon everyone is clinking glasses and the champagne begins to take effect.

"Here's to Natalya, God's Messenger," says Lucy.

"To Leo," says José.

"Happy Birthday, darling!" says my mother.

"Happy Birthday!" says my father.

"To Lucy and José!"

"To palm-readers everywhere!"

"To the future!"

Only my Aunt Rita has yet to take a sip. "Here's looking at you, kid," she says, raising her glass to mine. Like mercury, like stage fright, a shiver of excitement rushes through me as our glasses meet.

At exactly seven fifty-five, Vera clears away the paper plates, turns out the overhead light and waves us back into the shadows. My aunt adjusts her turban. Sasha motions Leo to the damask-covered table and sets a lighted candle at each end. In the glow of

the two ivory tapers, we can see the sweat beading on his forehead.

From the shadows, the rest of us watch mesmerized as my aunt
glides toward the table with a white rose in her glass.

Suddenly there is a knock at the front door. My father and José
Delgado leap to their feet. It's the reporter from *The Star,* complete
with lisp and camera.

"Someone said there was a special session here tonight," he
slurps, pressing his way in.

He must have seen our faces freeze. "Have you no shame?" Vera
shouts as Sasha looms toward him from the shadows. "This is a
private occasion!" The reporter slinks back toward the street. "I'm
sorry," he murmurs, already out the door. "I didn't realize . . ."

The light within the crystal ball is soft and white, as if a fine,
powdery snow has begun to fall inside the room. My aunt takes
Leo's hand and turns it so the palm is facing up. For a fleeting moment, their eyes meet. She runs her right hand toward his wrist and
holds it, feeling for his pulse as she scans his palm with the fingers
of her left. I see him nod, and she nods back; they are both ready.
My aunt cups her hands around the crystal ball and circles it three
times. Before we know it, she has begun to speak.

"I always said this was the last hand I would read, but here we
are. Why did I succumb? My opponent waged a magnificent campaign. Long ago, I frightened him away. We won't go into all the
reasons. The point is, he left, and his hand took up residence at other tables. But this hand is a hero—it came back. The second time it
was my turn to be afraid. I had never seen a hand so eager to be read.
And then, as you all know, the messages began."

My aunt looks up. It is clear from the rapt faces in the room that we are hanging on her every word. "It was the gloves that finally did the trick," she says, then stops, cradling Leo's hand in hers.

"That last one—because this is a hand of many gloves—reached out and shook me to the ribs. It was a clamor no one could forget, one to admire. So here we are, cracking open the safe, the tried and true."

Something has come over her, and we all know it. She turns away from Leo and peers out at the rest of us, shielding her eyes with her white arm.

Once again she cups her hands over the crystal ball and circles it three times. In the pool of light, I notice a small bulge.

Is it just my imagination, or is there something up her sequined sleeve?

There is no subterfuge in Leo's hand; unlike his mother's, it holds no high brick walls, no heavy drapes, no gates. At first, my aunt is mystified. A gentle breeze floats up from his warm palm, the sound of curtains moving, or of leaves. Then it dawns on her. She had said so herself from the beginning: if she looked, Leo's hand would be an open book.

It is all there.

Page after page, the episodes unfold. The years roll back, then forward, then back again to a time when Leo's father was a boy living by the sea. The place is Russia, the name Odessa, and the water is alive with creatures both frightening and delicious. There are caravels and freighters, trawlers, yachts and ships ferrying passengers to Venice, Istanbul, and Barcelona. Even America.

Another page. Another country. Memory pulls the grown man on. In water up to his neck, a child is struggling with something heavy. He wades back in, but this time he gives up. The body is too heavy. It is his father, weighed down by stones.

Inside La Pasionaria, the wind dies down. The only sound is the click of the meter with its bright red flag. And Leo speaking to a passenger in the backseat. "I got there just as he was pushing off into the waves. I ran down the beach and dived in after him. I tried to save him but when I felt the stones in his pockets I stopped. I couldn't go against his will. The third time he came up for air I let him go. I killed him."

His passenger looks up. "No," she says. "You saved yourself from drowning."

The face in the rearview mirror is my aunt's. In the depths of Leo's hand, she has seen herself as at the bottom of a well.

Now she understands. She reads quickly, skipping from place to place and time to time. Here is Spain, and here is Vera, the years darkening over a brilliant sky. Here is Leo as a boy, haunted by the fear of dying, and here as a young man, haunted by the fear of living.

And here is Carmen, remote and passionate as Spain itself, crossing the street, the ocean, the room. Carmen flinging herself on Leo like a shawl, drowning him with dark and light.

Effortlessly turning, the pages slow, speed up, as if propelled by their own motor.

Leo behind the wheel, singing at the top of his lungs in heavy traffic. Leo leaving a lawyer's office, granting power of attorney to his mother, scrawling one last note and begging one last time to be forgiven. Leo in a garden in Mexico with Margarita, cradling their infant daughter. "Rita," he says, his eyes brimming with proud tears.

My aunt reads on. She sees Frieda Kaplan sighing as she walks from room to room, stopping to check for dust along the edge of a gilt frame; Mrs. Callaghan on Sixty-eighth Street devoutly watering Leo's begonias; Vera whispering across the table at the Village Diner: "We need you to do something important."

My aunt is speaking faster and faster and I see her squinting toward the glass, and it seems to me the room grows dimmer as she grasps the crystal ball between her hands. "We learned the hard way," she is saying. "You can't turn a bullet back once it's been fired, you can only change its path. Thread leads to thread, and everything we need to know is right before our eyes if we allow ourselves to see it."

And now she is speaking again, or maybe she's been speaking all along, about how work turned into weapons is life stolen from the young, how hunger leaves the alphabet unlearned, how what is taken from the earth demands its due. All life, she said, is this precious balance: salt into water into corn or wheat or rice; food into its brilliant flower, speech; and the ceaseless movement of the trace as it flows, invisible ink, from life to death, from grief to love, and from love again to life.

Leo—kind, predictable Leo—is moving rhythmically now, his entire body acquiescing to her words, saying yes, yes, the whole mysterious, elusive future is as close as our own hands.

She has spoken of loss and of gain, of death, of hopes eternally deferred and the changes that turn human beings into animals or saints. Rare, of course, she is saying; rare, and yet so present when it happens that—speaking of a time beyond all scandals, beyond the theft of dreams, beyond the weighing of one life against another in the name of trade, not wanting to see but seeing everything because this time there are no gaps, no openings at all, just lines of once invisible smoke and an endless multitude streaming from a blazing hole. Caravans of buses clog the roads, children howl, loudspeakers blare, and the human tide pours forward, red and black against the liquid sky. The ground beneath them seems to shift and sigh, but as my aunt bends down to look more closely she feels the colossal roar of an explosion and plumes of fire shoot into the air and everywhere she looks there is this molten, fiery, grotesque whirl of flame: her voice altered, shuddering, a time beyond . . . anybody's . . . red hot . . . burning . . . nightmare . . . c h u r n i n g . . . t u r n i n g . . . a n y b o d y ' s . . . w i l d e s t . . . r a d i o a c t i v e . . . d r e a m s . . . earth/air/trees/clouds/plants/grass/cows/milk the first reports will never say exactly where my aunt sees smoke drifting over Poland and the Rhine, hears Geiger counters ticking in the woods near Kiev, detects contamination spreading upwind into Sweden south to Italy and France, the palm before her become a fresco of destruction sees Mississippi burning, Auschwitz burning, Hiroshima burning, the world collapsing like a house of cards sees everything we are or were turning to ash, Guernica, Dresden, Nagasaki, all the living and the dead, all the lies and all the crimes, Sharpeville, Tlatelolco and My Lai, sirens wailing, everything they hoped for and believed in high above the roaring chimneys past the empty streets of Shtebsk all her loved ones acrobats of death flailing floating drifting falling tumbling across the sky: poets doctors students lovers peasants dreamers children mothers and above them all, her white hair tinged with fire, an aged mermaid dancing in the courtyard of the Café Royale, and Chaim, mute violin beneath his chin, serenading her forever as their long-lost shtetl goes up again in smoke. ". . . but nothing," she is saying, "nothing vanishes without a trace—"

Suddenly my aunt looks up, and I know instantly what has occurred. She wipes her eyes with the hem of her white dress, but again they fill with tears, the world a blur except for Leo's face across from her—ecstatic, reassuring, large. She tries once more, but again his palm is blank.

She looks around the room; everyone she loves is here. She sees us all, sees the silver hair on Leo's arms, olive as moonlight in the dusk. She jumps up, peers at herself in the mirror, readjusts her satin turban, returns to her seat, asks Helen for her hand, then Vera, then Lucy, then Sasha and José. One by one they file up. One by one, their hands are blank. Blank as Abey's, as her own, as mine. "All blood relatives," she is saying as she rushes out the door, as I reach for Leo's outstretched palm. No one has thought to reassure him.

The summer stoops are packed with people; dozens of children are flying through the hydrant. Confirming her worst fears, every passing hand is blank. There are no loose images. My aunt leans back against the wall. She sees Jacob and Flora Bloom walking slowly toward the corner, stooped and rigid as two canes. She sees Lucita Delgado playing hopscotch with a friend. Then she turns back toward the group inside.

Her face is flushed, exalted, intoxicated with the meaning of what she has just seen. She looks at Leo, and Leo, unaccountably, looks at me. "We all belong to the hour of our birth," she says, extracting the key to the storefront from her sleeve. "Our dreams are tethered to the world we know. To hope is to imagine, but also to remember. And so each generation has to hope anew. We plant the roots, then pass the torch, and long after we're gone the trace remains of what we knew."

As my aunt bends to kiss me on the head, I release the hand that, without realizing, I have been squeezing hard between my own. When I look down, the triangle in Leo's palm has begun to flood with images.

"And remember, darling," a voice says behind my ear, "always feel the pulse before you start. The pulse will tell you if they're going to believe the rest of what you say. If it's fast they will. If it's slow they won't. It's the middle ones you have to watch for: they expect to hear something interesting."

ABOUT THE AUTHOR

Magda Bogin created and directs the translation program at the City University of New York. She has translated a broad variety of literary works, among them *The House of the Spirits* by Isabel Allende. Her articles on poetry, culture, politics, and women's issues have appeared in such publications as *The Village Voice, Ms.,* and *Parnassus.* She lives with her daughter in New York City.